MOSCOW SKY

A DAK HARPER THRILLER

RELIC RUNNER BOOK 5

ERNEST DEMPSEY

JOIN THE ADVENTURE

Visit ernestdempsey.net to get a free copy of the not-sold-in-stores Sean Wyatt short story *The Moldova Job,* plus six short stories that comprise *Dak Harper Origin Story*.

You'll also get access to exclusive content, private giveaways, and a chance to win signed copies.

While you're at it, swing by the official Ernest Dempsey fan page on Facebook at https://facebook.com/ErnestDempsey to join the community of travelers, adventurers, historians, and dreamers. There are exclusive contests, giveaways, and more!

Lastly, if you enjoy pictures of exotic locations, food, and travel adventures, check out my feed @ernestdempsey on the Instagram app.

What are you waiting for? Join the adventure today!

For Mattie

1

An explosion rocked the ground outside Kyiv's National Museum of History. The Russian commander didn't even flinch.

It took more than a distant blast to shake Nikolai Morovski. He'd seen war in multiple theaters—some known to history and the media, others redacted and erased from any possible public awareness.

Colonel Morovski stood by the armored personnel carrier, surrounded by ten of the best warriors the elite ranks of the Russian army could offer. Even with the thick-plated steel of the vehicle, and ten pairs of eyes sweeping the area nonstop for trouble, the determined leader would have had a tough time finding a place of graver danger for a man of his standing and rank.

Two generals, men he knew, had already been killed in action by the drones continuously launched by the Ukrainians. Many other high-ranking officers had fallen to sniper rounds. One had even been taken out during helicopter transport in what had been previously considered a safe zone.

Despite all this, Morovski stood tall, out in the open air with thick columns of black smoke rising from various parts of the city to meet the churning gray clouds overhead.

Specks of snow drifted around him, some blown from the ground around them, and some falling from the sky. Resolute, the man never shivered. He'd experienced worse cold than this on assignment in Siberia—a frigid hell to which he swore he would never return.

He stared at the building with disgust, despite its impeccable neoclassical design.

While architecturally beautiful, the three-story structure wasn't huge by any stretch of the imagination. Six columns held up the triangle-shaped roof and façade over the front steps. The middle section was hugged by two wings on either side, both angled inward slightly as if to funnel visitors through the heavy wooden doors at the entrance. Three cypress trees stood together on the left-front side of the building in an overgrown patch of grass.

"Their entire history is contained in this unimpressive structure," Morovski said with disdain, to no one in particular. "Pathetic." He shook his head.

He spit on the ground near his boots and crossed his arms.

"Sir," his second-in-command said from his right, "we should get inside."

Morovski looked at the blond man, who stood an inch taller than him. Kostya Arshavin didn't fear his leader, but he didn't want to disrespect him either. He knew better and had been loyal since his assignment to the colonel's side.

Morovski's eyes displayed irritation, but he spoke with the calm assuredness of a psychopath. "I want them to sweat," he said. "Before they suffer."

The second offered a curt nod and returned to scanning the area for threats.

After one more minute, not a second more or less, Morovski gave his own nod. "Kostya, shall we take a tour of the museum?"

"Yes, sir," the second responded. "Clear the building," he ordered to the rest of the men. "You four, take point. You four," he said, indicating another cluster with an index finger, "take the rear." He looked at a stocky brown-haired man to the left of the colonel. "Chevchenko, you're with me and the colonel."

Chevchenko nodded and tightened the grip on his submachine gun.

The group moved as one, swiftly ascending the steps under the towering portico at the entrance to the museum.

The building—designed like so many others from a Greco-Roman architectural influence—had somehow avoided every bomb and rocket the Russian army had thrown at the city.

While the Ukrainians may have considered this luck, Colonel Morovski knew it had nothing to do with good fortune. He'd made certain the museum remained entirely intact, for inside awaited something he desperately desired.

The point team passed between the columns, their weapons sweeping left to right and back again, with knees bent and eyes narrowed. They didn't expect trouble. Morovski knew the Ukrainian army was too engaged in too many places to worry about artifacts, art, and relics. Survival, to them, was paramount right now.

The colonel strode toward the front doors with confidence and a total lack of worry—the way Mike Tyson stalked into a ring in his prime.

The front four fanned out, two to each side of the main doorway with two hugging the frame—weapons at the ready.

Morovski appreciated their caution despite what he perceived to be an overabundance of it. He stopped eight feet short of the door and nodded to the two men closest to it.

The one on the left pressed down on the latch and pulled. It didn't budge.

The colonel rolled his eyes and looked back to one of the men in the rear guard—a soldier carrying a steel battering ram with a flat, square head.

He flicked his index finger at the guy, then pointed at the door.

The man took his cue and hustled to the front, hefting the heavy metal cylinder. He stopped close to it while his comrades waited on either side, ready to provide cover fire the moment the door burst open.

The rammer swung hard. The head smashed into the wood, and the door shuddered but didn't budge. He swung again, just as hard as the first time. Once more, the door resisted, but this time something cracked in the frame.

"Again," Morovski commanded.

The man with the battering ram didn't need to be told. He'd done this a hundred times, both in training and in the field. He swung again, harder than the first two times.

The instant steel struck wood, the door caved, bursting inward against its intent and design. It flung open, ripping the hinges off the frame, and fell to the parquet floor inside.

Within seconds, the first four men flooded into the lobby, sweeping the room as they'd practiced so many times before.

The first two aimed upward toward the alcoves and balconies, checking for threats from above, while the other two swept the main floor.

The colonel and his guards strode into the building and waited for two of the rear guard to follow. The last two men remained at the door as they'd been previously instructed—a preventative against an ambush.

He stepped between the first four men while the rest spread out, weapons ready.

The empty lobby only offered a single soul to greet the trespassers—a tall woman in black suit pants and a gray sweater. She stood in front of the information desk with her arms crossed, blonde hair pulled back in a tight ponytail. Her eyes shimmered like fiery liquid sapphire—a subtle yet unmistakable display of her disdain for the Russian invaders.

Morovski walked forward ahead of his men with Arshavin and the other guard trailing just behind each shoulder. He knew neither of them would give him an inch of space. They'd been trained to protect him at all costs without question, even if the only threat before them was a woman in fine clothing.

"You're going to need to pay for that," the woman said to the colonel as he approached.

"You should have left when you had the chance," Morovski replied in a tone as grim as the reaper's shadow.

"Better to die on my feet than on my knees."

The colonel tilted his chin up slightly at her spirit. Not that it would save her, but at least she had courage. "You're brave for a Ukrainian," he spat. "Foolish, but brave."

"Our people are the brave ones, Colonel. Your people don't want this war. Your president is the fool. This is a war you cannot win. And you know that."

Morovski put up his right hand to signal his two guards to hang back. He stepped closer to the woman. Arshavin's only protest was a sidelong glance at his partner, but he remained in his position.

The colonel stopped so close to the museum curator that her sweet perfume filled his nostrils like a summer walk in a field of wildflowers. He leaned in even closer, and sensed her breath catch—a revelation of her inner fear.

When he spoke, it was only loud enough for her to hear. "I don't care if we win," he whispered. "The president can have his war. My victory comes within these walls."

He returned to an erect stance and watched the confusion wash over her face from her porcelain forehead down to her dark red lips.

She swallowed and exhaled, resetting her resolve in a single breath.

"You're here to pilfer our heritage," she stated.

He chuckled and made a show of looking around the room as if he stood in a circus tent. The colonel removed his hat and ran his thick fingers through his thinning brown hair, speckled with strands of gray.

"I couldn't care less about this... pitiful heritage of yours," he sneered. "Your nation's true place is with the Russian Federation. Your history is our history. Your people would be wise to kneel. But if they want to die, it makes no difference to me."

"Bold words for a man who just said he didn't care if his army won or not."

Behind the colonel, Arshavin's eyebrows tightened at the statement, but he remained steadfast.

Morovski shrugged. "I am a bold man. How else would I attain my rank?" He raised his right hand and swept it around the room, pointing up to the balconies, and the display cases that encircled the floor. "You can keep your history," he said. "I'm not here for any of these trinkets."

She fought to keep the stoic expression on her face, but he caught the slight twitch in her jaw. "It may seem humble to you, but this is the history of a proud, resolute people. You may take these things, but the resolve will remain until you are gone from our land."

"Again, you think I'm here to take an old wooden wagon or a collection of medieval armor." He sized her up in two seconds. "You think me stupid?"

"Obviously."

The colonel laughed and looked back at Arshavin. "She has spirit. I'll give her that." He returned his focus to her, staring her in the eyes. "But you're a terrible liar." After a deep inhale, he crossed his arms and asked, "Where is it?"

"Where is what?" she asked.

Her game was so feeble that he could almost feel her heart skip a beat inside her chest.

"You know exactly what I'm talking about. Don't play dumb with me. My men know how to extract every possible ounce of pain from the human body. And they are not above torturing a woman."

She swallowed and clenched her jaw. "I don't know what you're talking about. Everything we have is here for all to see, Colonel."

He hummed shortly, amused. "That's twice you've called me colonel. That means you know who I am."

"You're a butcher. Everyone knows who you are. It's only a matter of time until one of our men kills you like they have some of the others."

"Perhaps," he allowed. "Every man dies sooner or later." He

inched forward. "But you know why I'm here. These things you offer me are of no consequence. So, I'll ask again. Where is it?"

The artery in her neck pulsed rapidly, another signal that she couldn't keep from him.

"I have no idea what you're talking about."

"Where! Is! The gold?" His voice thundered up to the vaulted ceiling and back down to the hardwood floor at their feet.

The volume and staccato of his voice startled her, and she shifted nervously. The curator inclined her head, stiffening her spine. "What gold?" she asked.

"You know exactly what gold."

She smiled, taunting him with the wide crease of her lips. "It isn't here, Colonel. Do you think we would be so stupid to keep our most priceless treasures here with you barbarians storming our gates?"

He gauged her carefully with all the wisdom of his decades in the military. Then he snorted. "You didn't move anything," he said. "Your people are too full of feeble pride to do something like that. Tell me where it is, and perhaps I won't have to put you through any pain."

"Search the entire museum," she offered. "You won't find it."

"Very well," he said. "Pain it will be."

He turned to Arshavin. "Squeeze it out of her."

She shook her head as the officer stepped toward her without hesitation. "You can torture me all you want. I will never tell you where it is."

Morovski cocked his head to the side. "I guess we will see. Won't we?"

2

Dak watched the alley from across the street from astride a black Triumph Thruxton, waiting like a fisherman for the line to jerk.

The bounty hunter he'd been tracking for the last week had finally slipped up, as Dak knew most of them usually did. Sooner or later, they made mistakes or got sloppy—usually as a result of frustration.

Through persistent patience and experience, he knew a hunter would always reveal themselves no matter how many times they tried to sweep away the breadcrumbs left in their wake.

It had been two years since the events that left Dak on the run from his former commanding officer, Col. Cameron Tucker. The betrayal by his brothers-in-arms had already been avenged, and Dak could have let it go at that had Tucker simply vanished into the sunset and never reared his ugly head again.

But the man seemed hell bent on his own vendetta. And had scoured the earth to hunt down and kill Dak, using every resource he had.

Dak still didn't know where the colonel's funding came from, though he knew it had to be from somewhere other than his military pension and savings.

With all his cunning and planning, Tucker never realized Dak had connections in the shadows, too. The bounty hunter nests, such as the one concealed in this dimly lit alley, were Dak's playground. He knew the people who operated them, and while they were sworn to silence, they knew the subtle difference between mercenaries with morals and those without.

Some of the proprietors—usually disguised as bartenders or underground casino owners—were as callous and shady as the operations they managed. Others, though, leaned to the side of right.

These were the ones Dak plied for information regarding Tucker's ambitions toward Dak's death.

So far, Dak had been one step ahead at each one of the man's attempts on his life. Now, Dak was two steps ahead.

He checked his watch and noted the time. It was nearly two in the morning in this murky area of Mumbai. Seemed like only days had passed since he'd been in this city. He hadn't anticipated returning so soon, even though it had been over a year. His practice was to never visit the same place twice within a few years' span, but doubling back this time had paid off.

Dak had received the encoded message four hours before and immediately locked down his position across the street. He'd stood up a few times to stretch his legs and alter his position so as not to look too obvious. But through the course of the night, and now early morning, he maintained a consistent watch over the nest's exit.

His quarry went by only one name—Murinho. Dak had rolled his eyes at first, wondering if the guy's true ambition was to be a Brazilian soccer star. He'd tempered his mocking, though, because Dak knew the man was as deadly as he was arrogant.

From what he'd learned, Murinho was former Brazilian special forces—a group without international recognition compared to those from the more developed nations of the world—a fact Murinho, no doubt, leaned on whenever he executed one of his marks.

Nothing like a mercenary with a chip on his shoulder, Dak thought.

The door in the alley abruptly swung open, and a figure appeared. The slender man wore a faded denim jacket and tight black jeans. He walked briskly toward the street, paying no mind to Dak at first. Or so it seemed.

Dak took nothing for granted, flipped up his visor, and proceeded to pretend to answer a text message. He allowed the bounty hunter to step out onto the sidewalk, only watching through his periphery as the man turned to Dak's left and continued down the block.

Dak checked his right rearview mirror and saw the guy stop at a black, two-door Jaguar F-Type.

"Well, Murinho. You have great taste in cars. But those skinny jeans... What is it with dudes wearing those." Dak chuckled at his own comment and waited until the taillights of the Jaguar glowed red before he fired up the motorcycle's engine.

Still watching in the mirror, Dak allowed the target to pull out and make a left at the next intersection before steering the bike out of the parking spot and onto the road.

Dak veered around the corner at the light and saw the coupe far up the street, adding distance between the two as the bounty hunter sped through the city.

"I guess you don't care about traffic laws," Dak muttered.

He twisted the throttle. The engine roared a throaty, guttural sound through the pipes. Dak felt the machine surge forward underneath him as he leaned forward to minimize drag. The wind whistled through the helmet and flapped against his Killers T-shirt. His drab, olive cargo pants also whipped against his calves as he picked up speed.

Dak only slowed when he felt he was getting too close and made sure to keep the mark far enough away that he could see where the man was going, but not so close that Murinho would notice. He hoped.

The car veered right and disappeared from view. Dak took the cue and twisted the throttle a little more. Again, the motorcycle lunged ahead with renewed vigor. Dak squeezed the bike with his thighs as the speedometer climbed.

He reached the turn in time to see the Jaguar cut to the left into a parking garage next to an unimpressive, ten story gray apartment building.

Dak slowed down to wait for the car to pass through the automatic gate, which he believed the driver was awaiting to open.

Then the bright red taillights dimmed, and the back of the coupe disappeared into the garage.

Dak gunned the engine again and turned into the garage. He slowed down enough to swerve around the white-and-red bar blocking the way in and slipped by it without even grazing his arm.

No guard stood in the guard shack, though Dak did notice the security camera attached to the top-front corner of the little building.

He remained unconcerned regarding his apparent parking violation. The signs read Resident Parking Only. Dak only planned on being there a few minutes, just long enough to get what he needed out of Murinho.

Dak knew the motorcycle's engine would give away his presence in the concrete parking deck and quickly turned into a spot around the corner, just out of sight from the guardhouse.

He killed the engine before it stopped rolling, shoved out the kickstand, and hung his helmet on the throttle.

While the apartment building stood ten stories tall, the parking garage only ascended three levels.

Knowing he had to pursue on foot, Dak felt grateful because the only way up was the stairs. He sprinted over to the stairwell and threw open the blue metal door, ducked inside, and hurried up the first flight.

He stopped at the next landing marked Level 1 in big blue letters painted on the concrete and eased the door open.

He poked his head through, drawing the subcompact pistol from his belt. He listened, and heard the sound of the F-Type's engine growling from somewhere in the garage. It was distant, though, which meant Murinho had gone up to the next level.

Dak let the door go, and by the time he heard it click closed, he was already nearing the second-level landing. He breathed hard at the sudden burst of energy required to move so fast, but he couldn't let the Brazilian get away.

Dak reached the second level and cautiously pulled open the door. Again, he looked through the crack and heard the Jaguar's throaty engine echoing through the parking garage.

He saw a blur of red at the other end of the deck and watched as the coupe's rear end disappeared around the corner and up the ramp toward the third level.

"Third floor," Dak grumbled.

He released the door and flew up the stairs, taking them two at a time until he arrived at the third level. Thankful he didn't have to go up any more steps, he pressed his ear to the door and listened, doing his best to calm his breath from the interval of exertion.

The Jaguar's engine gave away its driver's position as it passed by the stairwell entrance. Dak looked through the steel-wire-reinforced glass window above the door latch and saw the coupe slowly roll to the middle of the parking garage before it pulled into a spot along the inner wall.

The lights flashed, signaling the driver had shifted it into park.

Dak eased the door open, wary that even the slightest creak would give him away.

He had to cover one hundred feet, give or take, to get to Murinho, and with only a few dozen cars parked at random intervals in the garage, Dak had to be careful.

He ducked low and rushed to a red sedan parked along the outer wall, slipped around in front of it, and stopped on the other side to make sure the Brazilian hadn't noticed.

The Jaguar was out of view from this angle, so Dak kept going, crouching as he moved hurriedly across the concrete deck to the next vehicle—a black Mercedes C-Class with dark window tinting.

Dak skimmed along the grill of the German sedan and stopped again. From there, the next car that could provide cover sat five spaces away—a lot of room to cross completely exposed.

From his vantage point, he watched as Murinho climbed out of his ride and surveyed the room. It looked way too casual for Dak, especially for a guy whose livelihood brought no end of suspicion and trouble into his world.

The Brazilian turned away and started walking toward the elevator at the other end. From there, Murinho would have the advantage, or at best disappear for good.

Dak made his move and hurried forward into the open, only sixty feet away from the killer.

He focused as intensely on not allowing his quarry to hear a sound as he crossed the parking deck, narrowing the distance between himself and Murinho.

When Dak was only twenty feet behind the man, he straightened up and raised his pistol, then closed the gap to fifteen feet—well within range, even with a subcompact firearm.

"That's far enough, Murinho," Dak ordered in a calm voice. He didn't want to startle the guy. Doing that to a professional killer could have bad consequences. The kind that involved the mark turning around with guns blazing, which would force Dak to dive for cover while firing his own weapon—a less than optimal outcome.

Thankfully, the Brazilian didn't make a sudden move, or any move, for that matter.

"You're a hard man to find, Dak," Murinho drawled.

"I like to play hard to get."

Murinho's shoulders shifted as he chuckled. "I'm sure you do."

"Turn around. Very. Very. Slowly. If you twitch wrong, you die."

The Brazilian hesitated for two seconds, then slowly nodded. "No need for that, Dak." He put his arms out wide without being asked, and gradually twisted around until he faced his captor.

The first thing Dak noticed was the glaring lack of concern in the man's mud-colored eyes.

"Not smart, Dak," Murinho taunted. "You should have killed me when you have the chance."

"Had. You mean had the chance. If you're going to screw with me, you could at least practice your English."

Murinho sighed, amused. "Doesn't matter."

"Words do matter, Murinho. And now you're going to use yours to tell me where Tucker is."

"That's your plan?" He laughed and looked off to the right, his eyes locking on nothing in particular for a second before he brought his gaze back to the American. "You think you're going to torture me into telling you where Tucker is? Come on, Dak. You above anyone else should know that isn't going to happen. I don't know where he is. That's part of why this system works. We don't know where the contract comes from."

"And yet you seem oddly familiar with the man's name." Dak took two steps closer and reaffirmed his stance, twisted slightly with the pistol extended with his right arm.

Another, less exuberant laugh escaped the Brazilian's mouth. He bobbed his head with the noise. "I don't know where Tucker is. You think he'd be stupid enough to stick around and wait for you to show up?"

"Thought crossed my mind. He was stupid enough to stab me in the back."

"Perhaps. But you were stupid enough to walk into my trap."

Dak's brow furrowed with concern.

"Drop it," a voice said from behind.

Dak didn't recognize the deep baritone with what he thought to be a Dutch accent, but that didn't matter. He'd walked right into the ambush.

"You didn't think I make it that easy for you, did you, Dak?"

Dak rolled his eyes. "Would. Didn't think I *would* make it that easy for you. Jeez. If you're going to speak it, at least take the time to learn it first."

Murinho shook his head, unconcerned. "De Jong there could have already killed you. Tucker promised a sum that is truly life changing for your head. But he also said there's a bonus if we bring you in alive."

"I'm aware of the contract details," Dak sneered. "Maybe you didn't realize I'm in the network."

"Are you?"

"He's stalling," De Jong said, his shaggy blond hair swishing to the side as he snapped his attention to Murinho.

"Yes, thank you. I know that." Murinho took a wary step toward the American. "I believe my colleague here ordered you to drop the weapon."

Dak nodded. "Yeah, he did. But see, here's the thing, Murinho." Dak rolled his eyes again. "You have to have a last name, right? I mean, that's just ridiculous. One name? How many of y'all are there out there doing that? Must get confusing. What if every American just went by the name *John*. You know how ridiculous that would be?"

The Brazilian cocked his head to the side, either not understanding the point or not caring.

Dak continued. "Sorry, got distracted there. It's just, pick a last name already. Anyway," he glanced over his shoulder to see De Jong for the first time. "You should probably know that I didn't walk into a trap."

Murinho puzzled over the statement, lowering his eyebrows as he twisted his head back and forth in denial.

"Yes. You did, Dak. And you either drop the gun, or my friend here kills you and we take Tucker's first offer."

"Not gonna happen. Tell your boy to put his gun on the deck and kick it over to the rail. Or he dies first."

Murinho stared into Dak's evergreen eyes, trying to extract whatever game he was playing.

"I'm going to count to three, Dak. Then De Jong kills you."

"Just let me do it," the Dutchman said.

"No need to count," Dak countered coolly. "Seeing how badly you screw up English, I'm guessing math isn't your strong suit, either."

"One," Murinho spat.

Dak didn't move, keeping the gun leveled at the enemy.

"Two."

Dak's lips creased into a broad grin. "I tried to warn you. Will, would you mind?"

A voice responded in an earpiece tucked into his right ear. "With pleasure, my brother."

Dak didn't see the right side of De Jong's head erupt in a pink mist, but he heard the sound of the bullet zip through the air—and the man's skull.

He did, however, see the color drain from Murinho's face at the sight.

The Brazilian's right hand snapped down toward his belt. That was as far as it got.

Dak's pistol popped, echoing through the garage.

The bullet tore through Murinho's shoulder, severing the necessary muscles and tendons required to control the appendage.

The American stalked forward.

"That looks like it hurts," Will said into Dak's earpiece.

"Yes, it does."

Fury swept across Murinho's face. His eyes blazed with disbelief and rage—a cocktail Dak had seen more than a few times.

He grabbed the contract killer by the collar and pressed the pistol's muzzle to the back of the man's head, then shoved him toward the railing.

Halfway to the wall, Dak kicked him in the tail, sending the man sprawling forward.

Barely able to catch himself with his one good arm, Murinho stumbled ahead until he slammed into the three-foot-high concrete barrier.

"I won't tell you where he is," Murinho spat.

"Oh, so you do know," Dak stated. "I thought you might."

"You won't know if the place I tell you is the right one or not. For all you know, I'll send you into another trap."

Dak nodded. "Yeah, I considered that. But it's worth a try anyway." Dak aimed at Murinho's good shoulder. "Now. Where is Tucker?"

The Brazilian shook his head. A snakelike grin creased his face. "You don't have the—"

The gun report reverberated through the garage as the bullet shattered bone and tissue in the man's previously good joint.

He screamed this time, unable to withstand the urge any longer. Amid the howling were what Dak figured to be obscenities.

"I'm sorry," Dak offered, his tone full of mocking. "My Portuguese is a little rusty. Was that Tucker's location, or were you praying for mercy?"

The killer swore in English at Dak, who only shook his head in response.

"There are a lot more places I can hurt you, Murinho. Spare yourself the pain. Tell me where Tucker is, and I'll kill you quickly. Or I can make it last. The choice is yours."

Murinho breathed hard, his nostrils flaring with every exhale. He stared down at the ground as if trying to recall the answer, then met Dak's gaze.

"There's a bar. Not far from here. It's an underground place. He rented a flat above it on the third—"

The gun blasted again, this time sending a round through the man's thigh.

He screamed again, unable to clutch the wound with his flaccid hands.

"I told you what you wanted!" Murinho protested, rocking back and forth.

"You told me what you wanted," Dak replied. "And the eyes never lie. Now," Dak said, moving the sights of his pistol so they lined up with Murinho's right knee. "I hear that a knee shot is one of the most painful places to take a bullet. How about we try this again, and this time with the truth."

Murinho swallowed hard. The realization in his eyes betrayed the truth. He knew he couldn't lie to Dak Harper. If he continued, the pain would only get worse.

"Okay. Okay. Take easy."

Dak sighed and looked up to the ceiling for a half second, irritated. "Take *it* easy. Take *it* easy," he repeated. "I should shoot you on principle alone."

"No. No. Enough." Resignation filled the man's face. "The Majestic," he managed. "He's staying at the Majestic."

Dak inclined his head, staring through the man's eyes welling with tears. This time, Dak didn't find a lie behind them.

He lowered his gun and regarded the man's wounds with a passing glance, then stuffed the pistol back into his belt and pulled his T-shirt down over it.

"You should get those wounds looked at."

Murinho frowned. "You... you're not going to kill me?"

"I wouldn't have even shot you if you had told me what I wanted to begin with. Those injuries are self-inflicted, Murinho. And for the love of all that's good and decent, pick a last name. Seriously. It's weird."

Dak turned and started walking back toward the stairwell.

"You think that's wise?" Will asked in the earpiece.

"I'm not in the business of killing unarmed men."

"Was that some kind of a dad joke?"

"What?" Dak said, looking back over his shoulder at the wounded assassin. "Because he can't move his arms right now?"

"You know it is."

Dak chuckled. "No. That one was an accident."

Murinho squirmed, trying to get up while pressing a thumb into the bloody hole in his leg.

A look of sheer disbelief covered his paling face as he stared at the American.

"It's not smart to leave him alive, Dak," Will advised. "I can take him out right now. Clean. It'll be quick. Like the Dutchman."

Dak noted the body of the man on the other side of the garage with a look over his opposite shoulder.

"Perhaps," Dak said. "Maybe it's a bad idea. But there may come a day when we need our little Brazilian's help."

"You think he's gonna help you? He's a killer, Dak."

"So am I." He reached the door to the stairwell and looked back one more time. Murinho struggled to cross the parking deck, dragging his injured leg behind him.

He looked like a zombie that hadn't fully transformed yet.

"It's easy to pull a trigger, Will. It's harder to make an ally from an enemy."

"When did you get all philosophical on me?"

"About three minutes ago." He stepped into the stairwell and let the door close behind him. "Meet me downstairs. We have one more stop to make here in Mumbai before we head to Poland."

3

D ak's phone buzzed as he and Will stood in the holding room, waiting to be cleared.

Just after finishing his last job, Dak received a call from his 13-year-old employer, Boston McClaren, with information about another gig—one that had the potential to be the most dangerous he'd ever taken.

The teenage video game millionaire had come across a story regarding the Russian invasion of Kyiv, and despite the imposing peril this mission threatened, Dak couldn't turn it down.

Which led him here, to one of the seedier places in Mumbai. Fortunately, he knew the proprietor.

The burly man guarding the entrance to the underground casino looked like the kind who had been in every bar fight that had ever happened. While his intense stare and unwelcoming disposition might have intimidated others, Dak knew the man wouldn't harm him.

He stood next to the metal door with arms crossed as the slender, pastier man in the cage to Dak and Will's right confirmed their presence with the lady in charge by way of the cell phone glued to his ear.

"You sure this was a good idea?" Will asked, leaning toward his friend. He kept his eyes on the bouncer standing watch by the door. "I mean, shouldn't we have checked the hotel first?"

"I thought you didn't believe Murinho," Dak hedged.

"I didn't say I believed him. But you got the information you wanted."

"I know. We went over this in the car. We had to come here first."

Will shook his head, eyeing the guard with a ladle of suspicion. "He'll get away—if he's still there."

"My guess is the colonel is already gone. He never sticks around for long. That whole 'don't poop where you eat' thing seems to be his modus operandi."

"Okay," Will half agreed with an arched eyebrow that showed his suspicion. "Then why'd you bother? And why not check?"

"Who said I didn't check?"

"Okay, Harper. She said you're good," the guy inside the cashier cage shrieked. His tinny voice matched his skinny physique.

"Thanks," Dak offered.

The guard stepped aside and pulled the casino door open for the two guests.

"Have a good time, Dak," the bouncer said in a deep baritone as the two passed.

"Wish I was here for fun, Rocco. Next time."

"All right," the man said with a smile.

Will could only look on in confusion as they entered the casino. The robust, earthy smell of high-end cigars tickled their nostrils, overpowering the few who smoked cigarettes. The odors blended with other sensations: sounds of slot machines dinging and donging, chips shuffling, dice rolling, and roulette wheels rattling the white ball between frets.

An applause erupted from one of the three craps games as the roller—a guy from Korea—raised a fist in celebration.

The door closed behind them, and Will finally faced his friend. "You seem pretty popular around here. Why the security checkpoint if they know you?"

Dak clapped his friend on the shoulder. "You of all people should know, caution above all else." He grinned at the still-astonished Will and then headed off down the short flight of stairs onto the recessed game floor.

Dak turned the corner at the bottom and looked across the room, back up a similar set of steps, and saw the casino's proprietor —Tamara.

She noticed him immediately, and a pleased smile crossed the blackberry shade on her lips. Her black hair draped down over her right shoulder, covering a thin red strap doing half the work holding up a crimson silken gown.

Dak admired her for only a second, unwilling to give her that much power—and certainly none of his affection. That belonged with another woman, a lost love he hoped someday he could regain. The thoughts of his ex, Nicole, stirred his heart for a moment before he regained his composure.

Will sidled up next to him and stared across the room. "Is that her?" he asked, pointing without regard to poise.

"Yes, and stop pointing," Dak said. "She doesn't like it?"

"How do you know?"

"You like it when people point at you?"

"No," Will stammered. "I guess not."

"Come on," Dak said, letting it go. "Shouldn't keep a lady waiting."

"She is definitely a lady."

"Don't get any ideas, Will. She'll eat you for breakfast."

"Hey, I'm just admiring the view."

Dak rolled his eyes. "You need a girlfriend."

"Too much hassle," Will argued.

They reached the bottom of the steps and ascended between the two guards standing at either side. The men merely nodded at Dak, recognizing him from his previous visits. Their expressions of respect weren't lost on Will.

"What did you do to make everyone here like you so much?" he whispered as they reached the top of the stairs.

"I'm charismatic."

"It sure ain't your sense of humor."

Dak ignored him as Tamara stood up from her plush, blue chaise lounge and extended a hand toward Dak, palm down.

He took her hand and raised it to his lips, kissed it gently, and passed her his charming, effortless grin. "Good to see you again, Lady Tamara," Dak said.

Will took a step forward as if to repeat Dak's greeting, but she paid no attention to him. Her eyes remained fixed on his friend, the way a lion fixed its gaze on a wounded gazelle.

"The pleasure is all mine," she flirted.

Dak felt a tingle slither across his skin, sending goose bumps from his elbows all the way up to the back of his skull.

He didn't flinch, not on the outside, but forced himself to steer her away. "This is my friend, Will," Dak said, letting go of her hand despite her gripping protest. She turned her head and looked him up and down, then smiled as she might to a stray puppy.

She extended her hand in a more businesslike fashion to Will. "Nice to meet you. Any friend of Dak's, you know."

He took her hand, twisted it, and extended the same old-school courtesy Dak had. "Enchanted," he said.

"As you should be," she replied.

Dak couldn't fight off the chuckle that rose up from his gut. He nearly full-on belly laughed.

Will took the comment in stride. "As all should be in the presence of such beauty."

That one disarmed her, and both men saw it.

She blinked twice, twitched her right cheek, and caught her breath.

Will had done something few could. In a tennis match of hard-to-get, he was Rafael Nadal.

Tamara turned her head and eased back into her chaise lounge, motioning for the two men to have a seat next to her on the plush white sofa and the matching club chair across the glass-and-brushed-steel coffee table.

The men obliged, Dak taking the sofa spot—a subtle move at

corralling his friend away from the woman so they could talk business.

They weren't here to flirt, no matter how much Will might have wanted to.

"To what do I owe the pleasure?" Tamara asked, crossing one leg over the other as she propped her head up with palm to chin.

"Right to it," Dak answered. "I like that about you."

"You're a man who doesn't concern himself with the common pleasantries of sociability. You need something from me. The sooner you tell me what it is, the sooner we can enjoy each other's company."

Will's jaw nearly hit the coffee table's surface.

Dak merely replied with a smile at first. Then he leaned back and ran his fingers through his thick, dark brown hair. She stared into his green eyes, lost in them, and he wondered if she would hear anything he said or if Tamara was too distracted.

Her mind was clearly somewhere else. As aloof as Dak could be with women, even he could easily sense the flirtation with this one.

"How is your relationship with Lesma?" Dak asked abruptly.

Her chin inclined, and she tilted her head back. But she never took her eyes off his. "That *is* an interesting question." She picked up a drink on the table and took a long, sensual sip—letting her lips brush across the rim for an extra second as if the act might seduce him right then and there.

"I have no problems with Lesma. Ever since his son's... accident, our relationship has been good. He stays out of my affairs, as I have always kept out of his." She lifted her right eyebrow. "Why do you ask?"

"I need his help with something."

She chuckled and set the drink back down on the table. "You? Need Lesma Lebedev's help? Have you decided a life of crime is your new path?"

Dak offered a demure grin in response. "Not yet," he teased. He crossed one leg over his knee and folded his arms across his firm chest. "I'm looking for something—a lot of somethings, actually."

"And you believe Lesma can help?"

"He offered his help to me before. Said if I ever needed anything to give him a call."

"Then why are you here?" Her eyebrow twitched flirtatiously with the question.

"I don't have his number."

She burst out laughing. One of her guards by the top of the stairs turned his head slightly at the sudden sound, then returned his gaze to the gaming floor and the many patrons spilling their money onto the tables or into the machines.

"That's a good one," she said, pointing at him as she reached for her drink again. Tamara drew another sip, and this time decided to keep holding the beverage. "So, you need his number. I can give you that."

Dak didn't like the way she said the last sentence. It sounded like there was going to be a favor required before she would give him what he wanted. That's how things went with her last time—Dak scratched her back, she scratched his. But she'd wanted hers scratched first, and likely would again.

"What will that cost me?" Dak demanded.

"Cost you? No, darling. You don't owe me anything. You helped me before. And I know that if I ever need it, you'll do so again. Won't you?"

Dak felt the temptation to shift nervously, but he remained a statue.

Will managed to keep quiet despite wanting to jump into the conversation, but he found himself mesmerized by the way the two danced.

"Of course," Dak hedged. And meant it.

"So, tell me. What could you possibly need Lesma's help for? Run into some trouble with the Mumbai underground?"

"No. Nothing like that. This is much worse."

"Worse?" Her forehead wrinkled, and her eyes widened. "Do tell."

"You're aware of the war going on in Ukraine," he stated.

"Of course. Who isn't." Tamara waved a dismissive hand.

Someone on the gaming floor yelled in celebration. Her eyes

wandered to the craps table where a dozen people surrounded the game. One man, a multimillionaire from Thailand, raised both fists as he turned to the other players on both sides, smiling in triumph.

The outburst barely drew a smirk from Tamara. Players winning now and then was good for business, despite the temporary setback in revenue. The sense of invincibility that came with every small win also came with inflated risks.

Tamara continued when the noise settled down with the next round of betting. "Are you looking to go to Ukraine? Perhaps you should wait until the conflict is over. Surely, whatever your employer wants can hold off for a while."

Dak shook his head. "Normally, I would agree with you. Going into a war zone isn't exactly my idea of a good time."

"You can say that again," Will grumbled.

"So, you are going to Ukraine?"

"When the Russians invaded, they made a beeline for Kyiv, taking out other cities and towns along the way."

She nodded. "Yes. I've been trying to avoid the news lately. It's all smoke and mirrors anyway, but I know about the invasion."

"When the Russians took over sections of the city, one area they invaded happened to be the location of the museum of Ukrainian history.

Tamara leaned her head back, interest swelling in her eyes. "So, they attacked the museum?"

"Not exactly," Will interjected, unable to hold back any longer. He wasn't one for sitting on the sidelines waiting for game time. "They broke into the museum."

"Ah," Tamara realized. "So, they're not only thieves of land but also of historical items. How interesting. I didn't realize their president was such a fan of history."

"I don't know how much he knows about it," Dak said. "It could have been a rogue commander. I've had personal experience with that sort of thing." He glanced over at Will. "Whoever did this took every item of both monetary and historical value. We're talking

Scythian artifacts, many of them solid gold, along with several other pieces."

"Barbarians."

"What's worse," Dak added quickly, "is what they did to the curator."

"A woman?" Tamara asked.

"When the Russians first entered the building, they didn't know where the loot was. Apparently, the curator and her staff had the presence of mind to hide it. They tortured her for the information, which she didn't give up."

"Gotta admire that," Will chimed.

"Yeah, but they ended up finding it anyway. The newly appointed 'curator' discovered the treasures hidden in boxes in the basement. Apparently, while they'd been wise to hide the stuff, they weren't clever as to where they hid it."

"Interesting. I wonder, who relayed this information?"

"A staff member managed to record everything and send it out to the Ukrainian military leaders. But they had bigger concerns at the time."

"Human lives are more important than anything, even priceless relics from a nation's history," she demurred.

"We have to find her," Dak stated. "Whatever the cost."

"Assuming she's still alive." Tamara took another drink. "Which is doubtful. I have no qualms with Russian people, but their leaders— especially in the military—are some of the most ruthless I've ever met."

"You know Russian military officers?" Will asked, surprised.

"My dear," she drawled, "I get all kinds in here. And when you give a man enough vodka, his ego tends to reveal itself. While I've never been made privy to any tactical secrets, I've heard enough stories to be able to filter the truth from the bravado. And I can tell you... the ones I have had the displeasure of hosting in my casino are some of the lowest of the low."

"That's a reflection of leadership at the highest level," Dak included. "I hope you took their money."

"As well as their dignity, or what little of that they had left."

Dak allowed a sly grin to crease his lips.

She downed the rest of her drink and raised the empty tumbler. Out of nowhere, a slender man in a white button-up shirt and black bow tie appeared and snatched the glass from her, instantly replacing it with a full one.

"Talk about service," Will commented.

She ignored him, which Dak felt she did intentionally just to press Will's buttons. "Jafar," she called in the direction of the guard nearest the stairs.

The man turned at the sound of his name and stepped closer immediately. "Yes, Lady?"

"Tell the front that Lesma Lebedev is going to be arriving soon."

"Of course, Lady."

The guard snapped around to his left, returned to his post, and touched the radio earpiece with his right hand.

"What makes you so certain he'll show up?" Dak asked.

"He owes me one," she teased and raised the glass to her lips, letting it linger there for two breaths.

"And what do I owe you?"

"I believe I mentioned this before, but you don't owe me anything. You are in my circle of trust now. Friends don't keep score. They look out for each other."

Dak saw in her eyes that no untruth lingered beyond the veil. He'd done her a favor before, and apparently it was much more important than he realized.

"I knew I had a good feeling about you," Dak managed. "So, you want to call Lesma or should I?"

"My man at the front is already making the call," she said after a flicker of a glance to her guard. "Lesma doesn't refuse an invitation from me."

"He's not busy?"

"Not at this time of night. Probably at home, watching his shows."

Dak and Will both snorted.

The former's brow tightened in humorous curiosity. "What kinds of shows does a Russian mob boss watch?"

"He loves reruns of *The Office*," Tamara said. "The American version."

Dak laughed harder. "Really? Big Steve Carrell fan?"

"Who isn't?" Her tone was as dry as the gin in her drink.

"Good point."

"Anyway, he should be here within the hour. I'm sure he'll be glad to see you again. While you're waiting, feel free to spend some time at the tables." She reached over her right shoulder and plucked two casino chips off an end table behind the chaise, then tossed them to Dak. "It's on the house."

Dak noticed the $1000 printed on the two black discs. "House always wins, right?"

She smiled seductively, brushing her lips against the rim of the tumbler. "Always."

4

A cold draft cut into Colonel Morovski's eyes. He blinked it away and kept walking in the same determined way he always did. His stride portrayed confidence to anyone who saw it and left no question his unrelenting mind.

Half of his stalwart disposition came from his upbringing—the other from his time in Siberia. He'd kept his sordid childhood from everyone he'd ever met, never telling them about the beatings, the relentless and unrealistic pursuit of perfection that hung over him, and the way his abominable father finally met his end.

There were nights, though few and as far between as the galaxies of the universe, when the colonel considered the "teachings" of his father to be a blessing in his adult life. He'd learned not to compromise when so many others eagerly gave up what they wanted or needed in exchange for a tepid peace. Most importantly, young Nikolai learned to abolish weakness from within himself, and to dominate it when he sensed it in others.

"The perimeter is secure, sir," Kostya informed after a quick touch to his radio earpiece.

Morovski wasn't surprised by the statement. Of course the

perimeter was secure. His men were some of the best in the Russian army—handpicked by the colonel himself.

No one had questioned him on the selection of his unit. Not even the highest office in Russia. While other men occupied what some might have considered more powerful positions in the military, he wielded an influence that everyone in the Kremlin either respected or feared.

His shiny black shoes clicked with every step on the smooth concrete underfoot. Empty hooks hung from rails that ran along the ceiling ten feet above the floor, but the smell of death still lingered in the abandoned slaughterhouse.

Pale lights glowed dimly from the walls, fixed with steel cages around them. One flickered to the left, its bluish-white hue giving off a horror-movie vibe.

The colonel barely noticed. His gaze remained fixed on the black metal door straight ahead.

With the lights on and the frigid air tingling his cheeks, the colonel wondered who'd been paying the electric bill in the defunct business. His men hadn't orchestrated that, or if they had, none of them had reported it to him.

Those thoughts gave way to the building itself—a strong concrete-and-steel structure built during the Soviet era. It would have made a good bomb shelter for the Ukrainian people—had they considered it.

Or until his men cleared them out. In hindsight, he supposed it was wiser they had *not* used this facility—for their sakes.

Morovski stopped at the door and waited while Kostya hurried and pulled the latch to open the way in for his commander.

A warm cloud of air radiated out with the odor of cured meat that he figured was now a permanent fixture in the huge refrigeration unit.

The colonel blinked a few times, then stepped into the walk-in cooler. He immediately noticed that the huge refrigeration unit's interior matched the temperature in the rest of the building, which he felt grateful for. No need to keep his loot colder.

Inside, he stopped and surveyed the contents of the room.

More than a dozen boxes lined the walls on both sides—some stacked two or three high. He sauntered over to a container to his right and paused, then peeled up one of the flaps.

A yellow glimmer caught his eye from within the box, and for a fraction of a second he caught himself staring in wonder, admiring the treasure.

Within the box, atop a cushion of loose straw, sat a golden necklace from the Scythian Empire. Several flat gold rectangles attached to the matching loop. Each of the ornaments displayed a figure of a god or hero. Morovski wasn't sure which. And he didn't care.

All he cared about was the revenue it would bring him.

He strolled around the room, casually inspecting other items until he'd seen everything he felt compelled to.

Kostya stood in the open doorway looking like a chef staring at the toughest critic in the world, hoping for a scrap of approval.

"Looks like it's all here," Morovski stated. "Well done, Arshavin."

Kostya didn't display the relief he felt course through his body. Instead, he stiffened with pride. "Thank you, sir."

"You've chosen an excellent location to hide these things until we can make an arrangement with the buyer."

"Do you have a time frame yet?"

The colonel shook his head, looking down at the concrete floor with its many stains, scuff marks, and gouges. "No. I wanted to make certain everything was intact. Not that I doubted you for a second, Kostya."

He used the man's first name to disarm any doubts that may have lingered in Arshavin's mind.

"I would expect nothing less, sir. You are thorough in every task you take on. Why would this be any different."

Morovski offered a smile and walked toward the man. He patted him on the shoulder and looked into his eyes. "That's why you are my second," he said. "The greatest military leaders in history had dependable right hands, men such as yourself. You're an invaluable asset, Kostya."

"Thank you, sir," Arshavin said. As hardened as he was, through countless battles in war, he blushed at the kind words from his commander.

Kostya had been at the man's side since he'd finished officer training. He couldn't imagine being assigned to anyone else. He knew the weight of the words uttered by Morovski. The man didn't hand out compliments to everyone.

"Soon," Morovski said as he stepped out of the cooler, "we will be rich men." He pried his eyes from his second-in-command and panned the room, making eye contact with the rest of his guard who'd accompanied them into the building. "We will all be rich."

His head bobbed with intense sincerity. "Every one of you has remained loyal to me. We have bled together. Lost brothers together. And you have never questioned my command. Not once." The colonel paused for a second. "Despite the fact that what we do here is off the record."

When the colonel chuckled at his statement, the rest of the men joined in. The Russian Federation president had no idea what they were up to, nor would he. Morovski's men had made a pact. No one outside this unit would know what they'd done, and what they were going to do.

The men trusted their commander, and he—in turn—trusted them.

Technically, they hadn't done anything illegal. Their mission had been to take the city. Was it wrong for the colonel and the men under his command to take a little detour?

None in the room thought so.

Morovski turned to Kostya. "Set up a patrol around the clock. I want this building watched every second of the day. And make sure this place doesn't take any friendly fire. The last thing we need is to get blown up by our own."

"Yes, sir. I'll divide up the men into shifts right away."

The colonel bobbed his head once. "Excellent." He looked out at the rest of the men next. "Find the warmest room in the building to bunk down for the next few nights. I don't anticipate any trouble getting the buyer to confirm a rendezvous, but due to the nature of this foolish war, we may have to wait for the opportune moment."

The men all nodded their understanding.

Most of them didn't want to be in Ukraine. None had ever vocalized dissent against their president's orders, but Morovski could see it in their eyes. So could Lieutenant Colonel Arshavin.

Morovski wasn't sure how many of the men knew the true motive behind the president's audacious plan. But he and Arshavin knew exactly what was going on. It didn't take a genius to see the long play here.

The egomaniac had attacked a sovereign nation, unprovoked. While Morovski had no love for the Ukrainian people, as he'd displayed several times in the last few weeks, they played their part in the grand production unfolding on the international stage.

Their country provided much-needed resources to the entirety of Europe, including Russia.

Morovski found it baffling that so many millions, especially in Western Europe and North America, couldn't see the motive.

By cutting off Ukraine from the rest of the world, Russia could effectively starve Europe into submission.

Submission for what, Morovski did not know. He had a few guesses, but none of that mattered. By the time it was all over, he would be retired with commendations, and a payday that would last the rest of his life. He huffed at the thought of the pittance of the military pension he'd be paid compared to the wealth he'd soon have after fencing the wares they'd stolen from the museum.

Meanwhile, Europe would descend into anarchy as the many flaccid governments failed to feed what would be their millions of starving people. Social unrest would erupt into all-out violence. The leaders would beg the United States for help. Being the largest agricultural producer in the world, America would normally have the resources to ease the suffering.

Except recent economic instability in the States had caused skyrocketing inflation. Gas prices continued to rise as well, in no small part due to Russia's incursion into Ukraine.

While the majority of Europe starved to death, the Americans would sit on their stores of grain and meat and recite the immortal words of Marie Antoinette, "Let them eat cake."

It was, Morovski thought, ironic.

Starvation had been the unseen ally that spared Moscow from invasion more than once throughout history. Now it would be the tool of their triumph.

At least the president's triumph.

The colonel knew that, eventually, Europe would turn on its American allies. Their requests would turn to demands, and those demands would ferment into threats. Eventually, they would all be at each other's throats. More importantly, they wouldn't have the supplies or the money to mount an assault on Russia. By the time they figured out the game, it would all be over.

Morovski and his men would be heroes. And the president would never know of his minor indiscretion here in the heart of what used to be called Kievan Rus', the motherland of motherlands for many Slavs. Not even when he and his men were sipping vodka on a sunny beach somewhere far away.

The colonel turned to Kostya. "I'll call the German and set up the meeting. Hopefully, it shouldn't be more than a few days."

"He'll want us to deliver the goods," Kostya said.

Morovski had already considered that probability. He agreed with a grunt. "Yes, I'm sure he will. Men like him are too soft for the horrors of war. Still, I would prefer to keep the stash here. Less chance of an incident that way."

"Agreed."

"Then again, we may not have a choice. It isn't as if the market for these things is vast. Only a few people would be willing to take the risk, and spend the money."

"Yes," Kostya added. "No public exhibits for stolen Ukrainian artifacts. Private displays only."

"Correct. You and the men get ready for nightfall. Get the patrols organized, and have the men get set up where they can eat and sleep." His eyes narrowed as he gleamed at Arshavin. "We won't have to eat the army's prepackaged food much longer, Kostya. Soon, we'll be dining like the tsars themselves."

5

Dak hovered over the blackjack table for half an hour, cautiously spending the money he'd been given by Tamara so it would last longer.

He didn't particularly enjoy the game, nor did he hate it. For the time being, the table merely offered a perfect view of the door so he would know exactly when Lesma Lebedev appeared.

Funnily enough, Dak was up four grand when the stocky Russian walked through the door. Will, on the other hand, was already sitting on the sidelines at the bar. He'd blasted through his thousand in less than ten minutes at the craps table.

Dak scooped up his chips after winning one more hand to make it a cool five thousand in profit, then steered away from the game as Lebedev surveyed the room with two of his goons next to him—one on either side.

The second the big Russian spotted Dak, a grin spread across the man's fleshy face. His eyes squinted with the smile, and he immediately left his entourage behind to descend the stairs and make his way across the gaming floor.

He met Dak in front of the steps leading up to where Tamara seemed to perpetually sit.

Six feet away, Lesma approached with his arms wide. "Dak Harper," he announced—a little louder than Dak would have preferred. "It is so good to see you again, my friend."

Lesma embraced Dak with an engulfing hug and clapped him on the back three times. Dak returned the gesture. Thankfully, Lesma didn't do the kissing-on-each-cheek thing that Russians and many other Europeans offered upon greeting someone.

The two stepped back from each other. Lesma sized up his friend. "You look good. Keeping in shape, I see."

"Always on the move," Dak confessed.

Even though Lesma was a mob guy, Dak knew him to be honest—as honest as a criminal could be. He had a strange trust with the man —a bond that had been forged in the most unusual of circumstances.

Dak had watched as Lesma ordered the execution of his own son —a degenerate gambler, woman-abuser, and all-around bad seed. While the action may have been extreme, Dak understood it from the Russian's perspective.

He ran a business, one that required his enemies to respect him. His son was ruining his reputation, and rivals were starting to notice.

Lesma had given his son every chance to change his ways, but in the end the spoiled brat refused. And so, in a long-standing Russian tradition, he took an unexpected swan dive from the window of his apartment building. At least that's how the cops saw it—a suicide of a tortured soul.

Of course, many of them were on the take from Lesma's organization, so getting them to turn a blind eye to the incident required little effort.

"What brings you to Mumbai, my friend? And to what do I owe the pleasure of your request?"

"You didn't waste any time responding to Tamara's message."

He laughed from his big belly up to his jaw. "I am a powerful man, yes. But no one refuses Tamara. And besides, it is always good to be on the side of a strong, beautiful woman, huh?" The laughter continued and he jabbed out with his left elbow as he might if they were standing by a water cooler on their coffee break.

"Words to live by."

Will left his perch at the bar and sauntered over to the two men, arriving at the same time as Lesma's two guards.

"Lesma, this is my friend Will," Dak said. "If you ever need high-tech weaponry, he's your guy."

Will flashed a *come on, man* look at his friend as he extended his right hand out.

Lesma looked at Dak, wondering if he was serious. Dak merely pouted his lips and nodded.

"Really?" Lesma grasped Will's hand and shook it vigorously. "I will remember that."

"He's joking," Will said, pointing his glowering eyes toward Dak. "Aren't you." It wasn't a question.

"Oh, sure. Joking," Dak said with a wink to the big Russian.

"Ah," Lesma said. "Yes. Joking." He returned the wink.

"I hate you," Will chirped at Dak, then withdrew his hand.

Dak scanned the room, particularly the nearest tables. "Perhaps we should join the lady up there to continue our conversation."

Lesma nodded in agreement. "Of course. It would be rude not to say hello to our hostess."

The sounds of the casino accompanied the five men up the stairs where Tamara lounged with her usual drink in hand.

She offered a quaint, almost insincere smile at Lesma as he approached.

"Lesma," she said unceremoniously.

He, in turn, grinned back at her as pleasantly as possible. "It is good to see you again, Lady Tamara."

"I'm sure it is."

The taunt blew right over Lesma, and he helped himself to a seat on the sofa to her right.

Dak and Will took seats in the club chairs while Lesma's guards took positions near Tamara's by the top of the steps.

No telling what those four could talk about, Dak thought.

Tamara called her drink runner over and ordered a vodka for Lesma and a couple of neat whiskeys for the two Americans.

"You have to love a woman who knows your drink," Lesma blurted happily to the two seated men.

Tamara rolled her eyes, tolerating the oaf with a visibly herculean effort.

"So, he's here, Dak. You going to tell him what you want?"

Lesma looked to Dak, his grin fading, the eyes glazing over with wonder.

"Right into it then," Dak said. "Sure." He faced Lesma and leaned forward, planting his elbows on his knees and clasping his hands together. "About a month ago, as I'm sure you're aware, the Russian military invaded Ukraine."

Lesma snorted. Derision in his eyes mirrored the response. "Foolishness. I have no fondness for the Russian president. He's part of the reason I left."

"I wondered. And I'm glad to hear you say that."

"Oh?"

"During the attack on Kyiv, one group of the Russian army was tasked with an unusual mission." Dak paused for three heartbeats before he continued. "This unit detoured to the Ukrainian national history museum."

Lesma's brow furrowed. "Why would they do that? A museum isn't a military target."

"Like that matters to them," Will piped up.

The big Russian agreed with a grunt and a nod.

"The unit wasn't there on any kind of tactical mission. It was a heist."

Lesma's expression changed to one of curiosity. "A heist? What were they trying to steal? A bunch of old bowls and utensils?"

"Unfortunately, there was more in the museum than that. Which, by the way, are still extremely valuable." He glanced at Will before going on. "The Russian unit captured the museum curator and tortured her for information."

"Information?" Lesma asked. "What kind of information could a museum curator have that the military would want?"

"What she knew had nothing to do with military intel. The

museum housed some of the most valuable artifacts and cultural relics from Ukraine's history. We haven't been able to figure out exactly *what* was stolen, but the Russians took everything."

Lesma considered Dak's words for nearly a minute before he spoke. He rubbed his chin and lower lip as he thought.

He drew a deep breath and exhaled slowly. "This does not surprise me," he said. "The regime currently in power has many of the same qualities we've seen in tyrants before. The Russian president is mad with ambition. Stealing another nation's treasures—especially a nation he doesn't consider legitimately sovereign—is fair game for someone like him."

"You'd think it would be some kind of war crime," Will said.

"You'd think," Dak agreed. He turned back to Lesma. "We need your help finding the treasure that was taken from the museum."

Lesma huffed. Then he looked at Will, laughed, then returned his gaze to Dak as if waiting for the punch line. "Are you serious?" His face soured.

"Yeah. Dead serious." Dak only waited a second before continuing. "We need someone who has connections in the underworld, someone with international ties."

"Particularly to Russia, huh?"

"Da."

The response in Lesma's native tongue caused the slightest of smirks to tick the right edge of his lips.

"I'm sorry. Are you suggesting that we"—he extended an index finger and circled it around in the air between the three of them —"take on the Russian army to try and locate a treasure they stole from Ukraine?"

"Yep," Dak said.

"I suppose I'll get to keep some of the treasure."

"No, but I'm sure there will be a sizable reward in it for you. Along with the gratitude of the Ukrainian people."

"Pfft. Yes, I'll sleep so much better at night." He chuckled. "That was sarcasm right there, Americans!" He clapped his hands together and laughed at himself while Tamara rolled her eyes behind his back.

"Yeah, you... laid it on pretty thick. This is important, Lesma," Dak steered. "We need to find the stolen artifacts. A woman's life depends on it. Heaven knows what she's already been through."

Lesma's expression softened. "Yes. The military, they will do things... horrible things to people."

"All armies are like that," Will chimed. "Not every soldier, but armies. Yeah." A distant torment raged in the depths of his eyes.

Dak noticed it, but he already knew what his friend hid deep down inside.

Lesma agreed with a nod. "I suppose you are right." He let out a sigh. "I still know some people in the military. One of my cousins is an officer. I can find out where he's located. Last I heard, he was in the southern part of Ukraine. If he's still alive, he may know something about where the artifacts were taken. But it's a long shot, Dak."

"Better than no shot," Dak countered with a smile.

"I have some contacts in Ukraine who are nonmilitary, you might say. Perhaps they've heard something. I know a few who deal in just about everything. I will check with them first thing in the morning."

"Thank you, Lesma," Dak offered and bowed his head. "I appreciate it."

"I will help you, Dak, but even if I can get you the information you need, you'll still have to find a way into Ukraine, or if the artifacts already made it into Russia," he chuffed, "then you're looking at a different problem."

"What? You don't think we should waltz into Moscow and demand the Ukrainian artifacts be returned?" Dak smirked as he finished the sentence. As if on cue, a roar from one of the blackjack tables thundered through the room.

Lesma looked at him like he was crazy for a second, then laughed. He turned to Tamara while pointing at Dak. "This guy is funny."

She merely offered a demure smile and a slight nod.

Dak continued. "It's highly possible the artifacts are already in Moscow, but we need to follow the breadcrumbs first, which means Ukraine."

"Which means potentially diving headfirst into a war zone," Will grumbled.

"Your friend is right," Lesma agreed. "Very dangerous place right now, Ukraine. I would not advise going there." He laughed again. "I don't even like visiting there when there is no war."

"I know it will be dangerous," Dak said. "Normally, I would navigate this sort of thing on my own. I'm used to conflicts. Especially the warfare kind." He flicked his eyes from one man to the other and back.

"But you have connections in Ukraine that I don't have," Dak continued. "In any mission I ever ran in the Army, I did everything I could to utilize locals for intel. You're as local as I can get. And I trust you, Lesma. That's why you're here."

He saw the humility flash through the big Russian's eyes a second before the man set his jaw and stiffened his spine.

"You are an honorable man, Dak Harper," Lesma said. "Not many people trust me in this world."

"Same here," Will added. "Not a lot of love for gunrunners going around, even if we're selling weapons to the good guys." His head bobbed. "I'm in for whatever you need, too."

Dak smirked. "I didn't realize you were on the fence."

Will snorted. "You didn't tell me what we were doing."

"Had a lot on my mind."

"I don't have any connections in Ukraine," Tamara interrupted. "But you know you can count on me for whatever you need, Dak."

"I appreciate that. From all of you." Dak met each pair of eyes with a sweeping glance. "I have a contact in a covert agency who can lend us a hand. She's in Poland right now, mostly observing the situation in Ukraine and making sure no one sneaks around via the Polish border."

"Covert agency?" Lesma asked? "CIA?"

Dak shook his head. "No. She's in a different building. Different state, actually. Her branch is preventative and reactive counterterrorism."

"Reactive?" Will wondered.

"Yes," Dak said, a grim tone shadowing his words. "As in if someone hits us, we retaliate in kind. Such retaliations cause enemies to think twice. But the larger counterterrorism operations also keep an eye on suspicious characters."

Will shifted uncomfortably. "How suspicious?"

Dak flashed him dark expression. "If you have to ask, then you're that kind of suspicious."

Will swallowed hard.

"I'm kidding, buddy. Relax. They're not watching you." He waited until Will's expression eased, then added, "Yet."

Dak swept the group again with his shamrock eyes. "She's going to get us into Russia. After that, we're on our own. That's where you come in, Lesma."

The big Russian nodded. "Okay. Let's do it. I've never had a chance to be a hero before. Sounds like an interesting plot twist."

Dak chuckled.

Will rolled his eyes. "If you can get us in there, I can get us the guns," he said. "Gonna be weird being on the receiving end of my own product."

"I have access to a private jet," Tamara offered. "I'm not sure you can fly it into Ukraine right now, but if it can help you get to Poland, it's yours."

Dak hadn't expected that last bit. "Thank you, Lady Tamara. I appreciate it." He faced the others. "We leave tomorrow morning as soon as her plane can be ready. If that's okay." He looked to Tamara.

"I'll make sure it's ready."

Dak thanked her with a single nod, then addressed the two men. "Get a good night's rest, boys. Tomorrow is going to be a long day."

"I'll say," Will chimed. "By the way. Who is this contact?"

"She works for the Shadow Cell, a branch of Axis. Her name is Liz Morrow."

6

"I've been expecting your call, Colonel." The German's voice sounded colder than the walk-in cooler Morovski had left earlier.

He stood outside the plant as his men scurried around setting up tents and makeshift barracks on the inside of the facility's perimeter fence.

Looking out across the scene, he drew a breath before answering. "Yes, well, I'm sure you can appreciate that these things take time."

"Oh? I was under the impression you had already secured the goods."

"Collected, yes. But we wouldn't want any of our comrades to get wind of the stash. And there are the Ukrainians to consider."

"I'm surprised you're having such a hard time with them." The snide remark stuck Morovski like a dagger in the side, but he resisted reacting audibly to the barb.

"Yes. It would seem our president underestimated their defensive response. And the rest of the world is bent on keeping them an independent nation—sending them weapons and munitions every week."

"If the rest of the world really wanted the conflict to end," the German said, "it would already be over."

Morovski knew this to be true. The combined might of all the NATO nations, and others who lamented Russia's incursion, could have ended the war in weeks had they committed their formidable arsenals to the fight.

But the colonel knew that wouldn't happen. None of those countries possessed a spine anymore, even the United States. He knew that they, especially America, wouldn't send in their military. If they did, then China would respond in kind, or worse, invade Taiwan and thrust the United States into a war on two fronts.

The rest of the world followed that lead, happy to slap the Ukrainian stickers on their cars or perhaps hang the flag in their windows, but when it came to actually doing something—sending their loved ones into a war—none had the stomach for it.

"I didn't realize you wanted to talk about military strategy on this call," Morovski detoured.

"Now, now, Colonel," the German replied. "There's no need to get testy. I know you don't agree with the invasion and its purpose. I would assume your men feel the same."

"We are one," Morovski answered resolute.

"As you should be. And I am glad for it. We mustn't have any loose lips for this... arrangement."

"There are none. I've made sure of that. Every one of my men is loyal to me. Not the president or anyone else. And they will be well compensated for their loyalty."

"I'm glad to hear it. So, you have the gold?"

"Yes," Morovski said, irritated that the man even asked. He wouldn't have called if he didn't have the gold. "It's in a safe location."

"Are you still in Ukraine?"

"Our location is undisclosed."

"So, that is a yes. I'm curious why you haven't attempted to relocate the goods to somewhere less dangerous."

Morovski had expected this and was prepared. "This area hasn't seen battle, and I doubt that it will. Resistance here is thin, at best. The locals would rather run and hide than fight. Most of them left town in the days leading up to the invasion. Any who stayed joined the Ukrainian army and went off to support other cities. There is nothing of strategic value here, other than a staging point for more attacks on Kyiv."

The German hummed thoughtfully. "I must admit, I have wondered what your president's plan is. You took the Ukrainian capital, then withdrew. Strange."

Morovski kept his thoughts to himself. He knew exactly what was happening. The plan was never to completely occupy Ukraine. Russia didn't have the resources or the manpower to take over that entire nation and maintain it as the Soviet Union had done for decades. Doing so would stretch the Russian forces and its economy to the breaking point.

But setting up a military embargo against Europe; that took far less effort. Sure, some soldiers died. And while the rest of the world called Russian leaders bullies, denouncing every atrocity, the food on their tables dwindled, as did the oil fueling their cars and transport trucks.

Perhaps the German was one of the billions of fools out there who didn't know what was really going on. Morovski had a hard time believing that. From what he knew about the German, the guy was a savvy businessman. Beyond that, he had connections to some of the most powerful people in the world.

So the stories went, anyway.

"Who knows what the president is up to," Morovski misled. "Fortunately, I've been given a long leash. Which brings me back to the point of this call. We need to set up a rendezvous."

"So it would seem," the German agreed. "I'm sure you understand that I have no intention of coming to Ukraine to make the pickup."

"I assumed not."

"And I'm certainly not going to meet you in Russia. Too many uncontrolled variables there as well."

"Agreed. Not to mention the last place I want to see right now is Moscow."

"Yes," the German purred. "I doubt your president would appreciate you stealing a treasure from Ukraine and not letting him take a cut."

"He wouldn't take a cut," Morovski argued. "He would want it all. He's greedier than the tsars of old."

"Yes. I believe you're right. So, where then shall we set our little meeting?"

Morovski had been thinking about this ever since they removed the artifacts from the museum. There weren't any good solutions. The surrounding borders were on high alert against any incursion from Russian forces and would treat even the most benign entry as an act of hostility.

This meant he and his men would have to find a way around the usual entry points—wherever they chose to go. It wasn't as if they could simply put on some disguises and walk across the border. And planes would be tracked.

Poland wasn't an option. Every centimeter of their border was being watched around the clock, and by more nations than just the Poles.

He knew people in Belarus, but his connections there were also connected to the Russian president. And the Belarusian leader's loyalty to the Russian president was well known to most.

Moldova was an option, but there too were too many people loyal to the Russian president. Not to mention that the border there had effectively been reverse-blocked by the invading army to prevent escape by the Ukrainian refugees.

He'd pored over maps, both in his mind and with his eyes, and it seemed there was only one option. It was one he didn't like, but there weren't many options at this point.

"I suggest that we meet in Romania," Morovski offered. "Their border is more difficult to monitor, particularly in the mountains. A small unit like ours can get through on the trails, then find transport once we're in."

"You'll go on foot?" The German sounded surprised.

"If we try to take the roads, we'll be spotted. Flying isn't an option. Once we're across the border, we won't have to go far to get vehicles."

"It sounds as if you've already decided your entry point."

"I have." Morovski thought the man might offer some assistance in providing the aforementioned transportation, but the German added nothing else. "From there, it's up to you where you would like us to meet."

The German thought silently for thirty seconds before responding. During the quiet, Morovski continued observing his men as they set up camp for the night.

"Budapest," the German finally said. The capital of Hungary was a stomping ground for underground arms deals and any number of other seedy activities. While on the surface it was a vibrant, bustling city, few of the citizens knew of what happened in the shadows, and the international players involved.

Morovski felt both relief and confusion. He'd been worried the man might suggest they drive all the way to Berlin, or whatever German town he called home. Budapest was less than halfway. But he'd said Romania.

"Hungary?" the colonel asked, just to be certain he'd heard correctly. "You'd rather meet there than in Romania?"

"Yes. I trust that is acceptable." He paused but didn't wait for an answer. "I have contacts in Budapest, more so than in Romania. And it's a good halfway point. While I do appreciate that Romania isn't landlocked, I don't trust the Russian navy in that region. Too risky."

"Understandable." Morovski's response was less than sincere. Romania was the perfect place to do a deal like this. And he knew for a fact that the Russian naval presence off the coast was nil, at least for now. But he was in no position to argue, not with the only buyer he had for his haul.

"I wonder, though," the German said, "how you think you're going to get across the Romanian border without arousing suspicion. You may encounter trouble."

"We won't be dressed as Russian soldiers. We'll be disguised as Ukrainian refugees. No one turns away refugees."

"Excellent. Then I will contact you with the details of the exact location and time. Do not be late."

"We won't."

7

The knock at the door sent everyone in the suite jumping out of their seats. Except Dak. He merely turned his head toward the door with little affect.

Lesma and Will had been on edge since they'd arrived in Warsaw, though Dak wasn't sure why. An inkling trickled through his mind that maybe it was because the men hadn't been on a mission like this before. Will had done stuff shadier than this, though, so Dak didn't understand his friend's trepidation.

Dak rolled his eyes and stood up, straightening his Doors T-shirt as he shook his head. "Would you two relax? It's just Liz."

"How do you know?" Lesma asked. "I knew I should have brought my men with me."

Dak snorted, making sure the derision didn't miss the big Russian. He hammered it home with a curious glare and two raised eyebrows.

"Your men would draw too much attention." He walked over to the door and unlocked the deadbolt. "Besides, she's the only one who knows we're here."

"You sure about that?" Will countered.

Dak did everything he could to keep from rolling his eyes. "Did you tell anyone?"

Will stumbled over his answer. "No. Obviously."

"I have also told no one. Not even my men. They only know I left the country on business."

Dak opened the door wide to reveal a tall woman with magma-colored curly tangles hanging down to the black jacket covering her shoulders. She pinched a blue folder in her fingers.

Lesma caught himself staring at the beautiful woman, from her matte-black boots all the way up through the matching leggings to the top of her head.

"Sorry," Dak offered. "My friends are a little paranoid."

He stepped aside and stuck his arm out behind him as if to show the way.

She replied with an understanding grin and entered the room with the graceful ease of a ballerina, but her purposeful stride gave hint to the woman's true and lethal nature.

"Thanks," she said, her accent brushed by her Southern upbringing.

Dak closed the door behind her and locked it again. When he turned around, he caught his two friends gawking—probably accidental, but gawking nonetheless.

"Excuse these two," Dak said as he shifted to her side. "There's clearly something wrong with them. I'm Dak Harper. Thanks for coming on such short notice."

She shrugged and tilted her head to the side at the same time. "Happy to help out. Any friend of Emily."

"Emily?" Will blurted. "Who is Emily?"

His voice implied something romantic.

"Don't be an idiot," Dak replied, immediately returning his focus to Liz. "If you're working with Axis, then I know you're the best. And for this gig, that's exactly the kind of help I need."

"Then what are these two doing here?"

Dak's lips cracked into a grin. His shoulders shook as he giggled, but he couldn't contain it and outright laughed within three seconds of the comment.

Will crossed his arms over his chest. His head sagged toward the right shoulder. "Oh, so she's got jokes."

Lesma appeared lost. "Jokes? What is the jokes?"

"Nothing, Lesma. She's just messing with you."

"Messing with me?"

"So," Liz said, planting a palm on each hip. "You're Lesma Lebedev."

"I am," he took a step forward and offered his hand.

She took it and gripped it much harder than he expected, but instead of being caught off guard, he looked pleasantly surprised. "A strong handshake from such a beautiful woman. It's a shame you have a job. I could use someone like you in my organization."

"Yeah, I try to avoid criminal activity when it's not endorsed by the government."

He chuckled. "All government activity is criminal."

It was her turn to snort a laugh. "Touché."

She turned to Will and tilted her head to the side, letting her auburn hair drop over the right shoulder. "And you're Will Collins. Nice to meet you." She offered her hand.

He hesitated. "Did Dak tell you who I am?"

"No," she answered with a shake of her head. "He didn't need to. We know who you are and what you do."

His eyelids stretched open a little.

"Don't worry," she said. "You help the good guys. So, you're not on our list."

His shoulders sagged with relief. He took the proffered hand and shook it firmly. "I guess with friends like you, huh?" Will flung a skeptical glance at Dak.

Liz surveyed the room with a passing look. "Nice suite," she said, noting the white drapes that hung from a window stretching from one side of the room to the other. The city spread out beyond the glass, people busily going about their day in their cars or on bikes.

Still more filled the sidewalks—the rows of them looked like disjointed serpents slithering along the concrete.

Inside the room, a black fabric couch faced a flatscreen on the wall. A king-size bed occupied the space near the window in the front corner.

Liz directed her attention to the black dining table, where four chairs were arranged around it. Maps of Europe, Russia, and Ukraine littered the surface, along with pictures of several different people.

She slid the folder onto the table in an empty spot and briefly scanned over the maps. "Looks like you boys started without me."

Dak smirked. "Wanted to at least look like we knew what we were doing, you being a pro and all."

She appreciated the compliment with creased lips. "You're a pro too, Dak."

"Not anymore. I left all that behind."

Liz passed over the table's contents once more then met his gaze again. "You're doing a bang-up job of that, too. From the looks of it, I'd say you've left nothing."

"Private enterprise now."

"Yeah?"

"I work for a... philanthropist." Dak wasn't lying, but it was the best way to describe his employer's role. "He pays me to recover artifacts that were stolen, or that turned up after being missing a long time."

"And drags us into it," Will added.

Dak snorted. "He's just mad because one time he got strapped to a chair with a bomb under it."

"A bomb?" Liz asked.

"Yeah."

"Mad doesn't even begin to describe it," Will interjected.

"You're here, aren't you?"

Will rolled his eyes.

"Was this the thing in the ocean I heard about?" Liz wondered.

"Yep. Good times," Dak said.

"No," Will argued. "Not good times. Not good at all. We nearly got blown to pieces."

"But didn't."

Lesma could only watch the exchange going back and forth like the most awkward and hilarious tennis match he'd ever seen.

"Anyway," Dak continued, "all water under the chair... I mean bridge, now."

"You think you're funny," Will jabbed.

Lesma laughed. "I think he's funny, too."

Dak let out a chuckle at the big Russian's honesty. "I don't want to waste your time, Liz. I know how busy you are monitoring a million things right now."

She nodded. "Yeah, we are really busy. The director sent me here as soon as word of a potential invasion came through the wire. We've been watching the borders since then. There isn't much we can do from the agency perspective. We take orders directly from the president, as you know, and she hasn't greenlit any operations in Ukraine."

"Greenlit?" Lesma asked, a perplexed look on his face.

"You don't want to know," Dak responded.

"Right now," Liz went on, "we're on guard duty." She sighed. "So, whatcha got for me? Em didn't give me much to go on."

"I didn't give her much to go on, either."

She perked up, suddenly excited. "You mean I'm going to know more about something than Emily Starks?"

"Don't get too jazzed," Will cautioned.

Dak ignored him. "When the Russians invaded Kyiv, one of their units broke off from the main group and veered here," Dak pinpointed the location of the museum on the map of the city. "This is where Ukraine's National Museum of History is located."

"Museum?"

Dak confirmed with a nod and kept going. "Questions after. They broke in and caught the curator, then tortured her."

Liz bit her lip to keep from interrupting again.

"They were after a treasure horde worth no telling how much.

She'd hidden the loot, but they found it anyway. Now she's missing, and so is the gold."

She listened until he was done, made sure he didn't have anything to add by waiting two seconds, then nodded. "So, a unit of Russian soldiers stole a bunch of gold from a museum. And you're going to try to get it back?"

"Yep."

"You realize the curator is probably dead, right?"

"I hope not."

Her right eyebrow flicked upward. "You can hope all you want, Dak, but you know as well as I do what happened to her."

"We don't know anything yet. Until we do, we proceed under the assumption that she's alive."

She sucked in a long breath and exhaled. "I like your optimism." Looking down at the map, she bit her bottom lip. "So, what do you need from me?"

Dak's eyes darted to Will, then Lesma, then to Liz. She caught the subtle gesture but said nothing.

"We need you to get us into Ukraine."

8

For a second, Liz didn't respond. Then her eyebrows slowly climbed, pinching together to wrinkle her forehead. "I'm sorry. For a second there, it sounded like you said you want me to get you *into* Ukraine."

"I did," Dak said.

"Dak, Ukraine is a warzone now. Getting in, while difficult, isn't the biggest issue."

"Getting out is. I know."

"Right. So, you see the dilemma."

Dak picked up a glass from the table, poured water into it from a carafe, and took a sip. "Yep," he answered after swallowing. "Which is why you're here. We need someone who can get us in, and make sure getting out is easy."

"I can't get you an exfil if that's what you're asking for." She kicked her right hip out to the side.

"We have that side of things covered," Dak explained. "Getting in is the problem."

"Oh? How do you have those things covered?"

The other two men listened closely to the conversation. It was Lesma who spoke first.

"I have connections in Ukraine. Once we're in, they will provide us with transportation."

"And I have a few tricks up my sleeves, too," Will offered.

Liz listened to them, but her doubts tugged on her eyes and jaw like bricks on strings. "Look, I don't doubt that you boys have some sort of underground contacts that can help you out with this, but you're forgetting one vital piece to all this."

"Which is?" Dak pressed.

"What if they're not in Ukraine anymore. It's entirely possible they went back to Russia with the loot. And if that's the case, there's no way you're going to ever get it back... or the curator."

"We've considered that," Dak said. "I don't think they're going to Russia."

Liz's face tightened into a frown. "No?"

"They can't risk it. If they go back, then all that treasure will be confiscated by the Russian president. He may claim it as a war prize or could very well simply try to auction it off on the black market. I don't think that's what happened."

"And what are you basing this on?"

"A hunch."

Surprise lifted her eyebrows again. "Seriously? You're basing an entire operation, one that could—no, will probably get the three of you killed—on a hunch?"

"It makes sense," Lesma defended. "Many of the Russian people do not agree with this war. They think it is foolish, led by the whims of a madman. I agree. This heist was not by order of the president. It was a rogue element of the army."

"Based on that insight," Dak continued, "we believe there are a couple of options. One, they find a buyer or already have one, and arrange a meeting in Ukraine. Somewhere quiet."

"Unlikely," Liz stated. "The reason I'm here is it's not easy to get in without clearance. Unless you're going in as a volunteer for the Ukrainian army. What's the other option?"

"They leave via one of the other borders."

Liz pondered that one for a good ten seconds, her eyes searching the white ceiling as if it would cough up the answer. "They can't go to the sea. Not in Ukraine, anyway. That entire area of Crimea is blocked by the Russian navy. No one is getting in or out. Including their own. Unless, of course, they bartered with an admiral or something."

Dak shook his head. "I don't think that's what they'll do. The fewer people involved, the better. They can't risk any loose ends. And people love to brag. Can't keep their mouths shut."

"True. So, where then? They're not coming into Poland; I can guarantee that. We've got that border locked down tighter than a chastity belt."

"What about Belarus?" Will asked. He pointed to one of the maps on the table, indicating the border between Ukraine and Belarus.

"I don't think so," Liz said. "That leader is tight with the Russian president. If anything remotely suspicious happens there, the Russians know about it."

"Sounds like the bully's annoying little sidekick from the school playground," Will chirped.

"So, Belarus is out," Dak said. He ran his finger down the map to the next country. "What about Moldova?"

Liz leaned over the table and inspected the borders while she considered the possibility.

"Maybe," she said. "It's an option, for sure. But the only way out is into Romania. No coastline if they're trying to get the goods out via boat."

"I wouldn't trust going by water," Will injected. "Again, Russian naval activity in that region makes things sketchy—even for merchant vessels."

"And the Russian president has many loyalists in Moldova," Lesma added. "Not as many as in Belarus, but it would be cause for concern."

Dak inhaled deeply and pressed his finger to the map. "That leaves Slovakia, Hungary, and Romania."

"The first two have smaller borders. And security is pretty tight there. Romania, on the other hand, has mountains along their border with Ukraine. Would be easy to disappear there and slip across. Once they're in Romania, tracking them will be difficult."

"Which means we need to find them before they get there," Dak stated. He looked to Liz.

"How do you propose we do that?" she asked.

Dak had been pondering that question since before she arrived. Tracking the rogue Russian unit would be like trying to catch a ghost. Ukraine wasn't a small country, and there were plenty of places the unit could have blended in.

But if the group of thieves was trying to stay hidden from the rest of the Russian military, they would be where the rest of the army wasn't. Dak also knew that play had a limited time frame.

The Russian high command wouldn't allow one of their units to simply break away and do their own thing for long—unless it was a condoned covert operation. Based on his guess, Dak didn't believe this was one of those.

These guys were trying to stay out of the spotlight as long as possible. A few ideas bubbled to the surface of his mind about how to locate the rogue squad. Satellites could be useful, but they'd have to cover so much territory that finding the Russian unit would be more difficult than finding a pebble in a gravel pile.

They needed a way to narrow down possible locations, preferably within a fifty-mile radius.

"I don't suppose Axis does any misinformation ops, do they?" Dak asked with a mischievous grin.

Liz crossed her arms. "What did you have in mind? Other branches are already doing that in Russia. News reports are constantly flooding the country with information about how badly the war is going—although that's hardly misinformation."

"I'm sure some of the info is being embellished."

"Of course," she said with a proud smile. "Never waste a good opportunity to turn a tyrant's people against him."

Dak nodded.

"So, what are you thinking?" she pressed. "I'm guessing you don't want to misinform the Ukrainian people. They're being given every positive piece of news possible."

"No, definitely not them." He inclined his head and rubbed his chin. "We need to flush out this rogue unit. My guess is they're hiding out somewhere, probably under the guise that they needed to chase down some Ukrainian militants. Maybe it's time we send a message to the Russians and let them know one of their own has gone AWOL."

Dak saw the spark light in her eyes. The light bulb flickered on in the faces of the other two, as well.

"Turn them on their own," Liz realized out loud. "I like the way you think, Harper. Not bad for an Army guy."

He snorted at the playful derision. "We have our moments."

"You wouldn't mind if I use your laptop, would you?"

Dak motioned to the computer sitting on the edge of the table's far corner. "Be my guest. VPN is already active."

"I would expect nothing less," she said in what some might have misconstrued as flirtatious.

Liz moved over to the laptop, Will stepping out of her way to let her pass.

She eased into the seat and ran her finger across the track pad to bring the screen to life. A moment later, it illuminated and displayed the Fox Sports homepage.

Liz turned her head deliberately toward Dak, a befuddled expression on her face. "Looks like you've been working hard on this case."

Dak shrugged. "Is it a sin to check the Predators score?"

She sighed and returned her focus to the screen. "I didn't take you for a hockey guy."

"Hockey. Football. Soccer. Baseball. Gotta pass the time somehow."

"And here I thought hunting down stolen artifacts was what you did for that."

"That's my job. No one wants to think about their job all the time."

"Fair enough," she surrendered.

She opened a new tab in the browser as the men crowded around
to watch her work.

"This is going to take me a while," Liz said. "And I'll have to call it
in, so you boys might want to turn on the television and watch some
of that reality television I know you love so much."

Dak laughed.

Will looked offended. "I don't watch that crap."

"You sure?" She eyed him with suspicion. "You look like a *Real
Housewives* kind of guy."

Dak's laughter only heightened. "She's got you pegged, buddy."

"What? You know?" Frustrated, he couldn't think of anything else
to say and so spun around and made for the sofa like a pouting child.

"Look. Now you hurt his feelings." Dak taunted.

Lesma couldn't keep from laughing.

"You guys are hilarious," Will said as he reached for the remote.
He turned on the television and muttered, "I'm an HGTV guy."

Liz snorted and looked over at him.

Will winked as he reclined back into the couch.

"Give me an hour," Liz said.

"Why so long?" Dak joked.

She merely raised her eyes to meet his and said, "I know. Couldn't
have done this forty years ago. Technology is great when it works."

"I look forward to the havoc you're about to cause."

9

Colonel Morovski stormed through the entrance to the factory, blowing by the two guards stationed at the door on either side, his own personal guards rushing to keep up.

He'd been drinking his morning coffee when Kostya called him.

He strode into the temporary war room—one of the old offices in the facility—where his second-in-command had set up several maps on a narrow table, and a secure radio in the corner.

Two laptops sat on top of a desk off to the left.

The tiny room looked like the rest of the place—a relic from the 1950s when the town was bustling.

"What is it?" Morovski demanded. "You sounded urgent."

"It is, sir," Kostya confirmed. "The Marshal wants to speak with you."

The statement sucked the color out of Morovski's face. "The Marshal?"

The Marshal of the Russian Federation was the highest military rank attainable. Morovski's station paled in comparison to the power that man wielded. If he was calling, then it had to be bad.

"He's on the phone in person?" Morovski clarified?

Kostya merely bobbed his head.

"Very well." Morovski calmed his nerves and put on a look of stoic professionalism. "I'll take it alone."

"Yes, sir."

Kostya stepped out of the way to let his commander slip by and then left the room.

When he closed the door behind him, Morovski picked up the phone by the radio and put it to his ear. "Yes, sir?"

"Where are you, Colonel?" The marshal's question, while not entirely unexpected, still sent a shiver down Morovski's spine. He knew the man would know if he was lying. There were only so many ways you could hide.

"Vinnytsia, sir. My men and I pursued a large contingent of militants from the city to this town."

"I don't recall giving you orders to do that. Did those orders come from someone else?"

"No, sir. I gave the order."

"I see."

Morovski didn't miss the hidden message in the man's voice. There was no mistaking—the Marshal did not approve.

"You and your men will return to Kyiv at once and join with Colonel Baranksy's group."

"But, sir, we have the militants surrounded. We only need a little more time—"

"Don't lie to me, Colonel. Do you take me for a fool?"

"No, sir."

"Do you think me stupid?"

"Of course not, sir. But—"

"We received word this morning of a raid on the Ukrainian Museum of National History. Apparently, several priceless items were stolen. This happened about the time you were in Kyiv. Then, mysteriously, you and your team disappeared."

"Disappearing is what we do, sir. You know very well that I have been given a wide berth when it comes to making decisions. It's how we operate. It's how we get things done that no one else wants to do."

"Yes. I'm aware. So, are you saying you know nothing of this theft?"

"That is exactly what I'm saying, Marshal. And I find it disconcerting you would accuse me of such."

The Marshal said nothing for several seconds, and the pause sent a cold chill through Morovski's body.

If the Marshal didn't buy the lie, then their evacuation of Ukraine would be made more tenuous, and much more hurried.

"I apologize, Nikolai. I didn't mean to wrongfully accuse you. We will discover the perpetrators of this and bring them in."

"I hope you do, sir. And apology accepted. If I can be of any assistance in locating this rogue unit, please let me know." Relief filled Morovski's gut.

"Yes. It seems they stole all of the gold from the museum. Of course, when the president found out about the theft, he demanded the unit be brought in. Those items are the property of the Russian Federation now—spoils of war. I assume he wants to put them on public display, but it's possible he will keep them in his private exhibit."

Morovski let the last bit go. There was no chance he'd comment on the president's greed and ego.

"I believe we will eliminate the problem here within the next twenty-four hours, sir. After that, we can double back and search for the traitors."

"Yes. That's what they are. Traitors. Carry on with your operation, Colonel. I expect a full report when it's done."

"Yes, sir," Morovski said calmly.

When the Marshal bade him goodbye, Morovski stood there for a minute holding the dead phone in his hand. His chest swelled and collapsed in dramatic fashion as he simply stood there staring at the desk nearby.

No one dared look into the room through the window partially hidden behind tattered blinds.

"Something isn't right," Morovski muttered to himself "It was too easy." *Or was it?*

He'd noticed the paranoia building up inside him had gotten worse the last few days.

Morovski and his men were in a unique and challenging position. They couldn't trust their own army brethren. And if they ran into the Ukrainians, that would be trouble, too. Without any allies, Morovski's band had no one they could trust except themselves. And that only dumped rocket fuel onto the paranoia flaming in his chest.

He shook his head when the thoughts poked into his mind. That kind of concern was never helpful, and he'd become adept at ignoring such wild thoughts—allowing them to pass from his consciousness into thin air.

Still, something didn't sit right with the way the conversation with the Marshal ended. There'd been a tone in the man's voice—something odd.

He'd spoken to the Marshal routinely. Morovski, while not a general, was treated as if he were the right hand of the man himself. The Marshal had been the one to order covert operations that only Morovski and his men knew about.

They'd carried out missions that would curdle the blood of an ordinary soldier. Shock and awe was only the tip of the iceberg for what he and his men had done.

In some instances, they operated with the rest of the army, as when the invasion of Ukraine began. But it had been the lack of special orders that gave Morovski the opportunity to branch out and raid the museum.

For too long, the fires of resentment against the Marshal's leadership had burned in his heart, and he'd waited patiently for the opportunity to find a way out.

When the invasion plans started coming together, his mind guided itself to areas of his previous expertise.

A brilliant tactician, he'd always been an avid student of history —particularly wars. This study brought him a vast knowledge of many great leaders throughout the ages, and the wars they waged.

The Scythians were one such group. While often disregarded as insignificant by more nationalist-minded Russians, the objective historians knew better.

But it wasn't the Scythians' military prowess that interested Morovski. He'd long considered carrying out an operation to extract priceless artifacts from a museum, an exhibit, anywhere his unit worked.

Until the invasion, that opportunity had never presented itself.

With the heist completed, he was on the doorstep of a new life. Never again would he have to endure a harsh winter under the Moscow sky. Warm beaches and beautiful women beckoned to his imagination.

He snapped his head to dispel the distracting thoughts and refocused his mind on the issue of the Marshal.

He'd known the man a long time. Morovski sensed a lie in the man's tone, and in the way he so quickly accepted the explanation Morovski had given.

An old sensation trickled through him. It was one he felt often, and one that most civilians didn't believe men like him could feel.

Fear.

Morovski knew that fear was the fuel of courage, that facing it and harnessing it was what made the best and bravest warriors.

But this fear ran deeper. He wasn't just facing bullets or bombs. The Marshal knew he was lying.

He took two long steps over to the door and flung it open.

Kostya stood just outside with one of the other guards, both men facing outward.

"Lieutenant Colonel Arshavin," Morovski said.

Kostya's head turned quickly to face the man, followed immediately by his body as he whipped to attention. "Yes, Colonel."

"We need to leave."

Kostya's face twisted in puzzlement. "Now, sir?"

"Yes, Lieutenant Colonel. Now." He rounded on the other guard. "Go tell the men to prepare for our departure. We're leaving immediately."

"Yes, sir."

"I also need you to get on the computer and pull up all of our forces within two hundred kilometers."

"Of course."

Kostya slid by the colonel and entered the office with Morovski close behind. He flipped open the laptop and waited a few seconds for the screen to bloom to life. Then he entered his passcode and typed in a few other parameters.

Morovski watched him work, pulling up a real-time map of the area with red markers indicating the positions of allied forces in the region.

"There are three groups within that range, sir." Kostya's frown deepened. "It appears they are on the move."

Morovski agreed with a single nod.

"It looks like they're coming this way." He faced the commander with concern in his eyes. As if from nowhere, flop sweat drenched his brow and upper lip. The lip below it began to quiver. "Why would they be coming this way?"

The colonel's narrow eyes burned with anger. "Someone must have told them."

Kostya turned his head to both sides. "None of our men would have done that. They are all loyal to you, sir."

"I know, but it was only a matter of time until word got out." He blinked rapidly as he thought then returned his focus to the screen. "They're flanking us from three sides—the north, east, and north-west. Only a matter of time until that group to the south moves up."

"I estimate they should be here within a few hours, sir."

"They already knew we were here," Morovski realized. "I should have anticipated they might track us." His eyes focused on the border of Romania. "It looks like we're going to Romania after all. It's the only option."

"Agreed."

Morovski shook his head. "I tried to tell the German to meet us in Bucharest, but he insisted on Hungary."

"We can still get there from Romania, Colonel. It is only a slight detour. And it might make crossing the Hungarian border easier."

Kostya thought for two seconds. "Unless you think he might reconsider."

"Yes. I think you may be right about the border, and no he won't reconsider. The man is accustomed to always getting his way. He's not the type people say no to."

Neither was the colonel, but in this situation, he found himself in the unusual position of the subordinate.

Morovski wiped the worry from his face and put on the stoic mask he almost always wore—cold, emotionless. "Get the prisoner ready. We leave in fifteen minutes."

"Are you sure we shouldn't just leave her here? Dead or alive?"

"No. She may still be useful to us. It never hurts to have a hostage if things don't go according to plan."

"Of course, sir. I'll make sure she's secured in one of the transports." That brought another issue to the lieutenant colonel's mind. "If they're tracking us, they might send air support."

Morovski wiped his chin with his thumb. "Yes. That's why we're going to split up into three groups. I just hope the trucks we've commandeered are tuned up and ready to go."

10

"Well, well, well," Liz chimed, her voice cutting through the silent hotel suite like an irritated parent who just caught their kid searching the freezer for ice cream. "Would you look at that?"

She picked up the cup of coffee sitting next to the laptop and took a sip.

The entire room filled with the aroma of the fresh brew mixed with warm pastries Dak had picked up from the shop downstairs.

Dak had been looming behind her, watching the screen like a pot of water simmering on the edge of boiling.

The other two lounged on the couch watching some random streaming show about an archaeologist who searched the world for undiscovered mysteries and treasures.

They both turned their heads simultaneously when Liz spoke.

"You got something?" Will asked, sitting up straight. Lesma only looked over lazily, obviously comfortable in his spot on the sofa.

"Looks like it," Dak announced.

"We have three Russian units converging on the town of Vinnytsia," Liz said, staring at the satellite images.

"The real-time footage is pretty, well, unreal," Dak admitted. "I don't recall having anything that high quality when we were running ops."

Liz looked up at him over her shoulder. "That's because this is classified tech. No one knows we have this."

"Most of the missions I ran were classified, and we didn't have this. Although we did get high-res images. Those were impressive. They could display a license plate from space, but video like this wasn't available."

She merely smiled proudly before returning to the screen. "Now we need to see if there's anything suspicious going on in Vinnytsia."

She zoomed in on the town and moved the camera around to see if they could detect any unusual movement.

Will dragged himself out of his seat and meandered over to the table. Lesma took considerably longer to pull himself out of the cushions.

"Looks like a ghost town," Will commented as he hovered behind her next to Dak.

"Yeah," Dak said, regret lacing his words. "All those people had to leave their homes and everything they worked for to try to escape this crazy war."

Will crossed his arms. "What I wouldn't give for two minutes with the Russian president."

"He's a puppet just like the rest of them," Dak said. "All marching to a single drum."

"The question is: Who's the drummer?"

"That's who you want two minutes with. Figure that out, and you change the world."

Liz cleared her throat. "Sorry to interrupt," she said, "but I think we have something."

She zoomed in on what appeared to be some kind of factory. "See those trucks?"

"Are you controlling a camera in space right now from your laptop?" Will asked, distracted by the power she apparently wielded at her fingertips.

"Yes. Now focus. The trucks."

"Sorry."

"Yeah, we see them, Liz. They look like delivery trucks."

She nodded. "Right. Six of them. But what are they delivering and to whom?"

The realization hit Dak and Will at the same time.

"Good point," Dak confessed. "Looks like they're splitting up."

"You think they might be the thieves?" Will wondered, never taking his eyes off the screen.

Lesma finally arrived at the table and squirmed for a spot close to Will, who shifted awkwardly to the left to give the big man some room.

"That is them," Lesma proclaimed.

"How can you be sure?" Will asked.

"It's what I would do if I was trying to evade the police. And I do try to evade the police whenever possible."

Dak snorted a quick laugh at the admission.

"If you want to catch a criminal, you have to think like one," the Russian continued. "Notice how all the trucks look different? If they were delivering something from that factory, shouldn't they all look the same?"

Liz looked up at him, impressed. "You know, maybe we need to hire you on at Axis," she said. "You seem like a guy who thinks outside the box."

Lesma beamed with pride but denied the possibility. "I don't want to be on any government's payroll. But thank you."

"We're going to have to make a decision," Dak interrupted. "We can't watch all three groups at the same time." He arched his right eyebrow. "Unless you *can* do that with your magical satellite thingy."

Liz chuckled. "Unfortunately, no. You're right. We have to pick one. But which one?"

"If they're all working together," Will said, "then they'll meet up again somewhere. My guess is dividing their forces is just a way to avoid being tracked. And you can bet the Russians are tracking them now, if they weren't before."

"Affirmative," Liz agreed. "Now we just have to wait and see where these trucks go."

"Pretty smart, actually," Dak said. "Leaving their military transports there will draw all those Russian units to an empty factory. Assuming that's what they're tracking."

"Should be. Why would they bother with a bunch of delivery trucks?"

"Follow that one," Lesma said, pointing to the second pair of trucks.

"Why that one?" Liz wondered.

"Those two are moving slower than the other four. Which tells me those are probably the ones carrying most of the treasure. If they were smart, they'd divide it up equally between the six trucks."

"You know, Lesma? I think she's right," Dak commented. "You would make a good covert agent."

He blushed and threw his hand up at the notion.

"It doesn't pay enough."

"You got that right," Liz added. "Okay, following group two."

They watched in rapt attention as the pair of trucks wound their way through the empty city streets until they reached the outskirts on the western side of the town.

"Looks like they're heading for Romania. Just like you said," Liz proclaimed. "So, maybe I don't need to get you boys into Ukraine after all."

"That's a relief," Will sighed.

"Yes," Lesma said. "But now I feel I don't have anything of value to help with your mission, Dak."

"You've already proved your worth five times over, Lesma. And I'm sure your resourcefulness will still come in handy."

The Russian shrugged, but he didn't look satisfied with the compliment.

Dak thought it an interesting trait for a criminal to have such integrity, but he appreciated that. Perhaps it was a little extreme at times—like when he had his own son thrown off the top of a building —but he drew lines. Dak had to give him that.

"So, what's the plan?" Liz asked. "I guess you want me to alert the Romanians about the Russian military group."

"That would be a good start, sure," Dak said. "But I'm going to the border, too. Not that I don't trust the Romanians, but there's a lot of line to cover there."

"And you think you can make a difference with that?" She semi scoffed, though she didn't want to sound insulting.

"Who knows? But I can tell you this: I don't believe for a second that this rogue unit is going to take one of the main roads into Romania. They wouldn't be that stupid."

"Okay, so what then?" Liz asked. "I don't think they're going to be able to commandeer a train."

"How long until they reach the border?" Will asked.

"A few hours. If the Russian military doesn't catch them first."

"They won't," Dak hedged. "Those three groups are heading to the factory. By the time they realize there's no one home, the rogue unit will be across the border."

"You sound like you don't think the border patrol is going to be able to stop them," Liz guessed.

"Correct. They'll do what they can, but let's be honest: too much to cover. We need to look at every side road and goat trail going between the two countries."

Liz bobbed her head. "Okay. Sure." Her fingers tapped the keys rapidly as she entered the parameters on the computer.

The screen changed to a map. Then she made a few clicks on the track pad, and it changed again, zooming into the area along the border of Romania and Ukraine.

White lines trickled across the terrain like streams flowing from one country to the other.

"These are the main roads that go through checkpoints," she said, pointing at the screen. "The rest are smaller roads. There will be security, most likely, along many of them if not all. But it won't be like what you see on the others. Sorry, but I don't think I can pull up the goat trails."

She smirked up at Dak.

He set his jaw as he considered the problem. There were so many ways in and out of the country. Even with the conflict going on in Ukraine, he doubted the Romanians were covering every possible point.

Dak assumed that refugees had been flooding the country through the main thoroughfares, which was probably keeping most of the border guards busy.

He knew he had to make a decision, and quickly. Every second that passed put the rogue unit that much closer to their escape.

"What would I do if I was in their shoes?" he asked quietly, but loud enough for the others to hear.

"You know, there have been a few times when we were running weapons to freedom fighters where I thought we were being tracked."

Everyone turned their attention to Will.

"What did you do?" Dak asked.

"Well, when you want to get across a border with a bunch of illegal guns, you don't take the main roads. But we've already crossed those off the list of potentials. Sure, some of the country roads might work, but those are risky too, especially with a war going on next door."

"So, what would you do?"

"If it was me, I'd go through those mountains there." Will pointed to the map. "Not sure how I'd transport all that stuff they got. I imagine a bunch of gold is probably pretty heavy. Might not be an issue depending on how many guys they have."

"They could use pack animals," Liz suggested.

"Like horses or mules?" Dak clarified.

"Yeah. I bet if we look there are probably some farms in this region. If the rogue unit stole even a few animals, they could easily divide up the rest of the artifacts with the men and make the crossing on foot. Once they're in Romania, they'll be much harder to locate."

Dak had the answer he was looking for, but the solution wasn't complete yet. "We need to get moving. We'll fly to the nearest airport to the border. Liz, I'll need you to stay a little longer if that's okay and see if you can pinpoint any farms along the border between Vinnytsia and Romania where those trucks stop."

"I can do that," Liz said. "Better than waiting around on babysitting duty. If I get the call, though, I'll have to head back, but we're not stationed far from here."

Dak looked to Will next. "We'll need guns. And if you can hook us up with some ordnance, that would be helpful, too."

"Explosives? What flavor?" Will asked with a gloating smile.

"Whatever you can get us. We're going to need all the firepower we can get."

"I'm sorry, my friend," Lesma interrupted. "Are you thinking of taking on a contingent of Russian soldiers—just the three of us?"

"I see your point, Lesma. And I agree. The odds are definitely in our favor."

The Russian scrunched his face in a confused frown. "No, I meant—"

"I know," Dak laughed. "I was kidding. But I'm not kidding about taking out that unit." He pointed his attention back to Will. "We'll need the explosives for a diversion. I don't want to try to hit them with that stuff. If the curator is still alive, then the last thing we want to do is blow her to pieces."

"Makes sense," Will said. "But there are probably a couple dozen guys with that unit. And we don't know anything about them."

Liz hummed in protest. She'd been typing quietly on the keyboard. "That's not exactly true."

The three men stared at her as if trying to pry whatever new information she had from her eyes.

She spun the laptop around so they could see the screen. "They're an elite special forces unit," Liz explained. "Led by a man named Colonel Nikolai Morovski. A lot of what these guys do is off the books. I've heard some of the stories. It isn't pretty. They're not only effective at what they do, but also known for their ruthless brutality."

"Ah," Dak sighed.

"These guys are no joke, Dak. I know you're good, but there are a bunch of them and only one you. And I'm willing to bet a lot of them have comparable training to yours."

He nodded. "Yeah. Better in some cases. And they've been active in ops more recently than me." It didn't hurt him to admit that. He knew he wasn't immortal, or the only person in the world who'd been trained the way he had. There were other branches of the military that boasted the best and the toughest, just as his former unit did. Every major government in the world possessed such assets.

That didn't mean this mission was impossible. It just meant they'd have to be careful.

"Will?" Dak rounded on his friend. "See what you can get us as soon as we have a location. Time will be tight."

"I'll work on it."

"Liz, let me know when those trucks are all going the same direction and where it looks like they're headed. That'll help us narrow things down." He looked to the men again. "Load up, boys. We gotta catch a plane."

11

The delivery truck rumbled along the highway like a log wagon, constantly bouncing and vibrating with every tiny crack or pothole in the asphalt.

It had been nearly two hours of this continuous irritation, but every second that passed was a tiny victory for the colonel. The more separation they could get between themselves and their pursuers, the better.

He knew what would happen once the Marshal's teams found the factory premises vacated, along with the army transport vehicles still there.

They would send helicopters out looking, perhaps a spy plane, though he doubted that.

The choppers were close enough and fast enough to attempt to cut off Morovski's escape if they were able to come after them thirty to forty minutes sooner. But he knew their hunters wouldn't make it in time. As long as there were no delays.

Morovski looked across the cargo hold to the prisoner.

Galyna huddled in the corner, rubbing her shoulders and arms to keep warm—the sweater helping but still unable to prevent the cold from cutting her skin.

"What?" she demanded, sneering like an angry child.

"Nothing," the colonel answered. "I'm just wondering what to do with you once we've sold the artifacts."

She shook her head in disgust. "Those belong to the people of Ukraine. You're nothing but murderers and thieves."

He shrugged, the barb doing nothing to even scratch the surface of his soul. "I know what I am, woman. And I am not ashamed. Everything my men and I have done was because we were ordered to. I'm done taking orders. Once those artifacts are sold, we will be free men. Able to go wherever we want and start new lives."

Her look softened, but just barely. "Am I supposed to commend you on your new life choices?"

He chuckled and looked around the truck at the other men. Most of them were minding their own business—the stern, focused looks on their faces reflecting the conditioning that had been burned into their psyches. Morovski knew that each one of them was ready to spring into action at his command, so he felt comfortable sitting in the back of the truck among his men.

"I don't care what you think," Morovski snarled. "I only care that I get paid."

Her face took on a despondent look. "Then what do you have me for? Are you planning to sell me, too?"

"The thought crossed my mind. I'm sure our buyer knows people."

She spat at him. The wads of saliva struck his pants. A few droplets hit him in the chest and hands.

The rest of the men saw what happened and tightened their positions.

The colonel extended a hand as he would to a raging horse, keeping them steady.

The men relaxed, though only slightly, as Morovski drew a handkerchief from one of his pockets and wiped his clothes and hands. He rubbed the back of one and then the other to finish the job before replacing the rag.

"Please do not do that again," he warned. "There is still a way that you get out of this alive. But if you do that again, I assure you I will kill you myself and dump your worthless body out the back of this truck."

He saw the fear streak through her eyes—a sign that she knew he meant every word.

"Yes," he drawled. "I'm a bad man. I know this."

"Why do you need me if you're not going to sell me? Just let me go."

To her credit, it was the first time she'd actually brought up her release. The colonel had anticipated having to hear her beg the entire ride from Kyiv. Either she didn't believe that was a real possibility, or she was too stubborn to ask.

Perhaps a bit of both, he mused.

"It never hurts to have a little insurance," he answered.

"Insurance from who? Are you afraid the Ukrainian leaders will realize what you've done and send a rescue team? Because I can assure you, I am not that important."

His shoulders rolled slightly, and he diverted his eyes to the cab wall for a second. "Perhaps. Perhaps not. But that is the point of insurance, isn't it? You hope you never need it, but if you do, it is good to have."

Her nostrils blared as she exhaled in frustration.

"Just try to keep in mind that I control your fate. So, it would be a good idea to be nice to me. What happens to you makes no difference to me—unless it helps me."

"How noble."

He snorted. "I never professed to be such a thing."

The truck's brakes engaged, causing everyone in the cargo hold to sway toward the front of the vehicle.

Morovski's brow furrowed as he turned to look through the window into the cab.

The vehicle jittered to a stop.

The soldier in the passenger seat turned around and opened the door before the colonel had to knock.

"What's going on?" Morovski demanded. He immediately noted

the concern on the young man's face.

"We have a problem, Colonel," the soldier replied and suggested his commander look through the windshield with a sideways nod.

Morovski peered through the glass and instantly felt a knot drop from his throat down to his gut.

"Problems, Colonel?" Galyna prodded.

"No problem," he sneered. "Only a delay." He swept the cargo hold with his eyes, meeting those of each of his men. "It seems our brethren have decided to try to stop us. We knew this could happen. I will go out to talk to their commanding officer. If it looks like they will not let us pass, be ready to take them out on my signal."

He realized he had just ordered his men to kill other Russian soldiers, but that did nothing to dissuade the resolve on the commandos' faces. They knew what they'd done, and what that meant they might have to do in the coming days. The rest of the army was their enemy now. They were the quarry, and the men they'd called brothers before were now the hunters.

Patriotism and loyalty faded in the shadow of self-preservation.

The colonel stood up and made his way between the men and opened the back door. He climbed out and dropped to the ground, landing on the pavement with a thud that jarred his joints from his ankles all the way up to his hips.

He remembered a time when such a short fall wouldn't have caused even a ripple through his thick muscles. But that was in his younger days. He wasn't the spry, young warrior he had been only a few short decades ago. While he wasn't old yet, things were beginning to hurt that never had before.

Nothing hurts when you're sitting on a beach, he thought.

The reminder further calmed his nerves, and he slowly walked around the back corner of the truck, giving a single nod to the driver of the truck immediately behind him.

The men in his vehicle would pass along the plan to the others, though Morovski sincerely hoped they wouldn't have to resort to that.

He cringed at the thought of killing other Russians, but he'd do what must be done.

The colonel used both hands to tighten his hat as he stepped into view of the soldiers positioned behind the roadblock.

Two armored personnel carriers sat at opposing angles, each blocking a lane, meeting in the middle. Wooden barricades had been set up in front of the vehicles—which puzzled Morovski. He wasn't sure why those were needed, though he did notice the use of the strings of spikes laid out across the asphalt in front of them. Those would render any vehicle trying to get through useless, even if they somehow managed to break through the two heavy carriers—which he knew wasn't likely.

The thick gray sky overhead wept snow flurries that fluttered around the colonel, settling on his hat and shoulders as he took in the scene. The mountains around them and beyond the barricade wrapped themselves in white with dense evergreen forests standing atop the ivory covering.

He strode toward the men pointing rifles at him as though they were water guns. He played a dangerous game, but it was the only option he had.

Morovski hedged that the three groups closing in on Vinnytsia had not likely reached the meat processing factory yet but would any minute. This group blocking the road was there to prevent Ukrainian fighters from attempting to flee, or circle around and flank Russian formations.

Unless he was wrong.

Four more armored vehicles sat slightly behind the two bigger personnel carriers. These Humvee-like copies were equipped with .50-caliber guns on the top, and each was manned by soldiers who kept their fingers on the triggers. Most of the other men were positioned behind the vehicles or the wooden barricades for cover—though the latter provided little.

The second the men saw a high-ranking officer approaching, they immediately relaxed. Even forty feet away, Morovski could see that.

One of the men manning a 50-cal. said something to someone on the ground Morovski couldn't see.

A moment later, a pale, slender man in an officer's uniform appeared around the corner of the personnel carrier on the right.

Within two seconds, the colonel heard the officer order his men to stand down.

The weapons lowered, and the men relaxed a little more.

The colonel walked confidently toward the blockade, carefully stepping over the spikes along the way.

The other officer came out to meet him and swung under the wooden fencing. As the colonel approached, the man saluted his superior.

Morovski noted the rest of the soldiers emerging from their cover, all standing out in the open now. Some lit cigarettes while others simply started up casual conversations—all signs that they believed there was no immediate threat.

"Sorry for the trouble, Colonel," the other officer said as Morovski stopped six feet short of the man.

Morovski noted the man's rank—a captain, and from the looks of it the rank was newly attained. The man's eyes mirrored the iceberg blue of the colonel's, but there was an uncertainty, a lack of confidence in his that betrayed his standing.

"What is the meaning of this?" Morovski questioned.

"We have orders to prevent Ukrainian fighters from trying to escape or circle around behind other formations to the north, sir," the captain answered.

Just as I thought, the colonel gloated to himself.

"How can we help you, Colonel?" the captain asked.

"We're undercover right now, Captain," Morovski said in a hushed tone. He added a furtive glance to both sides, scanning the fields beside the road to make it seem more convincing. "We have word there is a rogue unit who stole a treasure from a Ukrainian museum."

The captain mimicked the colonel's initial secretiveness, glancing to both sides before asking, "And you think they're coming this way?"

"That's why we're here, Captain. My men and I have orders to proceed to the Romanian border and scour the area. It's possible they already slipped by."

Morovski studied the man. From the looks of it, the captain bought the lie. *And why wouldn't he? He wouldn't dare question a colonel.*

"I see," the captain said. "I'm sorry for the delay, Colonel." I will get these vehicles out of the way immediately, sir."

"Thank you," Morovski offered. The gratitude felt cold and insincere, but the captain knew his superior officers rarely even handed out the most meager form of it, so he accepted with curt nod.

The second the man turned around, Morovski swiveled to also face the other direction when he heard footsteps trotting up from behind. He looked over his shoulder and saw an officer with a phone.

Morovski's blood chilled.

"Sir, you have a call."

"I don't have time for this right now," the captain snarled. "We need to get these vehicles out of the way."

"Sir," the soldier insisted, "they said it's urgent."

"Who's they?" the captain demanded.

"The Marshal."

Morovski shuddered on the inside. He shifted his stance to watch the captain take the phone from the radio man and put it to his ear.

"Yes, sir?" he said, greeting the Marshal. Then he listened. "I am, yes." He took a sidelong glance over at Morovski as the Marshal spoke. "Of course, sir. We will take care of it."

He handed the phone back to the radio guy and muttered an order under his breath.

Morovski saw the flash of fear in the man's eyes, and knew the game was up. He started to turn around and walk back to his truck, pretending as though nothing was wrong. He only made it one step before the captain's tinny voice pierced the air.

"Colonel?"

He stopped, albeit after another dragging step, then looked over his shoulder. "I'm just going to need to see your papers."

Morovski's eyelids narrowed. "What did you just say, Captain?"

The man swallowed but stiffened his spine. "I'm going to need to verify your orders."

The colonel spun on the man and took two steps toward him.

"Are you stupid? Did you not hear me tell you we are on a covert operation? My unit isn't the type to carry papers, boy, and you would do well to remember your rank."

As he lashed into the man, Morovski noted the men gathering behind the barricade, their weapons hanging in their hands, ready to be raised at a moment's notice.

The insult only emboldened the captain, who inclined his chin in an attempt to get the emotional higher ground. "I'm sorry, Colonel. But I'm going to have to ask you and your men to come with me. We have received information that it is you who are the rogue unit you described earlier. My men will search your trucks immediately. You and your men are to be taken into custody, and the treasure will be taken to Moscow."

Morovski noticed the man's right hand lingering over the pistol on his hip.

The colonel drew a deep breath through his nostrils, taking in the cold air laced with the scent of evergreens and dried wheat grass.

"I see," Morovski said with a resigned nod. "I was hoping things didn't have to happen this way, Captain. I really was."

The captain raised his left hand and flicked four fingers to the men behind him, signaling them to move forward.

"Tell your men to stand down," the captain ordered.

Morovski couldn't deny the irony, a man of his rank being ordered by this lower officer.

With another nod, he reached up and pinched the bill of his hat, removed it, and stretched his arm out to the right. He held it there for a second in an awkward pose, then dropped the hat to the ground.

Gunfire erupted from behind him. A fury of bullets tore through the captain's ranks, cutting some of his men down in seconds.

The men never had a chance to react. They were still operating under the assumption this would be a peaceful surrender. Not one of them got off a single shot.

As the captain twitched his head from right to left—watching his men die—he alone was shielded by the colonel, but that protection lasted only seconds.

Morovski drew his sidearm and aimed it at the captain's forehead just as ten soldiers rushed to the barricade to aid in the fight.

The captain didn't have a chance to draw his weapon. He'd been momentarily distracted—more than enough time for the colonel to get the drop on him.

"Tell your men to stand down," Morovski said.

The captain shook his head in defiance. "Tell your men to drop their weapons, or you die right now. And so do they."

The glimmering blue eyes staring back at Morovski betrayed the man's fear, and he saw it was winning the fight in the captain's mind.

He raised his left hand, again with his palm facing out. "Hold!" he barked. "Drop your weapons, men. Let these criminals pass. The Marshal will deal with him, personally."

Morovski saw the conflict on some of the other faces behind the captain, but one by one, the men begrudgingly laid down their arms.

Within two seconds, the colonel's men spewed out from their cover behind the trucks and rushed forward with rifles raised—each one with sights trained on targets.

The captain remained steadfast. He alone had kept his weapon.

Morovski sensed the man's reluctance, and he saw the misguided courage boiling in the man's eyes.

"What are you doing, Captain?"

The man said nothing. He didn't have to. His right hand hovered over the holster on his hip, but subtly lowered closer and closer to the pistol's grip.

The colonel had seen American western movies from the 1960s— illegal versions during the Soviet reign. He recalled the scenes where two gunfighters dueled to the death with small firearms.

He never imagined he'd find himself in such a position.

A cold breeze slithered across his skin as he stared at the captain. He absorbed every detail of the man's features, entirely focused on his opponent. While Morovski's men charged forward and began apprehending their former allies, he barely noticed.

An instinct deep inside him commanded his reflexes. It wasn't anything he'd seen out of the captain. Rather, an ages-old gut feeling drove him to draw.

The captain never even got his sidearm out of the holster.

Morovski pulled his pistol and fired.

The report echoed across the hills and mountains, reaching in all directions before fading.

For a second that stretched like twenty, the captain remained upright despite the fact he was already dead.

The dark hole just above his nose began to ooze crimson. Then his legs buckled, and he fell backward, surrendering to gravity.

Several of Morovski's men stole a quick look toward him at the sound, more out of concern for their leader than surprise.

The enemy forces stared in rapt horror at the execution of their commanding officer. Their eyes hung open with beleaguered, drawn disbelief as they looked across the scene of so many of their own—killed by their own.

The colonel stuffed his sidearm back in the holster and bent down to pick up his hat. Once it was firmly on his head again, he took a step toward the dead captain, who stared up at the sky he could not see.

"You could have just let us pass," Morovski muttered. Then he stepped over the body as he might a dead rat and walked over to Kostya, who held a submachine gun braced against his shoulder.

"What do you want to do with these, Colonel?"

Morovski looked into the eyes of the terrified Russian soldiers. They were only following orders, as he'd done for most of his career. But this was war. And his war was no longer with Ukraine or anyone else. The Marshal was to blame for this. Not him. And the Russian president above all carried the heaviest portion of this burden.

For the colonel, the decision was easy.

"Kill them," he ordered without a hint of remorse. "Kill them all, and move these vehicles out of the way. Then we head to the border."

Morovski turned and started back toward the truck. The sounds of gunshots rang out across the grim setting, bouncing off the gray sky above.

12

The van sped along the road heading east out of Sighetu, leaving the Romanian border town in the rearview mirror.

Will gripped the steering wheel tightly as he felt the same sense of urgency he knew likewise gripped Dak and Lesma.

Ahead in the distance, the mountains on the Ukrainian side of the border climbed into the sky with white caps shielding the peaks from the sporadic sun that poked through the clouds.

To the right, the Romanian mountains reached upward with similar snowy dressings.

Dak stared at the map in his lap, while Lesma looked over his shoulder from the seat behind him.

Liz had arranged for the van that could hold eight or nine people when the third row was in place. For their purposes, she'd requested the third-row seat be removed to provide more cargo space.

Dak pointed at the map, pressing into the paper. "My best guess is they'll come south through Rakhiv. If they haven't passed through there already. Then there are a couple of towns with names I'm not even going to try to pronounce before they get to Dilove."

He lifted his finger and smacked it down on the name. "That's where they'll cross. The last town before the Romanian border."

"You sound really sure of yourself on this one," Will commented. "What makes you so sure they'll try to cross there? I mean, other than your previous hypothesis."

"It's still the same. The nearest border crossing is in Sighetu. But they're not going to try that. It's on a bridge over the Tiszu River. They'd have no way to escape if they took that route. They'd never make it through the Ukrainian checkpoint."

"Right. I get that. But why not go farther west?"

"The farther they stretch out their journey, the more likely their chances of getting caught. Thanks to our friend's little hot tip she passed along to the Russians, now the Russian army is chasing them. Without air transportation, it would only be a matter of time until their comrades caught up."

"Do you think the leader of this rogue band knows they're being chased?" Will asked.

"By now I would think so. Maybe they've already been caught and this whole trip was for nothing."

The van fell silent, only offering the steady rumble of the road against the tires.

"You don't believe that do you?" Lesma asked.

"It's a game of uncertainty," Dak answered. "If the Russian army caught them, then it's out of our hands anyway. But if they didn't, we still have a chance to save the curator, and the artifacts. We have to take the play whether we like it or not."

"There is no bridge in that area?"

"Doesn't look like it." Dak ran his finger along the road heading south toward the river. "The Tiszu acts as the border between the two countries. South of Dilove is where it's shallow and narrower than in Sighetu. My guess is they'll try to either walk or ferry across. It's freezing out there, so I can't imagine them trying to do it on foot."

"So, we just look for a ferry crossing?" Will wondered. "Like it's 1872?"

Dak laughed. "Maybe. Or perhaps they already have something else in mind."

He took out the phone and looked at the photos from near Dilove.

"I'd be surprised if there were anything more than rafts used to get across this. It reminds me of the Nantahala back home along the Tennessee–North Carolina border. Maybe not as deep."

"What if they had waders?"

"Like fly fishermen use?"

Will nodded.

"I hadn't thought of that, but it's possible. But there's still the issue of their heavy cargo."

"If there were enough of them," Lesma argued, "they could split the load and make it across."

"Also true," Dak agreed. "Each man carrying a share for such a short distance isn't out of the question."

Will turned the wheel to the right and steered the van southward along the road. Signs along the shoulder told them the next village was a place called Lunca la Tisa.

Dak checked the map again after reading the sign and checked the distance to the mountain village of Valea Vișeului—due south of Dilove.

"You don't think they came through Chernivtsi?" Lesma indicated the Ukrainian city on the map.

"Too many eyeballs watching for suspicious traffic," Dak reasoned. "They probably want to stay as far away from midsize-to-large towns as possible. Coming down into this valley is what I would do if I was in their shoes. Sparsely populated. Lots of places to hide in the mountains. Dense forests. Easier to get lost here than anywhere else along the border."

"I understand, but why wouldn't they just cross the river while still in Ukraine, and then go over on the mountain passes to the east of the valley?"

Dak sighed through his nose and nodded, then rubbed his eyelids. "You're right, Lesma. I've been so focused on them staying along the road until they could get as close as possible to the border before crossing. But that makes more sense. Then they wouldn't need waders."

"Or a raft," Will said, clearing his throat.

"Right." Dak traced the road with his right index finger. "There's a bridge in Dilove. If they crossed there, they could take that road southeast for a mile, park their trucks, and make a break for the border."

"How far would they have to go once they park?"

"A mile. Maybe a little more. But it wouldn't take them long, even with their haul. It's all mountains and hills there. Without air support, we're going to have a tough time spotting them."

"When we get to the valley," Lesma said, "what is the plan?"

"We'll have to try to get the high ground," Dak replied. "From these mountains, we should be able to spot them more easily. But there's no guarantee."

"There never is with you," Will quipped.

"Touché."

"And you're assuming we can beat them to the border. It's possible they've already crossed and disappeared into the mountains."

"I know," Dak resigned. "But we have to take that chance. Besides, we didn't come all this way just to turn around and head home."

Will chuckled. "No, we did not."

The road wound through the hills dotted by Romanian hamlets. The villages' architecture represented a strange blend of the bland communist structures built during that time frame and the more aesthetic traditional Romanian homes from before.

Dak admired the latter as they passed by in the window.

Sharply sloping, high-rooftop barns, churches, and chalets reminded him somewhat of the old Norwegian style of buildings he'd seen in pictures—though he'd never visited that country.

The mountains and hills, thick with untouched forests, reminded him of his home back in East Tennessee. But there was something about this place that seemed even more natural.

He found himself hoping the war going on across the river to his left didn't spill over into this country and spoil something so beautiful as it had done in many parts of Ukraine.

The irony wasn't lost on Dak.

He was bringing the war here, though with only three guys on his side he hoped the collateral damage would be kept to a minimum.

Lesma's pudgy thumbs tapped on his phone screen as he stared at the device in the backseat.

Dak noticed the Russian's silence and intense concentration on whatever he was doing. "Keeping an eye on the family business?" Dak pried.

For a second, Lesma didn't even realize the American was talking to him.

Then when it hit him, he lifted his eyes and looked at Dak, who stared back at him over his shoulder.

"What?" He shook his head. "No. The business is fine. The boys know how to run things while I'm gone."

"Then what are you doing? Texting a girlfriend? You're not married anymore."

Lesma's lips curled with mischief. "I'm pulling my weight, as you Americans like to say."

"Yeah?"

Will flashed a glance in the rearview mirror at the big man.

"You said the convoy is probably going through Rakhiv, then Dilove."

Dak nodded. "Seems to make the most sense. It's what I would do."

"Right. Well, I have a cousin who runs a hostel there. Since your friend Liz doesn't have access to the satellite right now, perhaps some eyes on the ground can help us."

A look of utter astonishment splashed over Dak's face. Gravity dragged his jaw wide open. "What?"

Lesma chuckled in his usual, hefty way. "Yes. My cousin Vladimir lives there. He's what you Americans might call a hippie. His hostel is on the main road that cuts through the town. If a convoy of delivery trucks passes by, he is in a prime location to see it."

Will chortled at the revelation. "You didn't think to tell us this before?"

The Russian lifted his shoulders and dropped them. "I didn't know they were going through Rakhiv until Dak said it."

"We still don't know," Dak interrupted. "But that's awesome, Les. If your cousin could help us out, that would be great."

"You sound like the guy from *Office Space*," Will said.

Dak snickered and looked over at his friend. "Lumbergh. Classic."

"Who is this Lumbergh?" Lesma wondered, confused. He searched both men for the answer.

"I guess we'll have to watch that movie with you when all this is over," Dak suggested. "Would be a good way to unwind after all this."

"Yeah, for real," Will agreed.

Lesma's phone vibrated in his palm, and he checked the screen. "My cousin said six trucks just passed through twenty minutes ago. He said he wouldn't have thought much of it, but they looked like they were in a hurry."

Dak nodded. "Great work, Les," he praised. "See? I told you you'd be a huge help."

Lesma beamed with pride. "Glad to be of service, Dak."

Dak turned around and peered through the windshield at the mountains around and in front of them. "Now we just have to get into position and hope they walk right into our trap."

13

Morovski felt the truck slowing down, pulling him toward the cab wall. He leaned forward and looked through the window and windshield to see where his driver was stopping.

He'd already selected the spot based on maps he and Kostya analyzed. Through the glass he saw the surrounding Eastern Carpathian Mountains rising into the gray blanket above. The windshield wipers smeared wet snowflakes on the glass.

An old trail cut into tall grass led into the forest straight ahead before disappearing around a slight curve. It was the perfect place to hide the trucks, and for them to make their escape across the border.

The remote area wouldn't likely offer much resistance in the way of border patrol, even with the heightened number of refugees fleeing the country. In fact, with so many Ukrainians desperately trying to get out, Morovski reasoned that more of the patrols' focus would be at the legitimate crossings as opposed to random mountain passes.

The Eastern Carpathians also presented far more challenges and dangers to ill-equipped families attempting to make the crossing. The cold and occasionally treacherous terrain made fleeing via that route not only dangerous but irrational.

The bordering nations were processing entries as fast as they could, but Morovski knew the system was overwhelmed.

Out here, the only thing he'd have to deal with was the fence.

The driver continued down the path, careful to avoid slowing down too much lest they got stuck in the snow and mud.

Morovski felt relieved when they finally entered the forest at the foot of the nearest mountain. He couldn't see out the back of the cargo bay but knew that once they were behind the safety of the trees, no one would know they'd ever been there.

Russian aircraft would have difficulty seeing the vans from the air, and they'd have to scour hundreds of miles to find them. And even if that happened, gunners wouldn't be able to target anyone through the canopy.

The truck continued winding through the woods for another two minutes, going deeper into the trees until it came to a spot where a four-foot-high snowdrift blocked the way.

The driver stepped on the brakes and shifted the transmission into park before he banged his fist on the back window.

Galyna looked across at the colonel, questions filling her eyes. She'd been silent since the incident on the road earlier and hadn't even asked what happened. She'd heard the gunshots but had been held in the cargo bay by one of the soldiers who'd been ordered to watch her, threatening that if she tried to escape he would execute her.

"Time to go for a walk," Morovski said to her as his men piled out of the truck and into the cold.

The soldier closest to her grabbed her by the arm and tugged her toward the opening.

She resisted, but it was a feeble protest. She'd been fed, but only to keep her alive. Her pale face and the dark circles under her eyes indicated her weakened state, and any fight she had left before had since been drained.

Morovski was the last to leave the cargo hold, following the soldier who ushered Galyna out. When he landed in the snow behind the truck, he immediately surveyed the surroundings.

The smell of clean snow and evergreen filled his nostrils, and he took in a deep breath to momentarily appreciate the fresh air.

"It smells like freedom, doesn't it, boys?" he said to his men as they gathered around him.

Several of them nodded. A few others laughed jovially.

Morovski turned and looked up the slope. A quarter mile away, a rickety wooden fence draped with old razor wire and barbs blocked their way.

He almost laughed at the barrier.

He knew there were no alarms connected to the fencing, and without any guards in towers or on foot roaming the mountainside, not a soul would know they had passed through.

He rounded and met the eyes of his soldiers, determination flaming in his. "The next stage of our journey will be difficult, men. Divide up the cargo. Each of you carry as much as you can. I will do the same. On the other side of this mountain is a small town where we can find transportation. It's only a few miles from here. Once we get there, it's on to Hungary, where we will sell these things and spend the rest of our lives however we want."

The men cheered cautiously, as if afraid their voices would give away their position.

Galyna looked around at them with disdain dripping from her eyes. She clutched her shoulders against the cold—her sweater doing little to keep it at bay. Despite the anger in her head, she found herself utterly helpless.

Even the greatest fantasies of stripping one of the men of their weapons and killing all of them was beyond her grasp. So, she merely huddled there, her feet getting colder by the minute in the snow that ran up to her ankles.

The soldiers hurried back to the two vehicles that carried the loot and began unloading the boxes. They divided up as much as they could into their rucksacks, trading out ordinary clothing for the loot, stuffing the bags until they swelled with gold. Several of the relics were too large to fit in the bags, which meant some of the men had to carry them in hand with their rifles hanging across their chests.

While they didn't feel comfortable in what could be considered a combat zone, they also didn't sense an immediate threat. Each man agreed to take a turn carrying the bulkier items, which mitigated any complaints or concerns about anyone doing more than another—much like taking watch at an encampment.

Once the men had all the treasure accounted for, they lined up in a column and began the trek up the slope, Galyna positioned in the middle.

It was the one thing she could be thankful for. With half of the men in front of her, their boots beat down the snow to provide firm footing and prevented her feet from getting colder—if that was possible.

More than once she slipped as she struggled to keep pace with the men who'd clearly spent much of their adult lives training in and for conditions exactly like this. To them, it likely seemed like they were on a spring hike on a flat trail.

Up ahead, the fence stood in their way.

She wondered how they planned to get through it without being cut to ribbons, then noticed two of the men carrying bolt cutters and thick gloves hanging from their belts.

It appeared the colonel had thought of everything.

As the column continued forward, she looked back at the man. He'd ditched his officer's uniform as well and now wore a black beanie on his head, a gray winter coat, and olive-green pants.

They hadn't bothered offering her any additional clothing to protect her from the cold. Not that she expected such chivalry from a band of thieves and murderers—especially the kind who would execute their own.

She shivered as a breeze swept across the slopes, whistling through the trees as it cut against her exposed skin.

Galyna had experienced frigid winters her entire life, but she didn't recall a time when she had felt this cold.

The column slowed as the men in the lead reached the fencing.

The two with the bolt cutters slipped on their work gloves and moved to the front. They started with the razor wire that lined the ground along the chain-link fence, clipping it in multiple places. Two other men took on the task of pulling the wire away to clear the path to the fence.

Once a ten-foot berth had opened, the two with the bolt cutters set to work on removing the top layer of barbed razor wire from the top. While the pullers tore the scraps away again, the bolt cutters started in on the chain link.

The rest of the men stood watch—half of them covering the rear and the others the two flanks.

Morovski quieted his nerves so his men couldn't see. Kostya stood to his right, supervising the work the cutters did but also scanning the slopes for signs of trouble.

The colonel knew that until his men were through the border fence and on the Romanian side, they were still prone—even if it seemed no threat approached.

And then it did.

At first, the faint beating sound was little more than a pulse. But it swelled by the second, growing louder and louder.

His men heard it, too, and the ones watching the flanks turned toward the rear in search of the source.

Morovski didn't need to look even though he did. He knew what it was. The familiar sound of Russian helicopters was as unmistakable to him as good Russian vodka.

He only hoped the cover of the canopy would conceal their vehicles and the path long enough for them to get across the border. Here at the fence, they stood exposed out in the open in the twenty-yard gap between the two forest lines.

For a few heartbeats, he considered ordering his men back into the woods where they could take cover and wait until the choppers left the area. But if anyone in the air spotted the trucks, they would hover near the border and cut Morovski and his men down.

He looked back to the cutters.

They were nearly done. Only another few sections, and they could pull the fence clear.

The beating continued to swell.

Morovski couldn't see the helicopters over the treetops, but he knew they were close. Too close.

The pilots must have been pushing the aircraft to their limits. He imagined a convoy surely followed on the ground. If the choppers spotted the colonel and his unit, they wouldn't even have to fire a single bullet.

"Fall back into the forest!" Morovski ordered abruptly. "Fall back!"

The men with the bolt cutters looked over their shoulders at him, then the few sections of fence they had left to remove, then dropped the tools in the snow and retreated with the others.

Every man hurried down the slope, carefully navigating the snow-covered ground. Two of them assisted Galyna with arms under her shoulders, virtually dragging her down the hill.

The last of the men made it under the canopy just as the sound thundered overhead.

Then two aircraft appeared through the breaks in the evergreen branches. The tops of the trees swayed and shook under the down-force of wind from the rotors.

Morovski watched with the bridge of his hand against his fore-head to shield his eyes from debris as the two helicopters hovered above them. His men braced their weapons, ready to fire if ordered, though the colonel knew their gunfire—if not squarely placed on the right points of the choppers—would actually do more harm than good. Bullets hitting the aircraft would give away their position to the pilots and destroy any chance they had at remaining undetected.

From this vantage, they couldn't hit the men guiding the choppers, so the only play was to stay low and try to keep out of sight.

Snow dust swirled in the air, knocked down from the trees above and stirred from the ground around the trunks.

As luck would have it, the man-made snowstorm cut down Morovski's field of vision significantly. He could barely see the men around him as snow blew around them in a raging vortex.

The colonel stayed low, hugging a tree with his shoulder as he waited. Several plans ran through his mind, as was always the case when faced with adversity.

If the helicopters spotted them, they could retreat back to the trucks and use them for cover in a gunfight. But the vehicles carried fuel, and the shells of the cargo bays were thin. The men would be better served with the trees around them.

Morovski also worried that the pilots and anyone else on board the helicopters might spot their handiwork on the border fence, but with so much snow blowing around, he couldn't even see it from his vantage point a short distance away. If not for the snow, he and his men would be done for.

Despite all his loathing of the white stuff he'd grown up with and lived with his entire life, now snow was saving his hide.

The choppers loomed for what seemed like half an hour. In reality, the two aircraft spent a mere two minutes overhead before abruptly turning north and proceeding along the border.

The colonel imagined the men inside the aircraft scouring the earth below—knowing their prey had to be close, yet unable to find them.

Kostya took over his duties as the second-in-command and held up a fist signaling to the rest of the men to stay in place until he gave the order to move out once more. The lieutenant colonel kept his eyes locked on the helicopters until they disappeared around the mountain bend, then he looked to Morovski for confirmation. A curt nod was all he needed.

He jerked his fist down and barked at the men to return to the border, ordering them to hurry. The last thing any of them wanted was to stick around long enough for the choppers to return.

The men with the bolt cutters returned to the fence and quickly stripped away the remainder of the chain link that blocked their path.

Once clear, the men poured through the opening two at a time until they were clear of the Ukrainian border.

Morovski was one of the last to cross, making sure his entire unit was over the line before he took one last look back at the Ukrainian forest. "Take your war," he said, as if the president could hear him. "We are free."

Two soldiers ushered Galyna through the opening and into Romania before he followed. Once on the other side, Morovski threw up his hands in triumph.

"Congratulations, men. We are now on Romanian soil."

The men shouted the victory.

When they settled down again, he panned over the group. "Remember, we are Ukrainian refugees. So, if we encounter any Romanian citizens, we must keep our weapons concealed. Some of you carrying the larger gold items may need to sacrifice your coats for a short time to cover them. Nothing arouses suspicion like a refugee carrying a golden spear, eh?"

The men laughed at the comment.

"This next part will be the hardest. But beyond the mountain there is a village where we can find transportation. From there, we make our way to Budapest and a lifetime of luxury. And most importantly, no more cold. Unless you want it."

They group laughed again but added in more cheers with the vision they all shared.

Morovski turned to Kostya and nodded again.

The lieutenant colonel ordered the men to head out and make their way through the forest along the slope between two mountains.

No sooner had the men begun their march than a single gunshot echoed through the valley.

The man in the lead fell to the snow—a pink spray splattered on the white patch around him.

Before the men could react, another gunshot popped through the forest, taking out another man in the column with a shot through the chest.

"Take cover!" Kostya barked.

A third shot sent a round through his shoulder. The impact spun Kostya around in a circle and dropped him to his knees, wincing in pain as he grabbed at the wound.

Morovski hurried to his lieutenant colonel's aid. "Snipers!" Morovski yelled.

The men scrambled for cover, rushing to any tree they could find —unaware of where the shots were coming from.

The colonel looped his arm around Kostya's torso under his armpits and helped him up.

"No, Colonel. Leave me. I'm fine."

"You are wounded, my friend. Quickly. To that tree." Morovski indicated a thick evergreen about thirty feet away. Most of the other men had already found cover, but now two lay dead in the snow.

As they plunged through the deep powder, another took a round in the abdomen fifteen feet to their right. He dropped onto the ground, grimacing in agony as he covered his gut with both hands.

Morovski noted the angle of the shot and turned his head up the slope to search for the sniper.

At first, he didn't see anything unusual. But when the next gunshot erupted, he spied the muzzle flash.

"Almost there, my friend," he comforted Kostya as they neared the safety of the tree. "Cut to the left. I see the sniper."

"You see them? Where?"

"Tree first. Then I show you."

The lieutenant colonel agreed with his silence and a quicker pace. The two men ducked behind the tree trunk and sat down in the snow

Before taking another look up the slope, Morovski checked Kostya's shoulder. A hole in the jacket oozed blood. He imagined the muscle and bone damage inside, but hoped it wasn't as bad as his mind believed.

"Hold still," the colonel ordered. He unzipped his coat and tore off a strip from his shirt. "This is going to sting."

He formed a small snowball and wrapped the strip around it tightly, then shoved the rag into the wound, pushing hard against it.

Kostya grunted, but the big man didn't let out a whimper or scream despite every instinct begging to do so. Then Morovski tore a piece of cloth from Kostya's shirt and wrapped it around the man's arm, tightening down the cold piece.

"That will numb the pain a little until we can get you to a doctor."

Kostya shook his head. "No doctors, Colonel. We cannot risk it. You know that."

"And I cannot risk my second-in-command losing his arm. We will find someone who can remove the bullet."

He already knew it was still in there from the lack of an exit wound.

"Remember," Morovski added, "we are refugees. Everyone helps refugees."

Kostya chuckled through the pain. "Not ones with guns."

"Perhaps. For now, we have to take out the sniper."

As if on cue, another gunshot blasted from above. Morovski was even more certain of the shooter's position.

All of his men were behind the safety of trees now, but he knew that wouldn't last long, especially if the shooters had grenades.

That gave the colonel an idea.

With a last look at the four dead men in the snow, he set his jaw and shouted instructions to the rest.

14

Dak kept his right eye pressed against the scope. He focused his breathing on a slow, steady rhythm just as he'd been trained, and as he'd done when on missions with the military.

He and Will had managed to take out four of the Russian soldiers before the rest of the unit reacted and took cover.

Dak had to hand it to them. The group's response was immediate. Even bogged down by the snow, the soldiers managed to quickly find cover with minimal casualties.

Before he could take out any more, the enemy replied with a counterattack from positions behind trees.

He hated being spotted so quickly, but Dak had also planned for that contingency.

The second the gunmen opened fire, he and the other two slumped back behind the natural trench the mountain provided.

The ditch dipped three feet below the front lip, which Dak and his men had piled up with snow as they waited to spring their trap.

He motioned with his hand to Will and Lesma to move down the trench to the west. Dak knew this would open up the soldiers' flank again and give them additional chances to take clear shots, or at least partially clear.

Will and Lesma crawled through the snow. It crunched under their knees and elbows as bullets cracked the air over their heads and splashed in the powder up the slope. Tree bark splintered around them, but the men pushed on until the rounds were to their backs.

Once they were temporarily out of harm's way, Will looked back past Lesma to Dak, who gave a nod. The three took aim at the Russian column and fired again.

Dak hit his target in the side of the man's torso, felling him to the ground in a single shot. He pulled back the bolt on the hunting rifle and prepared to fire again even as his partners let a volley loose.

Two more enemies dropped to the snow.

The rest of the soldiers adjusted instantly—all of them twisting around the trees they used for cover as they realized the snipers had changed positions.

Once behind cover, the gunmen continued to pepper the trench and the air above with rounds from their weapons.

Loud pops echoed through the forest, and Dak wondered if anyone from the Romanian side of the border could hear the sounds of the skirmish.

He knew that was wishful thinking. The next village was on the other side of the mountain, and it was unlikely anyone heard the gun reports.

He recalled being in the little town of Ringgold, Georgia, on the Tennessee border when he was younger. The Army Reserve's weekend training facility near there came alive on Saturdays and Sundays as the reservists practiced out on the gun range. Occasionally, they worked with small artillery out there, which always rattled the Cherokee Valley with deep booms that shook the ground.

Snow exploded from the bank and splashed over Dak and his friends, but the bullets failed to pierce the earth underneath.

Dak motioned to the other two again, and this time the three shifted back up the shallow gulley toward where they'd fired from initially.

They continued beyond that point, pushing along the slope until they were fifty feet past it. Then, with the same signal as before, the three popped up from behind the snowbank and took aim.

This time, however, the Russians were ready.

The enemy had anticipated the shift, including the overcompensation to go past the place they'd first opened fire.

Dak took a chance on a guy's shoulder but missed just to the right.

Will and Lesma also fired, but no more soldiers hit the ground.

After another shot by all three, the suppressing fire on their position resumed, and the three were forced back down onto their hands and knees.

"Well," Will said, "looks like they figured out our plan."

Dak nodded. "Yeah. I guess so."

"What was your backup plan again?"

Lesma looked to Dak, his eyes calm despite the storm of bullets around him.

Dak reached into his rucksack and pulled out a homemade explosive device. The baseball-shaped ordnance was charcoal gray with a makeshift detonator pin attached to the top.

"I hope this works," he said. Then Dak lobbed the grenade toward the center of the enemy position.

He and the other two ducked down and waited.

Dak counted in his head, then heard the explosion below.

He reached into the bag and took out one more, repeated the process, and tossed.

Ducking down again, he waited for the second big blast, then raised up from behind the ridge and looked for another target.

He'd hoped the grenades would take out several enemies—worst case, two or three. But when he searched the area below, he saw no additional bodies in the snow.

Two black craters smoldered, sending gray smoke into the air that blocked his field of vision to the point he could barely locate any of the enemy soldiers behind the trees.

Then he saw one sprinting to his right.

Dak pressed the scope to his eye and fired rapidly, but the round missed the man's side and burrowed harmlessly into the snow beyond.

Will and Lesma rejoined the fray, each taking shots at the targets as they scampered to new positions.

None of their shots found the mark, and the enemies slid behind the safety of more trees.

Dak didn't like what he saw.

The Russians were dividing their forces to protect both flanks, leaving a few in the center to merely hold down that part of the battlefield. Their intentions were clearer than a Montana river.

The enemy would initially set up on both flanks, cutting off the three snipers' ability to shift up and down the line and try to pick them off one by one.

The Russian leader was smart, which Dak figured, but he found himself impressed with how quickly the opponent implemented the strategy in the field. These were clearly seasoned troops.

He squeezed off a shot at a gunman to the far left of the Russian formation, but the round missed, and then three replies came from the enemies below.

Dak ducked back down at the same time Lesma and Will retreated to the safety of the trench.

The three men breathed heavily from the exertion of the battle. Crawling up and down the line had taken more energy than Lesma could have expected, and even Will and Dak found themselves breathing hard.

"What now?" Will asked. "They have both flanks covered. And the center. Should we fall back and regroup? Maybe take them out in the valley?"

Dak clenched his jaw. This hadn't gone exactly according to plan, which didn't surprise him, but still sent a needle of frustration through his chest.

"Did either of you see the curator?" he answered with a question.

The other two shook their heads. "No," Lesma answered. "I saw her when we first started shooting, but I don't know where she is now."

"Same," Will added. "Saw her just before we opened fire. I don't think she was hit. None of us took any of the targets close to her."

"Right," Dak agreed. "She must have run off in the confusion."

"That is good," Lesma offered. "Perhaps she escaped."

"I wouldn't count on it," Dak said.

He realized they'd already spent too much time talking. For all he knew, the men below were already moving up the hill toward them. That would be their next play.

The Russians would push up the hill to the right first since it was the farthest from the snipers' current position. When Dak and friends turned their attention to that group, the ones in the center would open fire, and the enemies to the left would move up—gradually squeezing the three like a python around a mouse.

Retreating up the hill wasn't an option. Even with the many trees, the run between the trench and the nearest cover would take four or five seconds—more than enough time for an expert marksman to take them down.

Now that the funnel had been created, Dak didn't think risking another shot was a good idea either.

That left only one option.

Just to make sure, he removed a small mirror on a plastic stick from his rucksack and raised it into the air.

He'd painted the thing white and packed it away for just such a situation. A quick look told him his suspicions had been correct.

The Russian flank to the east was moving up the slope one man at a time to close off any escape in that direction.

That left only one move.

"We're going to have to retreat to the valley and see if we can find another spot."

"What about the curator?" Will asked.

Regret smothered Dak's face. "We'll have to come back for her. It's possible she can get to help, either on the Ukrainian side or over the mountain."

"Didn't look like she was dressed for a winter hike," Will commented.

"I know, but we can't help her if we're dead, too. I don't like it any more than you, man. But we have to regroup."

Will nodded. Lesma did, too.

"Follow me. We should have enough cover in this trench to get beyond the enemy's western line, and then from there we'll double back the way we came, using the trees for cover. We'll move in staggered formation. One goes while the other two cover. Got it?"

The other two men nodded.

"Okay, move out. And stay low."

15

___

Morovski's men moved with the precision of a German motor, each cog and gear operating in tandem with the other just like they'd done in so many theaters throughout his command.

And this wasn't the first time he'd faced a nest of snipers.

He counted himself fortunate that he hadn't been one of the first targets. It could have been anyone, but that "honor" had fallen to his friend Kostya. Though the lieutenant colonel was only wounded, the injury would slow him down and make him ineffective in battle.

The colonel knew that his second wouldn't stay out of the fight, wounded or not. And the truth was, even in a slightly hindered state, Kostya Arshavin was one of the toughest warriors Morovski had ever met.

For now, the bleeding had slowed in Kostya's shoulder, though the lieutenant colonel's paled face showed the man was far from okay.

Morovski didn't have the luxury of worrying about getting his friend immediate medical attention. They were under fire from the high ground.

Even with the element of surprise, he'd lost relatively few men considering. But even those sparse losses stung. Both tactically and strategically.

At first, the colonel worried that the enemy raining rounds down on them was from the Romanian border patrol or military, but after the first volley, he dismissed that notion.

The people firing at them were using hunting rifles, not military-grade weapons. He also realized they were bolt action based on the cadence of reports.

Upon retreating to cover, he managed to catch a glimpse of one of the shooters—a large man in a civilian coat. And as he suspected, a hunting rifle in his hands.

Whoever these men were, they weren't professionals. Not soldiers anyway. And after another quick check, he realized there were only three of them.

Morovski had to give them credit for their plan of attack. They'd managed to ambush an entire unit of elite Russian soldiers, but that would soon be punished.

Why were these men here?

That was the question that begged to be answered as he crouched in the snow. The only thing that made sense was that the men must have been hunters searching for deer or other wild game and happened to be in the right place at the right time.

Soon, it would be the wrong place at the wrong time.

But why would they attack his men?

For all the hunters knew, they were a few dozen Ukrainian immigrants trying to escape the war. Sure, they had weapons, but that didn't change anything. There was no chance the hunters assumed them to be anything else. Certainly not Russian soldiers.

Nothing added up. *And why did they have explosives?* They weren't grenades—not the traditional variety, anyway. Morovski wondered if they were some kind of overzealous Romanian militia set to protect their land from any invaders—including refugees.

The men on the colonel's left pressed up the hill one at a time, staggering their movements so the other men could provide suppressing fire.

Kostya clenched his jaw and stood up, as if ready to brace the gun against his shoulder and take aim.

"Stay down," Morovski ordered. "Wait until the left is in position. You're in no condition to lead the assault."

A pained look streaked through Kostya's eyes. "I can fight, Colonel."

"That's an order, Arshavin. You will fight again. But I have another plan for this enemy."

Questions replaced the insulted expression on the lieutenant colonel's face.

Morovski grinned, then turned to one of the men behind a tree ten feet away. "Grenade launchers. Fire above their position."

The man nodded once and turned to another just beyond where he crouched. The two readied their weapons—rifles equipped with the specialized launchers under the barrels—and prepared to aim.

The colonel turned to his left and shouted at the men advancing up the hill. "Hold positions! Suppressing fire!"

The men obeyed without hesitation. They pressed against the nearest trees, they braced their weapons and opened fire in steady, rhythmic staccato.

When he was satisfied the enemy was pinned down, Morovski returned his attention to the grenadiers and motioned with a flick of the wrist for them to fire.

The men stepped out from behind cover, aimed, and fired.

Explosions rocked the slope above the trench where the snipers took refuge. The men fired again in rapid succession, pounding the enemy position with deadly shells.

Several trees splintered and fell.

Then, the earth trembled.

Morovski frowned at the unexpected occurrence, and he immediately saw what happened. A raging white wall of snow roared down the hill toward them.

The shelling had produced a small avalanche—either a happy accident or an egregious miscalculation.

"Take cover!" he shouted.

His men braced themselves behind the trees once more and waited as the snow wall churned faster down the hill.

Morovski watched as clouds of white dust pillared into the air. Trees shook. Some fell in the wake.

Then, when the charging snow hit the trench, it bounced up, broke apart, and sprayed down onto the men below. Their tree cover caught most of it, so the threat was minimal.

The forest fell eerily silent. Without the sounds of battle echoing through the trees, everything immediately took on a serene sort of quiet beauty. No birds chirped in the branches above. Even the wind seemed to cease its movement for a minute or two.

The men looked to their leader from behind their positions. They awaited the next orders, which Morovski was already contemplating.

He had learned a long time ago to always think ahead, always be two steps in front of the other guy—three if you could manage.

It was a trait he'd learned from his schizophrenic father, one of the only things he'd picked up in his youth from the deranged man.

His father had lived in perpetual fear and paranoia, always worried that someone was watching or listening. The voices didn't make anything better, and they often pushed him to do bizarre things until, ultimately, he murdered Nikolai's mother one horrific night.

Nikolai had heard everything from the next room in their little state-owned apartment. Then, as he cowered on his bed, he heard his old man shouting Nikolai's name, telling him to get in there.

When he refused, his father burst through the boy's door. He held a bloody hammer in his hand. His eyes burned with insanity—like a murderous character from some deranged Dostoevsky novel—the last scraps of the man Nikolai knew as his father, lost to the void.

Fueled by obscure anger, the man charged. It was a reckless, nearly blind attack, and he'd stumbled as he neared the boy's bed.

It was the only opportunity Nikolai had needed.

When his father leaned forward as he tripped, he still raised the hammer to strike a killing blow.

Nikolai had been sleeping with one of the kitchen knives under the mattress for months—a gift and a command from his mother.

As Morovski sat in the snow, he still recalled the sad expression in her eyes. She'd known what was going to happen and yet hadn't left. She could have taken Nikolai and run off to the countryside. His father would have tried to find them but would have eventually failed and given up.

But she wouldn't leave. She carried a sick sort of loyalty to Nikolai's father that he never understood.

Nikolai had held the kitchen knife behind his back just in case things went this way, and when his father started to swing the hammer, the boy leaped forward off the bed and plunged the long blade through his father's upper abdomen, just below the sternum.

In all the years Nikolai Morovski had fought in Russia's global conflicts, he'd never seen as much blood as what came out of his father on that night.

The man died in under a minute, gasping for help of all things.

After that, when the police were done with their job, the boy was sent to live with an uncle.

But the one lesson Morovski learned from his father stayed with him his entire life, and made him a great leader in the field.

"Did you mean to do that?" Kostya grunted.

Morovski's lips curled into a one-sided smile. "Would you believe me if I said yes?" He studied Kostya's face for a few breaths before chuckling. "No. That, my friend, was fate smiling at us."

"You think they're dead?" The lieutenant colonel looked up the hill toward the trench.

"If they aren't, it will take them a long time to dig their way out."

"Should we go check?"

Again, the colonel had already thought ahead. "No. If they aren't dead, we will be long gone by the time they emerge from the snow. But my guess is they're gone. We don't have time to stand around and dig them up to find out. Even a few feet off could mean hours of time wasted. We head to the village." He looked back at the dead men, their lifeless bodies lying still in the snow. Flurries settled on their clothes and didn't melt right away. The dead were already losing their body's warmth.

Morovski had seen that before.

He didn't expect to be attacked once they were over the border. It was the one thing he hadn't accounted for.

"Leave the dead," he ordered.

Kostya didn't question it. He knew there was no point in trying to bury the bodies, and they were against the clock.

Morovski gave the order to move out and to leave the dead where they lay. A few of the men looked uncomfortable with the notion but didn't disobey their commander.

They pushed forward, staying in formation, with one group taking the center, flanked on both sides.

The colonel helped up his friend with considerable effort. But once Kostya was on his feet, he steadied his balance and set his gaze on the forest to the east and the valley beyond.

"Let's move out, Colonel," he said with stout resolve.

The two marched forward in the middle of the column, both of them sweeping the woods around them and checking the sniper nest several times before it was out of sight. With no movement or signs of life, the group continued their march and disappeared around the bend.

16

D ak felt cold in a way he'd never imagined possible.
It stabbed at every inch of his body. And it felt as
though he'd been shoved into the tightest walk-in freezer
in the world.

The chill wrapped around him like an unrelenting ice blanket,
and he found it difficult to shake free of it.

For the first few seconds, he didn't know what had happened.

The explosions, he knew, were shells from grenade launchers.
He'd heard the familiar thumping sounds and expected to be in
pieces scattered around the snow. But the men had aimed high,
possibly because they didn't know exactly where to fire since Dak and
his crew had ducked out of sight during the shooting.

A wrecking ball of worry smashed into him: *Are Will and Lesma
okay?*

Dak could barely breath with the snow packed tightly around his
face, and the realization only caused his lungs to tighten even more.

He started shaking his head right to left, at first only millimeters
of movement, but as the snow crumbled from his skin, the gyrations
grew more pronounced. He did the same with his fingers and toes.
The snow tightly encased his entire body, and the only reason he

knew he wasn't upside down was due to the pull of gravity; otherwise, being so suspended would have been considerably more disorienting.

Dak kept shivering, pulling his thoughts toward a single thought —warmth. He imagined a blazing fire in the hearth back in his cabin in Tennessee. In his mind, he sat there with a hot cup of coffee warming his hands as he held it.

Another thought emerged, as he looked to his left and saw Nicole sitting on the couch next to him, curled up in a thick blanket with heavy winter socks on her feet. She nuzzled against his shoulder, and he felt her warmth radiating through him.

Dak kicked down against the earth beneath him and felt himself break free of the snowy bond.

His head burst out of the packed powder. He shook away the snow on his head and shoulders and freed his arms. It took another minute to dig out, but he finally crawled onto the surface, clumps of snow still clinging to his coat and pants, then pulled his rucksack out last.

He looked around, searching for his two friends. It didn't take long to locate them.

To his left, Will's boot and leg stuck up out of the snow, wiggling and kicking around in the air. Just beyond the leg, Dak saw Lesma. The Russian was only covered from the waist down with snow and had somehow managed to avoid being buried.

Dak quickly realized it was due to a thick tree only a few yards above that had taken the brunt of the avalanche and kept Lesma mostly above the snow.

The man shook off the clumps that had splashed onto him. As he brushed away more snow from his shoulders, he noticed Dak staring at him.

"Dak!" he exclaimed. "Oh, that was scary, yeah? I wasn't sure if you survived."

"You sound both relieved and yet not at all unsettled by that," Dak countered.

"Ah, I kid." Lesma waved his hand dismissing the notion. "I knew you would survive. That's what you do." He looked at the leg jutting out of the snow. "We should probably help your friend, though."

"Yeah."

Dak crawled over to where Will's leg flailed and started digging with his hands. Lesma joined him on the other side and likewise started pulling snow away until the other leg appeared.

"Grab one leg, and I'll get the other," Dak said. "We need to get him out of there before he runs out of air."

"Da," Lesma agreed in his native tongue.

The two men grabbed onto Will's legs and pulled, leaning back toward the slope for extra leverage. Their feet dug into the snow at first, forcing them to get a lower grip just below Will's knees.

They heard him shouting something, but the snow muted whatever cries for help or—as Dak suspected, profanities, he may have loosed.

"We need to pull at the same time. Okay?" Dak said.

Lesma agreed with a nod.

"All right. On three. One. Two. Three."

The two men tugged simultaneously on Will's legs. The combined effort jerked their friend out of the snow and sent them tumbling backward against the bank.

Will flopped around for a second, gasping for air as his arms and legs kicked in random directions. Then he rolled over onto his back and sucked in clean oxygen, finally able to breathe normally again.

Once he'd regained his bearings, he sat up and saw his two friends sitting on the snow with their backs against the slope. Both breathed hard from the effort of dragging him out of his frigid burial.

"What was that?" Will gasped, louder than he intended.

Dak quickly shushed him and looked around, suddenly aware that their weapons were buried, and the enemy could still be nearby.

He scrambled over to the edge where the lip of the trench had been before—now covered with fresh snow and tree limbs—and surveyed the area.

The avalanche had broken on the ditch and only sent a fraction of the snow and debris down below where their Russian adversaries had been before. Dak noticed the two black craters where his explosives had detonated, as well as the bodies of the men they'd eliminated, but there was no sign of the rest of the unit.

"Looks like they left," Dak realized, turning back to the other two.

"Where did they go?" Lesma wondered.

"My guess is they hauled off toward the next village."

"The one where we left our ride?" Will asked as he dusted himself off.

"Yeah." Dak looked that direction, but his view was partially obscured by a three-foot-high snowdrift. He rolled over onto his hands and knees and crawled to the hump, then peeked over the top. He muttered a complaint under his breath.

Three trails plowed through the snow and disappeared around the bend. Dak knew they couldn't be far away, but without weapons, chasing them at this point would be suicide. Then again, if they didn't catch up right away, the rogue unit would escape and be gone for good.

"They went that way," Dak confirmed. "We need to hurry if we want to catch them."

"But our guns are in the snow," Will argued. "And our gear. It'll take who knows how long to dig that stuff out."

"I know. But if we let them get away, we may not find them again."

"You are thinking we simply follow and watch?" Lesma clarified.

"Yeah." Dak turned his head back toward the valley, then to Will. "We can find more guns. It's not like I was in love with that hunting rifle, anyway. Plus, they're bulky. And we still have our sidearms."

"A lot of good pistols will do against that unit. We'd never get close enough for them to be effective."

Dak had already considered that. "Then we wait for the opportune moment. They don't know what we look like. I assume."

Will huffed. "You know what they say about when you assume."

Dak shared the chuckle. "I'm well aware."

"What?" Lesma wondered. "What is this about assume?"

The two Americans shook their heads.

"It's an expression," Dak explained. "When you assume, you make an ass of you and me."

Lesma's forehead wrinkled showing he still didn't comprehend. "You don't make an ass of me. No one makes an ass of Lesma Lebedev."

"That's right. And don't let anyone say otherwise."

The big Russian confirmed with a curt nod.

Dak stood up and looked out toward the valley again, just to make sure no one in the rear guard was doubling back. The trails remained empty.

The others stood, and he was about to give the order to move out when he realized something he'd forgotten.

"The curator," he blurted.

"What about her?" Will asked.

Dak stepped past his friends and looked down the slope to the place he'd last seen her. He swiveled his head around, now perplexed at the decision he had to make.

"We have to find her," he said.

"She could be long gone," Will countered. "We don't know which way she went." He threw his hands up. "Heck, they could have grabbed her before they left."

Dak spied the area where the Russian unit had been positioned during the firefight. Only a single trough of footprints trailed away from the tamped-down snow and the bodies littering the spot.

"No," he said. "They left in a hurry. I would have, too. All that gunfire, plus the explosions could have been heard by someone. If the Romanian border patrol showed up, they'd be finished. Disguises or not. No way they could have hidden that loot for long."

"If we go after her, we won't have a chance of catching up to the thieves," Will said. "You know that, right?"

Dak nodded. "Saving Galyna Kovalenka was always the primary objective," he stated. He remembered her name from the file he'd looked over before making the trip. "Retrieving the artifacts was secondary."

"That is a lot of gold," Lesma mused, as if his imagination took him to a place where spending it was relaxing under a tropical sun. "But Dak is right. We must find her."

Will sighed, but the expression on his face told that he agreed. "Okay. Let's head out. She couldn't have gone far."

The three trudged down the hillside toward the last spot where she'd been seen, and then followed the tracks.

"Well, this is the easiest tracking job I've ever had to do," Will commented as they waded through the snow.

The tracks led around the base of the hill, skirting close to the border fence, until they spotted a figure moving aimlessly in a zigzag pattern a hundred yards away.

"There she is," Dak announced.

She'd already put a considerable distance between herself and them, but she was moving slowly and from the looks of it wasn't dressed for this kind of weather.

"Come on," he urged.

The three picked up their pace with Lesma being the slowest and bringing up the rear.

When they were fifty yards away, the woman looked back over her shoulder and panicked. She started trying to run—apparently afraid they were part of the Russian contingent that had imprisoned her. She stumbled in the snow and fell face-first, then scrambled to get up and start moving again.

"Galyna!" Dak shouted. "Galyna Kovalenka! Wait! We're Americans!"

"I am not," Lesma said between gasping for air.

Dak ignored him and pushed ahead, pumping his legs harder. "We're Americans!"

The woman stopped in her tracks and turned around. She stared at the three men as they approached.

At twenty yards, Dak saw the concern on her pale face. She was freezing out here, and if she'd continued on along the border probably would have died from exposure.

He waved his hands over his head as he drew near to signal they meant her no harm. "See? We're here to help you."

The woman swallowed, and the last of her strength burned out of her. She wavered for a second, then her legs gave out and she fell onto her knees in the snow.

Dak slid to a stop in time to catch her torso and head. Will grabbed her by the shoulders and propped her up as Dak quickly removed his coat and handed it to his friend. Will wrapped the garment around her as Dak held her head and chin.

"Galyna. Can you hear me?" he asked.

Her eyes rolled, and an unintelligible word escaped her lips.

"Relax," Dak soothed. "It's okay. We got you." He looked down at her feet and noted the lack of socks. "Lesma, get her shoes off for me."

The Russian complied in an instant and removed the shoes.

Dak hurriedly ripped off his boots and pulled the socks off his feet. Then he stuffed her feet into them before putting his boots back on.

Then he slumped his gear bag onto the ground and unzipped the main compartment. He rummaged through and found the cord he was looking for, then removed a small hatchet from inside.

"What are you going to do with that?" Lesma asked.

"We need to build a stretcher," Dak answered. "Give her your coat, too, Will. Let her sit on that for now. Lesma, wrap yours around her like a blanket. Stay here with her while I get some wood for a stretcher. Will, see if you can find some dry wood lying around. Small sticks and some branches. We need to build a fire."

"That'll draw attention," Will argued as he stood.

"That's what I'm hoping. The soldiers are long gone by now. And they won't dare double back even if they see smoke. They're on a tight timeline."

The two Americans scurried up the slope to a stand of evergreens. Dak hacked off several limbs about three inches in diameter, then collected the bundle under both arms and made his way back down the hill. Will's job had been easier, and he'd managed to collect several pieces of wood and a small pile of twigs to get the fire started.

Dak dropped his load on the snow next to where Will was

working on building a little pyramid with the smallest of the sticks. Once it was ready, he reached into his rucksack and produced a fire starter—a little metal rod with a flat scraping tool attached with a black leather strip.

He set that on the ground next to the pile and set to work with a hunting knife from his left hip, shaving off bits of wood from one of the sticks until he had a little mound. Then he moved the twigs over top of the shavings and scraped the bar with the flat metal card.

It sparked several times until the slivers of wood flickered to life. Will bent over and blew on the tiny flames until they grew, then he arranged more twigs over top of them and continued to blow air onto the little fire.

Meanwhile, Dak laid out two of the longer branches of similar length and began strapping the shorter ones across it with the cord from his rucksack.

Lesma watched the two men working as he sat next to Galyna with his arm around her, occasionally checking to make sure she was breathing. The woman was half asleep, with her head slumped against his shoulder, but occasionally moving randomly in slow, uncontrolled twitches.

The Russian squeezed her closer.

"How's she doing, Les?" Dak asked as he finished strapping another branch to his makeshift stretcher.

"Alive," Lesma said. "But she is very weak. I imagine those animals didn't feed her much, if anything."

"Yeah. They were probably keeping her as a hostage. Or maybe hoped to sell her to someone once they got to wherever they were going. Or just as bad, maybe the leader of that group wanted to keep her for himself."

Lesma knew where that thinking was headed, and he shuddered. "I have done horrible things in my life," he confessed. "But nothing like that. Killing, sure. Stealing, now and then. But never that."

Dak knew the man detested such things. It was one of the reasons the Russian had killed his own son. For all his faults, Lesma respected women, and Dak could only wonder where that mindset had come from. He imagined Lesma must have had strong ties to his mother but had never asked and never would. Sometimes, it was best to let a man keep his secrets.

The fire began to crackle, and embers sizzled against the snow around it where Will had dug out a pit. He added more twigs and sticks, and within minutes the flames licked the air a foot off the ground.

Will moved over to Galyna and helped Lesma shift her closer to the fire as Dak finished the stretcher.

"If no one comes to help," Dak said, "we can carry her back to the village on this." He looked at his handiwork with grim satisfaction. Then he reached into his rucksack and pulled out an energy bar and a canteen. He handed the two items to Lesma. "See if you can get her to eat and drink something. She probably needs to."

The big Russian nodded and started unwrapping the bar, while Dak stood up and looked around the area.

He focused his eyes on the path the enemy had forged heading back into the valley, wondering where the rogue unit was headed next.

17

The remainder of Morovski's unit trudged wearily into the Romanian village of Valea Vișeului. He looked around at the sparse collection of houses, and even fewer businesses and administrative buildings.

A pale-yellow train station stood off to the side of the street. The rails were barely visible in the snow, sticking out like two rusty dark lines on a white sheet of paper.

He didn't imagine the rails were well maintained, despite the station looking as if it were.

The town nestled in the valley between the rolling mountains like a baby in a cradle, wrapped in a white blanket.

It looked like a village the rest of the world had forgotten, and the colonel wondered how people there made a living aside from agriculture. There were a few farms in the valley, but none covering the hillsides. For a fleeting moment, Morovski considered this a good place to disappear, but he knew that wasn't an option.

They had a date in Hungary that he wasn't going to miss, and from there, he'd go somewhere far warmer than this Romanian outpost.

Nowhere in this part of the world could offer the retirement he desired.

Morovski and Kostya led the way forward since none of them had any idea where they might find transportation in this one-horse town.

Upon seeing the few vehicles parked outside the train station, and next to a café in a gray building that looked like it could hold ten people, he spotted a white concrete block building with a dilapidated tin roof.

"Over there," the colonel ordered, pointing at the structure. "Looks abandoned. We'll hole up there until we can find some trucks."

Three of the men hurried in front of the colonel to take point.

The building stood sixty yards from one set of train tracks, and appeared as if it hadn't been used in years. What it was for, Morovski didn't know. And he didn't care. They needed to get out of sight for the moment. Twenty men carrying a load of unusually large bags looked beyond suspicious."

The column spread out and staggered in irregular formation to make themselves look less like a military unit and more like a pack of refugees, or travelers.

When the first men reached the front door of the building, they looked around to make sure no one was watching—even though they'd only seen a few people walking about aimlessly on the snowy streets. Then they barged through the door, bursting it open.

The rest of the men filed in, producing sidearms to sweep the interior and make sure no threats lurked within.

Morovski had little concerns about the derelict building, and that confidence was confirmed the second he stepped inside.

It had been a mechanic shop in its previous life. The single-bay garage door and worn-out hydraulic lifts beyond betrayed its original purpose.

The men spread out and set their gear down before turning their eyes toward their leader to await further instructions.

Two of them closed the door and stood guard on either side of it.

The colonel spoke quickly, and decisively. "I need three of you to go find us transportation. Three trucks would be optimal, but we can make do with two. Vans are also acceptable. Those would be tight, but we can make it work."

Every man in the room stepped forward. Morovski smiled at their willingness to volunteer. He selected three, and the men left through the door, taking only their sidearms underneath their coats.

"I need two more to find some medical supplies to help Kostya with his wound. We need something to disinfect it and clean it out so it doesn't get worse."

No one took a step back, and Morovski chose another two from the ranks to take care of that task. "There should be an apothecary somewhere around here. You all have some degree of field medic training, so you know what to get. They won't take any of our currency, so you'll have to pocket the goods while the other distracts the clerk."

The men acknowledged with a nod and made their way back out into the cold.

Morovski looked over at his lieutenant colonel, who sat huddled in the corner against the wall. The man pulled on his coat sleeves with both hands to protect against the cold. The colonel knew Kostya was colder than anyone else in the room.

He stepped over to Kostya and removed his own coat, then laid it across his friend. "There, that should help until we can get the wound cleaned."

"No, sir," Kostya protested. "That is your coat. I can't take that. You'll be cold."

"I'll be fine," Morovski insisted. "I'm plenty warm. Remember, I spent time in Siberia. An hour in the Romanian hills is nothing."

Kostya smiled his gratitude to the commander and offered an appreciative nod.

"The rest of you," Morovski said, "watch the windows and doors. It's possible a local saw us come in here. Perhaps they'll get suspicious. Perhaps not. Either way, be ready in case trouble comes knocking."

The men didn't have to be told twice. While they watched the windows and doors, they readied their weapons. Some cleaned their guns, while others checked munitions. But all of them were ready to fight if so much as a mouse peeped the wrong way.

And in this building, that was certainly in the realm of possibility.

The next hour went by with excruciating deliberateness. Each second that passed felt like the slow drip of the fabled Chinese water torture.

Finally, after pacing across the dusty floor for the hundredth time, the colonel was roused from his pensive deliberation by a short rap at the door.

The guard to the left of the door cracked it to check who was out there, and when he saw his comrades, opened it wide to let them pass.

The first two to arrive were the ones Morovski sent to find the apothecary. They carried nothing in their hands, but the colonel knew they'd been successful. Sure enough, one of the men pulled various first aid materials out of his coat pockets and carried them over to Kostya.

The other man reported to the colonel.

"There aren't many people out right now, sir. It didn't seem like anyone noticed us when we came into town. I explained to the clerk at the apothecary that I'd left my wallet in the car and would have to come back. She seemed to accept the explanation."

Morovski nodded at the young soldier. He was one of the youngest in the group—only twenty-two years of age, but his face bore the look of a fifteen-year-old.

The colonel had seen him use that as fuel to be twice as efficient, and often as ruthless in battle, as the rest of the unit. And Morovski appreciated the kid's mental fortitude.

"Excellent," the colonel replied. "Did you happen to see any viable transportation for our trip to Budapest?"

"No, sir. There isn't much here. I imagine in the summer there might be a few more people around, but not many. This area is pretty desolate." He quieted his voice so only the colonel could hear. "I would be surprised if the other three are able to find anything, sir. We may need to come up with a backup plan."

"Yes. I see," Morovski grumbled. "Thank you. Take a rest for a few minutes. I appreciate your effort."

"Yes, sir." The man spun on his heels and walked over to an empty spot on the floor next to some of the others and sat down to begin his routine of checking his weapons and supplies.

Within five minutes, the other three men arrived at the door. The colonel didn't have to hear their report to know what it was. He could read it on their faces.

Still, he tried, but he decided to receive the bad news outside in private, rather than in the building where all of his men could hear. The last thing he needed right now was any of them deciding this was a bad idea. Morovski wasn't going to let anything or anyone stand in his way.

He closed the door behind him and looked to the one who'd led the quest. He was a few inches shorter than the colonel but bulging with muscles from extensive training in the gym.

"Any luck?" Morovski asked.

"No, sir," the leader replied. "There aren't many vehicles in this town from what we gathered, and we covered most of the area where there are homes. It's like a ghost town right now. Must be the winter, although I doubt this place gets many tourists during the warmer months."

If the colonel was the kind of guy to let his heart sink at every little setback, this would have been the time.

But he set his jaw in a firm scowl and took a deep breath through his nose. "Well, that is unfortunate. We can't walk to Budapest."

"Perhaps there will be some delivery trucks coming through here in the morning, sir. It's possible."

"No. We don't have time to wait for that."

The man who'd been helping Kostya with the medical supplies

emerged in the doorway and closed it behind him. He had a bloody swath of gauze in one hand.

"How does it look?" Morovski asked.

The guy playing doctor turned around with a bloody swab of gauze in his hand. "Not great, but I think I can get the round out," he said. "They used a pretty standard hunting bullet. Fortunately, it didn't break apart on impact."

Morovski studied the man for only two seconds before saying, "Do it."

The soldier confirmed with a nod. "Yes, sir." Then he disappeared back into the building.

A frigid breeze swept across the valley, cutting into Morovski's skin like a blade of ice. The cold sent a shiver through his body, but he fought it off with sheer will, and imagined sitting by a beach on a hot day somewhere in the tropics.

"We can't wait until morning, Corporal," Morovski reinforced the message from before. "It has to be today."

"I can go back through the village again, sir. I'll double-check."

"No. Don't bother. I trust your judgment. If you said there was nothing, then it must be so."

"Then what are we going to do, sir?"

Morovski couldn't say he didn't know. His men expected him to always have the answers, even if one didn't seem apparent.

He knew it would be dark soon, and once night fell, they would be stuck. And the old shop offered little in the way of warmth and comfort. Even as tough as he and his men were, spending the night in this place in the middle of winter would be a test he didn't care to take.

But what choice did he have?

He was about to tell the corporal to order the men to prepare for a cold night when he heard a whistle in the distance.

His eyes flashed at the sound, and he turned his head in the direction he thought it came from.

Then a horn blared, and he knew his ears hadn't deceived him.

With the sound, the colonel found a renewed sense of hope. "Did you hear that?" he asked.

The corporal shrugged with a nod. "Of course. I imagine the entire valley heard it, sir."

"That is the sound of our salvation, son. Go tell the others to collect their things. We need to catch a train."

18

A ray of sunlight pierced the clouds outside the window and shone into the inn bedroom along the floor by the bed.

Galyna opened her eyes like a cat who'd been napping by a fireplace. The lids cracked slowly at first, then widened, closed, then opened fully.

Dak stood over her. At first, a look of confusion and surprise filled her eyes. Fear came next, but he smiled pleasantly at her to diffuse any panic.

"Galyna," he said as calm as an Appalachian stream, "it's okay. You're safe now."

He watched her process everything, but the look of worry didn't leave her face. "Where... where am I?"

"You're safe," Dak repeated. "You're in a Romanian village." The concern eased, and her facial muscles relaxed. "I'm Dak Harper, and these are my friends Lesma and Will."

The two men nodded to her.

Will leaned up against the wall by the door, casually standing guard. Lesma sat in a desk chair with black leather cushions.

"Sorry for the accommodations, but there isn't much here," Dak said.

"We're lucky we could find this," Will half complained. "There are like eight buildings in this place if you don't count the farmhouses."

Dak snickered.

Galyna started to sit up, but Dak put out both hands to slow her down. "Take it easy," he ordered. "You've been through a lot. You managed to eat and drink a little something before we brought you here. But you're still really weak. We'll get you some food shortly."

She did as instructed, bracing herself with palms against the mattress as she kept looking around the room, still unclear on so many things.

"Americans?" she managed. "Why are you here? Are you with the American government or military?" She didn't hide the doubt she cast at taking in Lesma's appearance.

He didn't notice.

"We're not with the military," Dak said. "Will and I used to be. But not anymore."

"We're retired," Will chimed.

Dak suppressed the urge to laugh at the term.

"So, why are you here?" she pressed.

"I heard what happened at the museum. I work for someone who pays me to find things when they disappear—or if they reappear in the wrong hands."

"The artifacts," she gasped. Hope filled her eyes. "Did you salvage the artifacts?"

Dak shook his head, despondent. "No. The men who took them and held you captive got away."

"We killed some of them, though," Lesma said with a nod and a wink, as if that would make her feel better.

She looked at him then back to Dak. "Those artifacts were Ukraine's history. The Scythian Empire was one of the greatest in history, and at its time was a world power." The last flicker of hope vanished from her face.

"I know," Dak said. "But our plan to take them out failed. They're a well-trained unit. I'll give them that. We're lucky any of us got out alive. But you were always the priority, Galyna."

Her eyebrows pinched. "How do you know my name?"

"That part wasn't hard," Will explained. "Once the story got out, your name came with it."

Dak could see the many questions still running through her head from the look on her face. All he could do was smile and try to keep her calm.

"I know it's a lot to take in," he said.

She nodded. "Yes. It is. But you saved my life. Thank you. Thank you all. I cannot believe you came all the way to Ukraine to rescue me. I will forever be in your debt."

"No debt," Dak said. "Just glad we could help."

She shifted in the bed and sat up a little straighter. The color had returned to her skin, and she looked visibly better than when the three men had found her.

"What happened?" she asked. "I remember the shooting. Then some explosions. The next thing I saw was... your face. Then... a fire?"

"The Russian unit caused a small avalanche. We were buried under it for a few minutes. Maybe ten. I don't really know how long, honestly. But I can tell you it was the coldest I've ever felt in my life." He laughed it off. "When we found you, you were pretty out of it. Will started a fire to get you warm. We hoped someone from the Romanian border patrol would find us. Eventually, we loaded you on a stretcher and started walking."

"Which was not easy," Will added, "but probably for the best. We'd have had to ditch our guns somewhere."

"Guns? So you were the ones shooting at the soldiers? Just the three of you?"

Dak shrugged as if it was no big deal. "I mean, we didn't have a choice."

"You are either very brave or very reckless," Galyna said with an awkward laugh.

"Amazing how often those things coincide," Will joked.

"I can imagine."

"My only regret is we weren't able to save the artifacts," Dak lamented.

"Do you think any of them were damaged in the fight?" she wondered.

"Hard to know," Dak said. "We were careful."

"Except for the explosives," Lesma chuffed.

"Right. I mean, I figured those were more of a diversion," Dak admitted. "But didn't really work out." He sighed. "Now all that history is lost, and we don't have a way to track them. They'll be long gone."

Galyna hummed pensively.

Dak's expression changed. Curiosity flittered through his shamrock eyes. "What?" he asked. "What was that?"

She stared at him for a few long breaths that seemed to suck the air out of the room. The three men collectively inched their heads forward as if to pry the information from her.

"Well, when I was being held hostage, the colonel wasn't careful with what he said. I guess he figured I wouldn't escape, so he didn't seem to worry about talking about his plans."

She stumbled over her words for a second, tears welling in her eyes as she relived the terrifying experience.

"He said he might sell me off, or keep me around as his pet. He teased me with the possibility of freedom, but I knew better. Men like him—wicked men—are as greedy as they are despicable."

The three men listened as she continued.

"But while he was talking to the others, he mentioned a buyer—a German."

"Did this German have a name?" Dak asked.

"I didn't hear the name. They just called him the German." She saw the disappointment darken their faces, and quickly added, "But I did hear where they are going."

Hope splashed into the men's eyes. "You did?" Will asked, stepping away from the doorway.

She nodded. "They're going to Hungary. They're setting up a meeting with the buyer in Budapest. I don't know where exactly, but if that can help you track them, we may still have a chance to recover the artifacts."

Dak's head bobbed as thoughts ran through his mind at breakneck speed. "I'll call Liz and see if she can help us out with that. If she can get access to the satellites again, we might be able to locate the Russian unit."

"How?" Will asked. "They probably stole some trucks and have been out of the area for a while now."

"Right," Dak agreed. "But there are only a few ways out of this little town."

He stepped over to his rucksack, pulled it up off the floor near a desk, and set it on top. Then he opened the zipper and pulled out a map they'd used when they were with Liz. He spread the map out over the desk and flattened it before running his finger along one of the roads.

The other two men moved closer to look over his shoulder as Dak stopped his finger on the little town where they now stood.

"There are only two roads out of this village," he stated. "Only one heads toward Hungary."

"So, we call Liz and see if she can spot a group of trucks driving down that road?" Will suggested.

"Right. You guys saw the area. There isn't much here. Three trucks running in a row from here would be awfully suspicious. This road runs right along the Ukrainian border, and it will pass through the town of Sighetu. There's border crossing there, so I bet the rogue unit is going to do all they can to avoid trouble there. Too many cops, military, all that right now."

Dak took out his phone and pressed the number for Liz's phone.

It rang twice before she answered. "You know you're supposed to wait three days to call a girl after she gives you her number, right?"

"I don't like to keep a lady waiting," Dak countered.

She laughed with an amused hum. "What can I do for you?"

"I'm not sure if you can score access to that satellite again, but we need to track some trucks."

"Again? What did you do to the last ones?"

Dak's lips creased slightly. "They left those in Ukraine. Crossed the Romanian border on foot in the mountains."

"Glad to hear your intuition was good. But they got away?"

"We were outgunned, as we knew we would be. But we rescued the curator. She's safe here with us."

"Oh, wow. That's wonderful news, Dak. I'll be sure to let the right people in Ukraine know that."

"The rogue unit still has the artifacts, though. We need to get them back. You think you could help us find a couple more trucks? There are only two roads out of Valea Vișeului. They'll take the one heading northwest toward Hungary. But they'll have to pass through Sighetu."

"That's a bigger town. If they've already reached it, they'll likely split up, and then finding them will prove much harder."

"I know. But can you try?"

"Let me check."

Dak waited patiently for two minutes while the others in the room watched him, expecting an answer any second.

"Dak?" Liz said as she came back on the line.

"Yeah. I'm here."

"I'll be able to access the satellite in twenty-two minutes."

He felt the wind blow out of his lungs. "By then, they'll already be in Sighetu."

"What I can do is watch the road on the other side of the city. It looks like the only road heading toward Hungary goes west, then south into Satu Mare. If you can get there to cut them off, you've got a chance."

"There's no way we can get there in time. They have a big head start," Dak reasoned.

"What if I could get you a ride?"

Dak's eyebrows lifted and his eyes widened with hope. "What kind of ride?"

19

"This city is a lot larger than I thought it would be," Dak realized out loud.

He watched the town of Satu Mare spread out beneath him, the city lights stretching in multiple directions.

The dark streets weaved around shops, flats, churches, and administrative buildings that looked more like palaces than ordinary places of government.

From the helicopter, he could see nearly the entire city except for parts that remained hidden in thickets of trees. The moon hung high in the clear sky with only a strip of a cloud stretching across its face to blunt the pale glow.

"Yeah," Will agreed through the headset.

Lesma sat against the window on the other side, his face glued to the glass while he watched the countryside give way to the city below.

"How will we find them here?" he wondered. "It will be nearly impossible."

"We don't have to watch the city," Dak reminded. "Just the road. Liz already called in a favor with the local police. They've set up a roadblock on the only road coming into this town from that direction.

If they're coming through here like we think, then they'll swim right into our net."

He looked over at Galyna, who stared out the window to her left. She sat with her back to the cockpit and hadn't said much since the chopper picked them up on the other side of the mountains.

"When we land," Dak continued, this time directing his words at her, "we'll find you a hospital so you can get checked properly by a physician. Just to make sure you don't have any lingering—"

"I'm fine," she cut him off, dragging her eyes away from the window to look across at him. "And there's no way I'm not coming with you three."

"We can't let you do that. It's too dangerous. You're lucky to be alive as it is."

"Maybe," she said. "But those artifacts are my charge. It is my responsibility and my life's work to preserve the history of Ukraine. I cannot simply stand aside and watch. So, you can give me one of those guns, or I'll just use my bare hands. Up to you."

Surprised by the woman's courage and stubbornness, Dak knew he should refuse her request, but he also knew that wasn't going to play out. She'd find a way to get involved one way or another, and if she wasn't with them, the danger would be far greater.

He reached into his rucksack and pulled out a 9mm Springfield pistol. He'd procured one of those to go with his .40-cal, the preferred sidearm that almost always accompanied him. But the 9 was extremely effective, compact, and perfectly weighted.

He handed her the weapon amid a shocked stare from Will and Lesma.

"You can't be serious," Will protested.

The pilot glanced back over his shoulder, also surprised at the interaction, but he quickly returned his focus to his task of flying the helicopter.

"You clearly haven't tried to win an argument with a woman," Dak countered.

Lesma chuckled. "He's correct, my friend. Fight the battles you can win. This is not one of those."

Dak handed her the pistol.

She took it and inspected it with a quick once over.

"Do you know how to—"

She immediately ejected the magazine from the well and checked it, then pulled the slide and caught the round that fell from the chamber. She looked at the barrel then the rest of the upper receiver before allowing the slide to move back into place. Then she shoved the chamber round back into the magazine, slid that into the well, and pulled the slide one more time to re-chamber the bullet.

"To use it," Dak finished. "I guess so."

"It would help if you had a holster," she said plainly.

"I suppose it would," he agreed and reached into the rucksack for a side holster. He passed it over to her, and she expertly fixed it to the belt around her waist. Then pulled the coat he'd given her down over it. "Better?"

"Much."

The pilot cleared his throat to get everyone's attention. "We're coming up on the blockade now. I'm going to set her down in a field next to the road. The Romanian authorities know you're coming. Still, I'd hide those weapons if I were you. Keep them out of sight unless you want them confiscated."

"Anything else?" Dak asked.

"Let the Romanians handle it. Last thing we want is an international incident with a couple of Americans, a Russian, and a Ukrainian with firearms."

"Until the firearms part, it almost sounded like the setup for a really bad joke," Will quipped.

The pilot apparently didn't see the humor. "Just make sure you hang back until their people apprehend the criminals. Once they do, you can introduce the woman to them. She can handle the requisition process from there."

Galyna cocked her head to the side and smiled as if to say, "Yeah, let me handle it."

Dak merely shrugged. "Fine by me. I'd prefer to sit back and watch on the sidelines for a change."

Will eyed his friend with suspicion, but he let it slide.

The pilot tilted the aircraft to the left and nudged the nose downward, then as they neared the ground, leaned it back slightly until it leveled off.

The passengers watched to the right where several police cars blocked the road leading into and out of the city. Cars leaving the town passed by sporadically without any fuss, but a line of vehicles stretched a quarter of a mile down the asphalt as the cops slowed down every one of them for a quick inspection.

The helicopter touched down, and Dak quickly opened the door to let the others out.

The passengers removed their headsets and hung them on hooks before exiting the aircraft.

Dak was the last one out. He slapped the pilot on the shoulder and said, "Thanks for the lift."

"No problem," the man said. "I was bored sitting around on the border."

"Keep a sharp eye. The world has gone crazy lately."

"You got that right, brother."

Dak hopped out of the chopper, closed the door, and smacked it twice to let the pilot know they were out.

He crouched low as he made his way over to the rest of his team. The aircraft blew snow around them in swirling funnels as it took off.

The group watched as the helicopter lifted up into the night. Within thirty seconds the blinking lights were high above the ground and sailing off into the darkness.

Dak slung his pack over his shoulders and indicated the roadblock. "I guess we should go introduce ourselves. Liz said they'd know we're coming. We just need to make sure we keep our firearms out of sight."

Everyone confirmed with a nod.

The group marched through the snow until they reached an old wooden fence that marked the property where they'd landed. The thought struck Dak as funny—that they'd just landed in someone's field, probably.

Dak crossed the fence first, then helped Galyna over. The other two followed. Dak led the way to the nearest police car, where two Romanian cops stood there chatting about something. Their breath blew out of their mouths in puffy clouds. It didn't appear they were concerned with anything; in fact, it looked as if one had just told a joke based on the laughter from the other.

Dak approached them with caution, waving to them with his right hand and keeping the left out wide so they wouldn't feel threatened.

"Hello," he said in a tone he hoped didn't startle them.

The two cops rounded on him, but neither reached for their pistols. They'd obviously seen the helicopter, and either were aware that Dak and his team were coming or assumed reinforcements had just arrived.

The cops didn't move. Instead they waited for Dak to stop a few feet short of them with the rest of his crew in tow just behind him.

"Nice roadblock you have here," Dak said as cordially as he could muster.

The cop to the right nodded. His thick black mustache bristled over his lips. The other guy, a younger man by at least ten years, shrugged.

"You must be the American we were told about," Mustache said.

"Yes, sir. We won't be any trouble. This is the Ukrainian curator from the museum the suspects robbed. We're only here to confirm the artifacts are safe and returned once you fellas handle business."

Mustache nodded in appreciation. "Good. You have influential friends...." He waited for Dak to introduce himself.

"Dak. Dak Harper. And this is Galyna, Will, and Lesma."

"You are the ones who rescued this woman from the Russians, yes?"

"That's correct," Dak said without an ounce of pride. "Not sure if you heard, but your border fence is going to need some repairs."

The two cops glanced at each other, puzzled. "What do you mean?"

"The Russian soldiers you're looking for cut a big hole in it. That's how they crossed the border. Don't worry about it. I'm sure the border patrol will take care of it." Dak changed the subject. "So, nothing yet, huh?"

"Not yet, and we have been out here for hours in the cold. This better not be a waste of time," the younger cop warned.

"It's not," Dak assured them.

"Do you have any idea what kind of trucks we are looking for?" Mustache asked.

"Probably something like that one," Dak said, pointing at a delivery truck rolling slowly up to the blockade. "Except I would imagine they'd have a couple of them at least."

"Mmm." Mustache nodded. "We have checked several of those in the last few hours. None of them contained anything unusual."

He sounded annoyed.

"You are certain they are coming this way?" the younger cop with the baby face asked.

"Only one road into this town," Dak reasoned. "From that direction, anyway."

"Well, you four stay back and let us do what we do. If the Russians are coming this way, we will find them."

"Sure thing," Dak agreed. He motioned for the others to follow him to a tent where a few more cops loitered over a table. He noticed paper coffee cups stacked on one side and a portable thermos in the middle.

"Wonder if they'd mind if we have a cup," Dak wondered to the others.

"Anything to keep warm out here," Will said. "It's freezing."

The cops at the table didn't seem to mind the visitors helping themselves to a hot cup of coffee, but they barely said anything.

It was evident, to Dak anyway, that the police were less than thrilled to be out here on such a cold night doing the bidding of a foreign agency—no matter who or what they were trying to catch.

"They don't seem happy to see us," Lesma noticed under his breath as he raised a steaming cup to his lips. The second the hot coffee scalded his tongue, he winced and struggled to swallow. "Ugh. Too hot."

"I wouldn't be happy to see us either if I was them," Will remarked. "These guys get asked to do enough already. Now they're being told to look for a rogue band of Russian soldiers who stole some artifacts that have nothing to do with the Romanians."

"That isn't entirely true," Galyna corrected. "The Scythian Empire reached far across this area, including parts of the mountains here in Romania. While most of their history is attributed to Ukraine, they did have a presence here."

"My mistake." Will put on a humiliated mask and turned the other way to sip his coffee.

Dak stood there with his arms crossed, staring at the slow-moving traffic as it crawled through the blockade.

Cops with flashlights shined bright beams into every passing car. Most of the vehicles were small, and only carried one or two passengers. The occasional family went through now and then, but nothing that even remotely resembled a team of Russian warriors.

Dak had considered the possibility that the rogue unit might split up into multiple vehicles, but that would have required them to find and commandeer several cars and trucks. Based on what he'd seen in Valea Vișeului, that seemed highly unlikely. There'd been few vehicles there, and he'd seen no trucks.

That last part begged his mind to question its reasoning. If there were no trucks available, that only left passenger vehicles. But if they weren't able to get enough of those, how on earth would they get here, and eventually across the border into Hungary?

A delivery truck rumbled to a stop at the checkpoint, and the police instructed the driver to veer off onto the shoulder where they'd created a makeshift inspection lane.

Dak felt his hopes climb a little as the truck pulled off onto the side of the road.

The cops instructed the driver to get out, and the man complied, but Dak knew right away that guy wasn't with the rogue unit. Unless he'd stashed twenty or so men in the cargo hold, this truck was another swing and a miss.

Four men in uniform ambled around to the back of the van and waited while the driver opened the cargo bay.

Dak couldn't see what was in it from his vantage point, but he could tell from the reaction of the cops that there was nothing of interest in there.

"What's the matter?" Will asked his friend, noticing Dak's unsettled demeanor. "You don't look happy."

"It's nothing," Dak lied. He turned and looked down the road leading into the city. The bright lights of the town blurred the dark sky overhead, dimming the twinkling stars.

"That's not true," Will prodded. "I know you, Dak. Something's bothering you."

Dak sighed and looked around again, his eyes falling on the cops hanging around nearby before redirecting back to the roadblock. The driver who'd been stopped climbed back into the rig and pulled away, merging back onto the road between cars.

"I'm not sure," Dak muttered just loud enough for only his friend to hear. He motioned with a flick of his head for Will to follow.

The two Americans stepped away from the table where Lesma tried his luck with the hot coffee again, while Galyna drank hers as if it caused no problem.

When the two were out of earshot, Dak glanced over his shoulder and then looked at his friend. He wore a conspiratorial look on his face that told half the story.

"What is it?" Will pressed.

"Something isn't right," Dak said.

"What do you mean? The cops have this place locked down tight. And like you said, this is the only way in and out of the city from where the Russians crossed."

"Right. I know I said that."

"And it's true. We all looked at the map. If they'd tried to come through over the mountain passes, off-road style, they'd still be out there somewhere." He pointed a finger to the dark peaks in the distance to the north.

"Yeah. I know. I know. But...." Dak faltered.

"But what?"

"Something doesn't seem right. That's all. It's just a hunch."

"Hey, this was the plan. We got here. Now let the cops do their jobs and find the perps. When they do, we'll collect the loot and send it somewhere safe until the war in Ukraine is over. Probably not the best idea to send it back right away." He snorted at the thought.

Dak chuckled a muted sound. "Yeah. Probably not." He looked over at the blockade again, trying to convince himself that this was the right move. But something deep down in his gut twisted in knots.

Will studied his friend for several seconds and shook his head. "But you're not believing that, are you?"

"It's just that... How long did it take us to get here once the chopper arrived?"

"I don't know," Will shrugged. "Forty-five minutes? An hour, maybe?"

"Right. And how long did we have to wait for the helicopter?"

"Are you thinking that they already got through before we arrived? Because if that's what's bothering you, these cops said they've been out here for a few hours already. Didn't they?"

"I guess so. The one with the mustache made it sound like they'd been here at least a few hours."

"Right. So, their response time was pretty fast."

"Yeah." Dak saw where his friend was going with this line of thinking.

"If the travel time from the town we were in to right here was about an hour, then there's no way that Russian unit got through already."

"I guess you're right."

"Darn right I'm right." Will raised the cup of coffee to his lips and took a sip. "Gah," he spat. "Why they got this coffee so hot?"

Dak laughed. "Because it's cold out?"

"Yeah, but come on. This is hotter than McDonald's coffee. And that stuff is like boiling." He shook his head but still went back to the well—this time with greater caution.

The cars continued to snake their way through the roadblock like a line of turtles heading toward a pond.

"Reminds me of when I used to take the train to school," Will continued. "My parents had this coffee pot that would make it so hot it would still be steaming thirty minutes later in an open cup like this. By the time I got to class, it was just about ready to drink."

Dak listened to his friend. Then, suddenly, a sickening feeling clenched his gut. "What did you just say?"

Will lowered his eyebrows, curious what caught Dak's attention. "What? I said my parents had a coffee machine that made it too hot. It was—"

"No. Not that part," Dak said. "The other part. You said you used to take a train to school in the mornings?"

"Oh, that. Yeah. My parents both had to be at their jobs. I mean, it wasn't like I was in grade school or anything like that. I was a junior in high school at the time. I could handle myself on the train."

"The train," Dak said, the epiphany swelling in his mind like a spotlight.

"What about it?" Will took another sip.

"They didn't take trucks. They took a train."

The curious look on Will's face turned to utter confusion. "What are you talking about? What train?"

Dak looked back over to the tent where Galyna and Lesma stood carefully sipping their beverages, then took out his phone.

"In the village, there was a small yellow train station."

"Right," Will tried to follow. "So?"

Dak waited three seconds until the realization hit Will in the eyes.

"Hold on. You're not saying you think the Russians took a train here, are you?"

Dak took off the beanie on his head and ran his fingers through his hair. "I don't know. Maybe."

"I'm going to need a little more than maybe, Dak."

Dak looked back over at the roadblock one more time, then into his friend's eyes. "I don't know why I didn't think of it before."

"Because a few dozen Russians with guns would stick out like a sore thumb on a train? How you think they're going to get through the Hungarian border with all that firepower? Not to mention all the stolen artifacts? Pretty sure someone would have seen that."

"You'd think. Look, I don't know how they would have done all that. But we can't help the cops here anyway. And they clearly don't want us bothering them and their process. So, what does it hurt if we take a little trip to the train station to see what we can find out?"

Will looked over at Lesma and Galyna standing under the pop-up tent. "She needs to be here if the Russians actually do come through this way."

"Make up your mind, Dak. It doesn't sound like you believe that's going to happen. And it isn't like you to be indecisive. You know she's going wherever we go. Right?"

"Yeah," Dak said with a nod. "I don't think we're going to be able to shake that one loose."

"Exactly. Besides. She's a smart one. She'll know something's up if we just dip out."

"True." Dak exhaled slowly, resigned. "Okay. We check the train station. If we don't find anything, we come back here."

"Good plan."

As the two walked back toward the others, Dak mumbled under his breath. "I just hope I'm wrong."

20

Colonel Morovski stood outside the train station with the rest of his men. They spread out along the platform to look like they weren't all together, even though there were only a dozen or so other people waiting on the next train.

He'd dispersed funds to the men so they could go in and purchase their own tickets in groups of three and four, sending them in intermittently so as not to arouse suspicion. Then again, that many men with Ukrainian passports all buying tickets to the same destination in Hungary should have aroused suspicion in even the most unwary ticket clerk.

When Morovski went in to buy his and Kostya's ticket, he was pleasantly surprised by the abject lack of security, and concern, by the people operating the station.

The colonel hadn't known where they might need to go next once they left Ukraine with the stolen goods. He only knew sticking around there wasn't an option.

He'd planned everything in great detail except for that. The last piece was left up to the German.

The Ukrainian passports Morovski had ordered would allow his men to pass through security here in this city's train station, but getting across the Ukrainian border into Romania would have been a much different scenario.

Things were tight at the main crossing in Sighetu. With so many refugees fleeing the war, everyone was being thoroughly processed for entry.

Morovski had ordered his men to stash their rifles in the derelict building before leaving Valea Vișeului. They stuffed them into cupboards and down in the hole underneath the hydraulic lift. While he loathed having to ditch perfectly good and proven weapons, he knew there was no other way. Aside from that, he hoped they wouldn't be needed going forward.

Now that they were out of Ukraine and safely in Romania—heading to Hungary—there would be no one threatening their passage. Still, he ordered the men to keep their sidearms just in case, with the plan that if they had to pass through metal detectors or additional checkpoints, they could drop them in trash cans before entry.

A short humph escaped the colonel's lips at the thought. He looked at the old train station with its faded beige brick façade and red-tiled roof. The building ran along two train tracks—one that conveyed the line running into Hungary and the other that took travelers to the south, deeper into Romania. The second's platform looked like it was made of earth with no concrete for passengers to stand.

It was that line Morovski and his men had taken to reach this point. Now, they could only stand and wait for the last train of the night heading to Hungary.

The journey to Budapest was a long one—around seventeen hours—and with multiple stops between Satu Mare and there.

The colonel didn't mind. He and his men could use the rest. They'd been pushed to the breaking point during the mission. Since leaving Kyiv, sleep had come at a premium, and as he swept his gaze across the motley band, he could see it in their tired eyes and drawn faces. It would do them good to be in a warm train for several hours.

He'd still have four men take watch for two-hour increments, but that would enable everyone to get a good rest.

Morovski looked over at Kostya, who leaned against the wall. The man looked exhausted, and weaker than he'd ever seen his lieutenant colonel. For a soldier built like a brick house, he more closely resembled the abandoned building they'd left only a few hours before.

After a quick look around, Morovski sauntered over to his friend and tilted over until his shoulder pressed against the wall.

"How are you feeling, Lieutenant Colonel?" he asked in a professional tone. With several of the other men standing nearby, he preferred to keep things professional.

"I'm fine, sir," Kostya said.

"You look like hell."

Kostya laughed. "I feel like it, too. If I'm honest. But I'll survive. Federov believes he got the wound cleaned. So I don't think I'll need to see a surgeon after all." He looked over at the makeshift medic and grunted. "He's terrible with the stitches, though."

Morovski snorted a laugh. "I wonder if you could have done better."

"I doubt I would do worse."

The two shared a chortle, then the conversation fell silent for a minute.

"You think we'll make it?" Kostya asked. He looked into his commander's eyes with the sincerest of hope.

It wasn't often Morovski saw the child within those eyes. He'd witnessed the lieutenant colonel wreak merciless havoc on enemy forces in the field of battle. Now, however, his humanity demonstrated itself in a way that the colonel could only imagine.

He'd buried his own humanity long ago. The only remnants that lingered were the parts that desired freedom.

"Of course, my friend," Morovski said without a sliver of doubt. He started to clap his friend on the shoulder then thought better of it with the injury still sending pain through the man's nerves. "The worst is over now. Soon, we'll be on a train to Budapest. When the German buys these treasures from us, we will be free men. We will live a life we could have only dreamed of before. But first, you will see a real doctor to make sure your shoulder is healing properly."

A snort escaped Kostya's nostrils. "I knew you would say that."

"We have known each other a long time, my friend. I would expect you to know what I would say. All the great military leaders of history always had a second that served as their right hand. No matter the battle, I know you will always act in the same way I would. That kind of leadership is difficult to attain."

"Thank you, sir."

"No, Kostya. Thank *you*."

A train horn blew in the distance, bringing the conversation to an end.

The men sprang to action, collected their gear and the illicit cargo, and made their way toward the edge of the platform.

The train lights emerged from the darkness around the bend about the same time brakes squealed in the cold night air. Then the huge metal serpent slowed as it approached the station.

Morovski waited patiently, but an old feeling twisted in his gut.

His eyes darted around—not paranoid but also not feeling safe just yet. Once they were across the Hungarian border, he'd have a glass of vodka in the bar car and take a deep breath.

He scanned the platforms for anything suspicious, but as the train pulled in and groaned to a halt, no threat appeared.

The men waited for the passengers to disembark before they began loading up. Morovski helped Kostya up the steps even though he knew the man wouldn't accept the assistance. It was more to allow him one last look around before he boarded.

With no sign of trouble, the colonel stepped onto the train and followed his lieutenant colonel down the aisle to the left. The two men settled into seats across from each other.

Several of the men laughed down toward the other end of the car. The collective relief they felt filled the space.

Morovski turned his head and looked out the window, patiently waiting for the train to get moving.

He saw a few other passengers climbing aboard on other parts of the train, but none of them looked like they were searching for him and his unit.

Kostya offered his commander a weary grin from across his seat. "Colonel," he said, snapping Morovski's attention from the window. "Relax, old friend. We're safe now. Only one more thing to do. Sell the treasure and disappear. Like you said."

"Yes," Morovski agreed. "We will be in Hungary within the hour. Then all of our troubles will be over."

21

Dak burst through the doors and into the train station, striding as fast as he could without outright running.

They'd seen the train approaching from a few blocks away.

He immediately spotted the ticket counter along the far wall and pushed his pace to its max as he crossed the tile floor.

Lights in unremarkable chandeliers illuminated the station lobby in a glow that was somewhere between bright and dim, as though only receiving half the power they needed to burn.

Will and the other two struggled to keep up with Dak but tailed along a few yards behind him.

When Dak reached the counter, he took a breath before planting his hands at the base of the window between him and the ticket clerk. "Hi. That train that just pulled in. Is it going to Budapest?"

The young black-haired woman in a crimson vest nodded while looking confused. "Yes," she answered. Dak could tell it took her a second to process the English. "It will be leaving in five minutes. You almost missed it."

"Thank you. I was wondering, was there a large group of men

with Russian accents that came through here tonight? They were probably taking the same train."

She puzzled over the question for several breaths, looking up at the ceiling at an angle as she tried to remember. The mere fact she couldn't recall told Dak everything he needed to know.

He'd been wrong. The rogue unit hadn't come this way, and they weren't taking a train.

"No, there was no large group that came through here," she answered.

Dak's face sagged at the confirmation. He'd taken a risk coming here. Now he only hoped that the cops at the roadblock didn't miss the Russian unit as they came through.

"But," she added, "I did sell tickets to far more men tonight than usual."

A spark of hope flickered in Dak's chest. "What do you mean?"

She rolled her shoulders. "Normally, we have an even mix of passengers. Earlier, though, several small groups of men came through buying tickets. They were in groups of three and four. They certainly sounded Russian, though they may have been Ukrainian. They looked like refugees from the war."

"And there were no women with them?"

The rest of Dak's crew leaned in closer to listen.

The clerk only had to think a second before she answered. "No. There were no women. Which was odd. Most of the refugees we see in here are women and children with a few men mixed in."

"No children in the groups, either, I assume?" Dak said.

"That is correct. In hindsight, if all of them were together, I don't understand why they didn't just buy their tickets at the same time. It seems odd to split up like that."

Without context, the young woman had no way to understand exactly why that procedure had been suspicious. She only saw it as strange.

"Do you remember how many of them there were?" Dak knew time was running out. The train would be leaving within the next few minutes, but he had to know. If he and his team got on a train to

Hungary and it turned out the rogue unit hadn't gone that way, there would be almost no way to find them again.

The clerk thought again, directing her eyes to the ceiling overhead as if the cracked and peeling white paint might lend more information.

Dak's patience burned away with every passing second. He wished he could speak the woman's native tongue, but Romanian was one of those languages he'd never even considered learning.

"It's hard to say, but I guess around twenty. Maybe a few more or less. We haven't been very busy tonight. The late train from here doesn't usually have as many passengers as the earlier trains. Most of the refugees take the earlier ones if they are trying to get to family or friends in Hungary."

That was all Dak needed to hear.

"I need four tickets, please," he said.

Arabic and Farsi had been at the top of his list in the military, and he'd picked up a few additional dialects from the Middle East—conversational at best. He knew a little Spanish from high school. And that was the limit to his foreign language capabilities.

"Okay," the teller answered. "Four tickets to Budapest."

She started typing on the computer and then clicked the mouse. "I need to see some identification, please."

Dak reached into his bag and pulled out a passport. Lesma and Will did the same. But Galyna didn't have any identification on her.

She alerted Dak to this problem by clearing her throat. He didn't catch what she meant at first. Then when he realized she wasn't holding anything, his heart sank into his gut.

He cursed himself for not thinking of this sooner.

A flurry of ideas rushed through his head. He had some cash. Maybe he could bribe the teller. But one look at her squashed that idea. Unless she had the proper visas or passport, Galyna wouldn't be allowed on the train.

Dak noticed the glaring lack of security at the doors—manned by a few men in police suits. But they weren't checking bags, and there were no metal detectors present. He couldn't imagine such a scene back home in the States.

"Oh?" he said, making a show of it. "Can you not find yours?" He directed the question at Galyna.

She pressed her lips together, panic bubbling in her eyes. "No. I must have left it at the hotel."

"Crap," Will blurted but quickly adjusted his facial expression so he didn't look so worried.

"Let me see if it's in my bag," Dak said. He began rummaging through his rucksack, fully aware that he had nothing of the sort inside. The act was merely to serve as a hinge of pity for the ticket clerk. Maybe she would have mercy on them if they looked desperate enough to not miss the train. He doubted it.

Lesma scowled at the problem for a few seconds. Then his face brightened. He opened his gear bag and started looking through it.

"I'm sorry," the teller said, "the train is about to leave. There will be others tomorrow, and you can see the arrival times on the board over there." She pointed at a schedule board to the right hanging over the doors leading out to the platform.

"Here it is, Natasha," Lesma said. "I forgot I was carrying some of your things, dear."

Galyna's face twitched with dubious curiosity.

"My wife," Lesma continued as he stepped up to the teller and set the Indian passport on the counter. "It was a short trip, so we only brought one bag."

"Ah," the teller said, seeming to buy the story. "And what were you doing here in Satu Mare?"

"Visiting my niece," Galyna said, jumping into the lie with both feet.

"How lovely. I hope you enjoyed your stay in our city." The young woman studied the passports. So, you are from India? You don't sound like it. Or look like it."

"I am Russian," Lesma explained, grateful to be able to tell the truth which was far easier than making things up on the fly. "She is from Ukraine."

The teller raised both eyebrows. "That must be an interesting relationship right now."

"Not really," Lesma coughed.

Galyna elbowed him in the ribs. "You sleep on the couch tonight," she warned.

"Wouldn't be the first time," he joked.

Dak paid for the tickets with a stack of bills he'd kept in his bag.

Once the tickets were bought, the clerk stamped their passports and handed them back to the group. "Enjoy your trip. You should hurry, or you will miss the train."

"Thank you," Dak said.

The four hurried to the doors and passed between the cops standing guard. The men barely regarded them as they passed.

Back out in the cold on the platform, Dak stuffed his passport back into the rucksack and slung it over his shoulder.

"Okay," he said, directing his full attention at Lesma. "Once we're on the train, you're going to have to tell me how you did that."

Lesma chuckled as he zipped his bag. "Certainly."

They climbed onto the train at the nearest car and got on board.

22

Dak led the group onto the train car farthest from the front. It was darker on that end of the platform where the light on the pillar had burned out.

If the Russian unit was on this train, he doubted they'd let down their guard and not watch for trouble.

Before walking out the door onto the platform, he instructed Galyna to pull the hood of her coat over her head, and to keep it low. If the rogue unit *was* watching, they would have trouble recognizing Dak and the other two men. But Galyna they could easily spot, so keeping her face hidden was paramount until safely on the train.

Dak internally rolled his eyes at the word *safely*.

There was nothing safe about this play. They were getting on the same train as a unit of elite Russian soldiers who had tried to kill them earlier, and had nearly succeeded.

The only advantage Dak and his team had was the element of surprise. The soldiers likely believed him and the others to be dead, and Galyna either the same or still out in the forest somewhere.

Either way, it was unlikely they thought she'd be a threat.

Dak found four seats at the back of the last train car and stood aside to let Galyna take the window seat facing the back of the train.

Lesma and Will spread out, as Dak had directed before boarding. Will took a rear-facing seat across the aisle so he could keep an eye on the exit. Lesma found a place one row up facing the front of the train.

Both ways in and out of the car covered, there was no way someone could get the drop on them.

The train car was nearly empty. Dak counted only eight other passengers spread out randomly around the seats. Most of them looked as though they were about to fall asleep at any second, and one already had—a man with thick, tousled brown hair leaning against the window.

Half of them looked like young travelers from other countries or perhaps other Romanian towns. Their bags gave away their travel plans—probably backpacking around Europe and staying in various hostels along the way.

Dak had friends who'd done that in college, and while he saw the appeal of taking a summer to do something like that, he'd never found the time. As he thought about it, he found it odd that these travelers would do something like that in the dead of winter.

To each their own, he thought.

The train jerked forward, causing everyone's heads to jerk slightly from the momentum. Outside the window, the old train station faded away—slowly, as though melting into the past.

Dak watched only for a few seconds and then refocused his attention on the door at the other end of the car.

The conductor's voice through a speaker system interrupted his thoughts.

The man first spoke in Romanian, which none of Dak's group understood. Then the conductor repeated the announcement in English.

He gave out the order of the stops the train would make—which were fewer than Dak expected, though he supposed that made sense since this was an overnight ride. He doubted many people would be catching the train in the early morning hours.

The conductor also mentioned that keeping the lights off would be appreciated in the main compartments.

Dak wondered how many private rooms there were on this thing, and if the Russian soldiers had purchased any of those—or if all of them had.

That would make finding them more difficult.

Then again, Dak wasn't sure finding them while on the train was the best move.

Up until now, his plan had been pretty fluid. If he was honest, there really hadn't been a plan except for getting the tickets and climbing aboard. Fifteen minutes ago, he wasn't even sure the rogue unit would be on the train.

The overhead lights dimmed as the conductor finished his announcement.

Dak looked across at Galyna. She stared out the window at the city lights as they grew sparser by the second.

"Are you okay?" Dak asked.

The question pulled her gaze from the window. Dark half-moons hung under her blue eyes. Even with a little rest before, and some nourishment, she still hadn't fully recovered from the ordeal with the rogue unit. Dak knew, probably better than she, how close she'd come to death.

"Just a little tired," she said.

"Get some rest," he ordered in a kind tone. "We'll be watching the doors."

"And what about you three? Shouldn't you rest?"

"We'll be taking shifts," he explained. "Don't worry about us. You've been through a lot. And you still need to recover."

"Thank you," she said. "But I'm not sure I can rest knowing the men who are responsible for this are on board this train."

Dak nodded. "I can understand that. I feel the same way. But they aren't on this car." He diverted his eyes toward the front and swept across the seats. "Nobody in here is with their unit. Just ordinary travelers."

"But they *are* on this train," she insisted.

"I sure hope so," Dak said, half joking.

It was a strange thing to say. Hoping the enemy was on board presented both danger and opportunity.

"What are you going to do?" she asked.

"I was just thinking about that," he confessed. "I didn't really have much of a plan except for getting on board." He glanced out the window to buy himself a few seconds. "There are other people in here, and throughout the other cars. Getting in a gunfight is not optimal. Innocent folks could get hurt or worse. I'd prefer to keep collateral damage to a minimum."

She listened to his explanation but found it unsatisfying. "So, what will you do?"

He sighed. "I guess the best thing is to do a little recon. Check out the other cars, find which ones they're on—if they're not in private rooms—and then go from there. All I need to do is confirm they're on board. Once I do, I'll call in the cavalry."

She didn't seem to understand that last line and showed her confusion by cocking her head with a puzzled expression.

"It means I'll call reinforcements," he explained. "When those Russian soldiers get off the train in Budapest, there will be an army of police and special agents waiting to take them into custody. They won't have anywhere to run."

Concern draped across her face. "You're going to just walk right by them on the train?"

Dak understood her worry. "I don't think any of them got a good look at us when we ambushed them at the border. We were at a good distance. They won't recognize my face. To them, I'll just be another passenger."

"I hope you're right."

"Relax," he said. "Get some rest. Will and Lesma are watching the doors. No one is coming in or out without them noticing."

She swallowed and looked back out the window. Distant thoughts filled her eyes.

Dak hoped whatever she was thinking about would lead to some sleep.

"Those men must pay for what they've done," she said, her voice somewhere else.

Dak leaned forward, his elbows on his knees. He didn't want to ask but felt compelled. "They didn't... do anything to you, did they?"

She didn't answer right away, and he worried that momentary silence confirmed his fears.

"No," she answered. "Nothing like that. Although I am certain that would have happened eventually. They were all focused on getting out of the country and meeting their buyer—whoever that is. The German."

Dak considered the last part, mentally reliving what she must have been through.

"You didn't get a name for the German, did you?"

"No," she said, feeling like she'd answered that one before.

Dak knew he wouldn't be so lucky. And even if she did know the name, the German wasn't the immediate problem. Still, he wondered....

"Sit tight," he said as he stood. "Get some rest. I'll be back in a few minutes."

She nodded absently, continuing to stare out the window at the outlines of black, skeletal trees and shadowy mountains standing against the ink of the night sky and the hazy glow of the fading city lights.

Dak stepped over to Will and leaned down. "Keep an eye out. I'm going to go have a look around."

"You sure you don't want one of us to come with you?" Will asked.

"No. That'll look suspicious. Best go alone. Besides, I highly doubt they got a good look at us at the border. Our faces were mostly covered. And they were too far away to get any detail."

"So, you're just going to walk to the front of the train and back?"

"Pretty much. We need to know for sure they're on board."

"What if they aren't?"

Dak flicked a glance to the front of the car. "Then we'll need to get off at the first stop."

"And if they are?" Will studied his friend's eyes.

"Then I call Liz. And when we get to Budapest, the Russians walk off the train and into the waiting arms of the authorities."

"You make it sound so easy."

"Yeah," Dak grumbled.

"And you know it never is."

"I know. But maybe we'll get lucky this time."

Will huffed. "I hope so. Try not to get into any trouble. Oh, and if you pass the bar car, grab me a bourbon."

Dak smiled at his friend. "If they have any."

He stepped away from Will and relayed his plan to Lesma, who accepted it without protest.

"I will watch the door," Lesma said. "No one will get in without me seeing." He patted his right side where a slight bulge protruded in his coat. Dak knew the man's pistol was concealed underneath. The big Russian seemed proud of it.

"You'll do just fine, Les. I'll be back shortly."

Dak left his team behind, walking unsteadily down the aisle toward the front of the car. The train swayed left and right, testing his balance. He used the overhead bin to brace himself with his hands as he passed the first few travelers on the right.

The young couple were looking at their phones, busily typing messages to friends or loved ones.

Dak kept moving forward. The wheels clacked on the tracks underneath in a steady rhythm as the train reached its top speed.

He passed another pair of travelers, two younger men in civilian clothing. Dak allowed an extra second of focus on those two before moving on, just to make sure they didn't appear to have weapons or anything suspicious.

He decided the better way to do this was to only inspect the other travelers on his way back here, and so he moved a little faster until he reached the door leading out into the walkway between the cars.

He opened the door and stepped out into the accordion-like area. The sounds were much louder here, and the air far colder without the climate control of the cars.

Dak reached out his hand to the next car, opened it, and continued through.

He made his way down the aisle, only taking note of the number of people in these seats as he passed but finding nothing suspicious.

In the third car, he found the bar where four travelers—two males and two females—sat drinking cocktails and chatting in Romanian.

With the dim, old-fashioned sconces lighting the bar car, Dak felt like he'd gone back in time and stepped into a murder mystery.

He continued by the bar and to the next door. Despite Will's request, Dak had no intention of getting any alcohol. The last thing any of them needed right now was to dim their wits.

He reached the next door and stepped out into a cold, noisy coupling tunnel once more. When he opened the opposite door and set foot inside, he immediately noticed far more people than he'd seen in any of the other cars. And many of them noticed him.

Half a dozen faces turned around and looked back at him, wondering who had just let in the burst of cold air and affronting sound.

Dak swallowed and closed the door behind him.

Most of the faces that stared back at him were men dressed in civilian clothing. Only a few women occupied seats with either their boyfriends or husbands. Thankfully, no children were aboard.

The couples seemed uninterested in Dak and turned their heads back around to continue doing whatever they had been before.

But several of the rough-looking men leered at him. Dak knew right away who they were. He'd found part of the Russian contingent.

Okay, he thought to himself. *Be cool. Just walk on by and get a head count.*

Dak did as his thoughts directed, ambling forward with his hands on the rails above each shoulder to keep himself steady.

The Russian soldiers turned back around one by one, apparently unthreatened by his appearance. As Dak passed, his eyes fell—however briefly—onto the bulging packs on the floor between the men's feet. He wasn't certain, but he thought he caught a glimpse of gold shimmering through the opening of one bag.

The men hadn't recognized him, as he suspected would be the case. Still, a trickle of relief snaked through his chest as the men turned around. The ones facing the rear went back to looking out the window—for the most part. A few still looked at him as he passed. Their narrowed eyes assessed him, and those assessments only further entrenched Dak's belief that these were the men he was looking for.

Beneath the disguises, these men were soldiers through and through, and to someone like Dak, there was no hiding it. He'd recognize military anywhere.

He kept moving, careful not to meet the eyes of any of them for more than a split second.

As he continued forward, Dak felt like he'd fallen into a pit of vipers—all ready and willing to strike at a moment's notice.

It took immense willpower not to turn around and check his six, and for a second he regretted not having Will or Lesma with him to watch his back. But he knew he'd made the right call. Two would have been more likely to arouse suspicion than him going it alone.

Just be cool.

He passed through the next interchange between cars without any trouble. When he opened the next door, Dak discovered a similar collection of men spread out through the car. But more of them.

Just as before, they turned around and inspected him as he entered, and having found nothing of interest with him, returned to conversing with each other or looking out the window.

Dak moved faster this time, more intent on getting out of the car and into the next. The slower he moved, the stranger it would appear. But if it looked like he was trying to get somewhere, then he'd just be another passenger on their way to Hungary.

After spotting a few more bulging packs on the floor with the men, he focused his eyes on the front of the car until he reached the door and then stepped out into the cold again.

When he opened the next portal, he found no more of Russian contingent. Only a handful of people occupied this car—an elderly couple, a few young couples, and a group of four young men who were laughing at something one of them had said.

"Okay," Dak muttered to himself as he slid into a seat in the left corner.

He'd counted a dozen men in the previous car. Combined with the car before that, there were eighteen.

Dak took out his phone and found Liz's number. It was late, and he didn't want to wake her if she happened to be asleep, so he typed out a quick text message.

The rogue unit took a train to Budapest. On board with them now. They didn't recognize me. Have a team ready to apprehend in Budapest.

He hit the Send button, but an error message popped up on the screen. He looked in the top-right corner of the device and realized the problem. There was no cell service.

He grunted in frustration and held the phone up in the air hoping that would somehow make a difference. It didn't.

Dak sighed and looked out the window at nothing in particular. He knew he had to sit there and wait for a few minutes. Going straight back to his car might arouse suspicion. Although he wasn't entirely sure it would make a difference if he waited or not. All Dak could do was hope that the Russian soldiers dismissed his passing as simply looking around or trying to locate a friend somewhere else on the train.

His gut twisted in knots as the hills passed beyond the window.

He checked the phone again but still no signal. Now he wished he had gotten one of those drinks in the bar car. Even a short one would have given him something to do as he waited for the seconds to tick by—and it may have calmed his nerves just a little.

Dak had become adept at handling the latter in most situations, but in this one he found himself in new territory.

"What's the worst that can happen?" he breathed, barely audible even to himself. *They aren't going to recognize you. Just relax. And if any of them bothers you, deal with it. It's not like they're going to start shooting.*

After what seemed like an hour, but was only ten minutes, Dak stood up and checked his phone again. Still no signal.

He exhaled, frustrated, but turned and exited through the door.

Seconds later, he stepped back into the car where the majority of the rogue squad rode and walked carefully toward the rear.

As he neared the midway point, he caught a glimpse of a man that was clearly older than most of those with him. The guy wore a gruff expression on his face, born from years of battle.

Dak had seen that kind of look before on the faces of commanding officers, and he knew right away this guy was the leader. The man was armed; of that Dak was certain, even though he couldn't see the weapon underneath the man's gray winter coat.

The officer looked up at Dak and met his gaze with a standoffish one of his own. In that moment, Dak remembered the man from the border shootout. Time froze, and Dak felt half-paralyzed as he tried to force himself to keep moving.

But there was no mistaking it. This man was the one leading the rogue unit. He'd seen the guy barking orders during the firefight and had watched as the man helped another take cover.

Dak wondered if the commander recognized him, but that was more paranoia than rational thinking. The American had had the benefit of using a scope, and the other had nothing but chaos and confusion. Still, the way the man locked eyes for two seconds with Dak's sent a chill through his spine.

The only thing Dak could do was offer a curt nod of his head—a cordial gesture he offered to strangers as if to say, *good day to you, sir.*

The conductor's voice abruptly crackled through the speaker system, nearly sending Dak jumping through the roof. "We are now entering Hungary."

It was the interruption Dak needed, and he immediately took another step forward toward the next door.

The Russian leader said nothing, offered nothing in return. He merely turned his head disinterestedly toward the window once more and continued watching the passing countryside in the darkness.

Dak waded to the back of the car and jerked the door open. Before he stepped through, he stole one last look over his shoulder at the commander's seat. A man a few years his younger sat across from him—his head leaning against the window, his right arm hanging limp across his lap.

Then Dak left through the portal and quickly made his way back through the next car, careful not to draw attention from the remaining Russian soldiers.

None of them paid much attention to him as he passed, just as they hadn't on his initial journey through. A few of them dozed with their heads against the windows, while the others talked or stared absently through the glass.

Dak didn't even breathe until he reached the next door and returned to the noisy cold again.

Then he took a deep breath and exhaled. "That was sketchy," he said to himself, and then reentered the bar car, thinking now might be a good time for that bourbon after all.

23

Morovski thumbed his chin as he stared out the window. There'd been something off about the man that passed earlier. He couldn't put his finger on it, but a needle poked his gut repeatedly ever since the guy appeared and disappeared.

The man looked healthy, and his skin's light tan betrayed someone who'd spent time in the sun—recently, perhaps.

There was none of that to be had here, not in the winter.

This part of the world had sunshine in the colder months, sure, but wintry gloom pervaded most of the time. Few bore the look that man had.

Probably an Italian, Morovski thought. People from the Mediterranean came through these parts on vacations, though not often during the winter. They usually traveled to the north of their own country to hit the slopes.

What had it been about the man?

There was something odd about him.

The colonel saw him pass by the first time when the stranger went through the car on his way to the one toward the front of the train. *What was he doing? Looking for the bar car, probably.* That reasoning made sense. If a person went the wrong way, they'd easily get turned around and miss that the bar car was two back from there.

And of course, maybe the guy was looking for a friend that was in another car. That reasoning didn't add up to Morovski, though, because the seats weren't assigned on this train. It was first-come, first-serve.

He chewed his lower lip as he looked outside, then scanned the car around him. The men who were on first watch sat upright at full attention—as he would expect. The others lounged, their eyes closed as they either slept or tried to fall asleep amid the motion of the swaying train and the sound of the tracks clacking underneath.

Kostya rested with his head against the window, eyes closed. Morovski had never seen his second in such a weakened state, but the color was already returning to his face—a good sign that he was recovering.

Still, the passenger that passed by a few moments before lingered at the front of the colonel's mind.

Something was off about the man. And the way he'd offered a simple nod. That wasn't an Italian gesture. It was more... of an American thing.

He'd encountered Americans many times over the years since the fall of the Soviet Union. He'd even served on a few missions with some when the decades of the Cold War had been left behind and the two nations flirted with peace.

Morovski knew he was being irrational. They were safe now, and several kilometers into Hungary. No one knew where they were—certainly not the Russian military, and no one knew where they were headed. They were safe.

He kept telling himself this over and over again in his mind, but he couldn't shake the paranoia.

He sighed and took out his phone to distract himself but saw he had no signal. He read the date on the screen as if to remind himself of the rendezvous arranged for the next day.

The colonel slid the device back into his pocket and looked around the car again. He tried to fill his mind with the peace and calm of the tropical beach he'd soon be on, sipping drinks brought to him by beautiful young women in bikinis. That vision always seemed to help calm his overactive mind.

He closed his eyes, confident that the men around him would handle any trouble should it arise. But there it was again—a thought of trouble.

You're safe, Nikolai, he thought to himself as if the conscious effort would soothe his nerves.

But the passenger's face kept popping into his mind like a demon possessing his every thought.

The man had locked eyes with him. *And did I catch the stranger looking down at the bags at my feet?* He tried to remember the moment, and the more he focused on it, the more he seemed certain the man *had* looked down at the packs.

Morovski checked the sidearm under his coat, both with his hand and with his eyes. It didn't appear to be obvious. No protrusion of the weapon stuck out, but now he became increasingly aware of it as if it would have been obvious to anyone passing by.

He twisted his jaw back and forth as he considered the problem, and a single solution kept brimming to the surface of his imagination.

With one last check on his sleeping friend, the colonel arose from his seat and looked back in the direction the stranger had gone. There was no sign of him in the car, which he'd suspected. Morovski heard the door at the other end open and assumed the man had continued on his way.

But to what end?

The colonel's eyelids narrowed—a quick, twitching motion. Then he turned to the men sitting on the other side of the aisle from him and took a step toward them.

The two on first watch stiffened slightly as their commanding officer bent over at the hips to address them.

Morovski leaned close and motioned them to do the same.

"Did you two notice the man who just came through here a few minutes ago?" he asked.

The two looked at each other as if asking for permission, then both nodded at the same time.

"Yes, sir," the one on the right said. "Male passenger. Dark hair."

"That's the one," Morovski confirmed. "Did you notice anything unusual about him?"

Again, the two glanced at one another. This time, they shook their heads.

"No, sir," they both whispered, taking the cue from the colonel that they should remain quiet on the subject.

Morovski straightened and looked down both ends of the car before bending down again.

"I want to know what he was up to," the colonel said. "He's probably just another passenger looking for the bar car. But there was something odd about him. Find him and make sure he's not up to anything suspicious."

"Suspicious, sir?" the soldier on the right asked.

"Yes. It's possible he noticed our unusual luggage. However unlikely, we need to be certain no one slipped up and left something hanging out of their bag."

"Yes, sir." The two men stood up.

"Check every car. When you find him, if he's minding his own business, then return at once."

"And if he isn't?" the one of the left asked.

"Handle it."

24

Dak entered the last car and spotted his friends in the back along with Galyna, whose head leaned against the window. Her long, wavy hair cascaded down over her right shoulder.

Lesma saw Dak reenter the car but waited patiently for the American to reach the back before saying anything.

When Dak drew near, Lesma's expression asked the question. Dak motioned to the big Russian to turn around and follow him.

Dak eased back into his seat across from the slumbering curator while Lesma took the seat across the aisle opposite of Will.

The three men leaned in close over the aisle as Dak spoke.

"They're all a few cars up. I count eighteen of them, six in the car nearest to us. A dozen in the car beyond. And I'm pretty sure that's the one their leader is in."

"Makes sense," Will said. "Protect the CO."

"Right." Dak looked down the aisle toward the front. "I recognized him from the border."

"You think he recognized you?" Concern flittered through the words.

"No. I don't think so. Like I said before, we were concealed. And too far for them to get a good look."

"What do you want to do?" Lesma asked.

Dak took out his phone and checked it again. "Still nothing. Either of you have a signal?"

The two men looked at their devices and shook their heads.

"In these mountains, we are remote," Lesma stated. "But we should have a signal when we get to the first stop."

"So we just have to hang out and hope the Russians didn't get suspicious," Will voiced. He glanced at Lesma. "I mean the other Russians."

"I take no offense."

"Yeah. I guess we don't have any choice right now. Just sit back and try to enjoy the ride."

"Fat chance of that," Will quipped. "Who wants to take first watch?"

"I will," Dak offered. "You two get some rest. There's no one coming from the back door here. I'll keep an eye on the front."

"You sure?"

Dak noticed movement through the doorway window at the other end of the train. He sighed as the realization hit him. He recognized one of the faces, even from that distance. It was one of the Russian soldiers. As the man swayed to one side, Dak saw another guy behind him.

"Great."

"What?" Will asked, then followed Dak's gaze to the front of the car. "Are those—"

"Yep. Ease back in your seats and be cool. They're probably just coming around to see what I was up to."

"I notice you didn't bring me that bourbon," Will chimed as he leaned back in his chair.

Dak forced a chuckle as he took out his phone and pretended to check messages.

The men entered the car through the doorway like two apex predators on the hunt for a meal.

Ignoring them entirely would have seemed unnatural, so Dak lifted his eyes from the device in his hands and looked down the aisle toward the men. He regarded them only for a second, then as if they were of no consequence, returned to his phone screen.

Every fiber of his being hoped this wasn't about to turn violent. There were other people in the car, though all eight of them were now asleep.

Dak looked up again as the train passed through a series of flashing red lights outside. *A railroad crossing,* he realized. The blinking red glow cast through the train's windows reminded Dak of horror movies where the villain stalked their prey down a corridor illuminated by a strobe light.

The crimson hue splashed over their faces, making them seem all the more sinister as they moved through the cabin.

The light show only lasted a few seconds. Then the feeble glow of the lights along the wall were all that illuminated the sinister faces approaching.

Dak steadied his breathing and watched the two men with his peripheral vision, looking up again only when the men were two rows away. As would anyone if two strangers were moving throughout a train cabin at this hour. It wasn't like they were looking for an empty seat.

When the men reached the back of the train where Dak and his crew sat, they stopped at the back door and turned around.

Dak had played the game long enough. He looked up at the two—both men he'd seen before on his trip toward the front of the train. They were young, probably in their early to mid-twenties. One had short blond hair, the other brown—and both cut in a military style.

The men peered down at Dak as if sizing up a cut of meat and deciding whether or not they wanted to eat it raw or cook it over a fire.

Across the aisle, Lesma and Will watched the exchange. Will's hand shifted inside his coat. Dak recognized the pistol's bulge around his friend's abdomen.

The last thing he wanted was gunfire erupting in the train's cabin.

Not only would it be unbearably loud, but it would send the other passengers into a panic.

If there was to be an altercation, it needed to go down the old-fashioned way.

"Can I help you?" Dak asked, looking up at the two men.

They didn't answer, but the blond one diverted his eyes to Galyna, who rested quietly—her head still against the window with her neck bent at a slight angle.

The soldier's eyes widened instantly. In that moment, Dak knew the game was up. He saw it in the man's reaction. The soldier recognized Galyna.

The blond started to stuff his hand into his half-unzipped coat—where Dak was certain a gun lay in wait.

Dak sprang into action, twisting out of his seat in a single fluid motion. He grabbed the blond's wrist in a tight grip, then drove his left elbow upward into the soldier's jaw. Dak both heard and felt the pop.

As the blond man fell back against the wall, the other guy reached for his own weapon. Before his hand disappeared into the folds of the coat, he felt a heavy thud against his shoulder as Will drove into him from the side. Brown Hair struck the corner of the door with his other shoulder, and his head smacked against the wall, dazing him for half a second.

Dak whipped his right elbow at the blond's temple to strike the knockout blow. Having already delivered a concussive shot, one more to the side of the man's head would likely drop him.

But the blond bent his knees and dropped beneath the swing, then drove his fist into Dak's gut. The punch slammed the air out of Dak's chest for a second, and he stumbled back two steps.

Will's opponent swung a fist to defend himself, but Will caught the punch with his left hand and delivered a hammer punch to the man's cheek. Brown Hair's head snapped around. He raised his fists to defend himself. He blocked the first and second blows from Will, who then adjusted and went for the groin with his knee.

The enemy swung low with his right elbow, pounding Will's

thigh. Will grimaced at the dead pain shooting through his leg. Then the opponent swung the bridge of his fist across Will's face. Will's head twisted hard to one side, and as he tried to regroup to defend the next blow, a huge bulk barreled past him and plowed into the soldier.

Will steadied himself in time to see Lesma run the man into the door and burst through it out into the open air.

A cold chill blew into the cabin amid a cacophony of noise.

Dak felt the blast hit him as his opponent chopped at his neck. Still trying to catch his breath, Dak could only offer a meager deflection of the blow that would have crushed his windpipe, but he couldn't stop the next fist that struck him across the jaw.

The impact spun Dak around, giving the enemy the chance to wrap his left arm around Dak's neck. The Russian soldier squeezed to the point Dak's larynx closed shut.

Behind him, Lesma pinned the brown-haired soldier against the railing at the back of the train. The big man swung hard at the soldier's face, landing one blow just to the right of the guy's nose. Brown Hair managed to raise his forearms high enough to block the subsequent blows, then used his shoulders on the rail for leverage and kicked out both feet hard into Lesma's midsection.

Lesma staggered backward into the back wall of the train as the soldier regained his balance and stepped toward the bigger man.

He cocked his fists ready to mete out punishment, but Will flew out the door with his right foot extended. The flying sidekick hit the soldier in the side of the head and knocked him toward the steps on the right side of the car.

Will landed on his feet next to the man and immediately straddled him. The trees in the forest on both sides of the tracks whooshed as the train sped by, and then suddenly the sound stopped.

The clacking swelled, and Will realized they were on a high bridge over a ravine.

He punched the Russian in the nose and felt it crumple under his fist. Blood spurted instantly, and Will felt he'd won the fight. But the soldier had one more trick up his sleeve.

Brown Hair rocked both legs up into the air and shifted his weight, throwing Will over the side of the train.

Lesma regained his footing in time to see Will go over. He roared like a giant, pale bear and charged the soldier as he bounced to his feet once more.

Lesma lowered his shoulder and smashed into the man before he could mount a defense.

The massive impact drove Brown Hair beyond the railing and over the stairs. He yelled as he tumbled through the air down into the canyon below, disappearing into the dark.

Lesma breathed heavily, immediately overwhelmed by despair from losing Will. Then, he saw something flicking around in the dark like a rag.

It was Will, holding onto the bottom edge of the stair railing with one hand.

"Little help!" he shouted.

"Will!" Lesma leaned over and grabbed Will's other arm as he extended it upward. He wrapped his meaty fingers around Will's wrist and pulled.

Will kicked his feet until the right one found purchase on the lower step, and then he pulled with both arms, using Lesma's strength to climb back up onto solid footing.

Inside the cabin, Dak struggled to free himself from the choke-hold. He had only seconds left before the lack of air would render him unconscious. Through blurring eyes, he saw some of the other passengers rousing from the sound and the sudden burst of cold air shooting through the back of the train.

None of them moved to help, though, probably assuming it was a drunken brawl by a couple of travelers who'd had a few too many from the bar car.

Dak wriggled, but the man's grip was too strong. The light faded around him, and darkness began to encroach in the corners of his eyes.

Desperate, Dak swung his elbows against the man's ribs. Right, left, right again. He felt the impact of all three and then missed on the fourth as the blond man arched his back to avoid further damage. It was all Dak needed.

In a last-ditch effort, Dak whipped the back of his head toward the man's face and struck him square in the nose.

The arm around Dak's neck loosened, and the American took a step forward, doubling over to catch his breath.

The Russian soldier's nose bled profusely, oozing crimson down across his lips and dripping off his chin. Furious, he charged toward Dak as he regained his breath, but something caught the attacker's shin and he fell forward, off balance.

Dak pivoted and caught the man with an elbow to the throat as he fell. The combined momentum and upward thrust of Dak's strike crushed the soldier's windpipe. Dak spun, wrapping his right arm around the enemy's neck—turning the tables. Then he started tugging the kicking man backward.

Dak looked to his right at Galyna, who'd stuck out her foot just in time to trip the soldier. Her eyes were wide with fear and anger but also a fierce determination.

The Russian soldier kept kicking, gasping for air that would not come.

When Dak reached the back railing, he saw they were over a ravine and knew exactly how to dispose of the trash. He ripped the man to his right, then kicked out with his heel, striking the soldier squarely on the tailbone.

The man managed a feeble yelp as he flew over the side and down into the darkness.

Dak fell to his hands and knees, the expense of the fight finally coming due. He sat there on all fours for a minute, catching his breath and running a self-diagnostic to make sure he hadn't sustained any significant injuries.

Then he felt a hand on his shoulder and turned around, ready to defend himself again with a raised fist.

He let down his guard at the sight of his two friends hovering over him.

"You two look like crap," he joked, still sucking in the cold air in quick, hard gasps.

Will and Lesma chuckled.

"You're one to talk," Will said.

Dak stood up and looked into the train. Galyna lingered in the doorway, staring out at the three men. The terrified faces of the other passengers stared back, uncertain what to think or say.

"It's okay, everyone," Dak announced. "They were Russian soldiers posing as refugees, but they're gone now. No need to worry."

It seemed his little speech did little to settle the travelers' nerves.

"Thanks," Dak offered to Galyna. "Well done."

"You're welcome," she replied. "Now what are we going to do about the rest of them?"

25

Morovski checked his watch for the tenth time in as many minutes.

What was taking those two so long?

The two he'd sent to the back of the train had been gone for nearly fifteen minutes—more than enough time to run a quick recon. Ten minutes more. The train wasn't *that* long.

Something was wrong.

He snorted hard in frustration and pushed himself out of his seat. He turned and looked toward the back of the car, staring at the rear door beyond his men that occupied the rest of the cabin.

Morovski waited thirty seconds, thinking that little extra amount of time would be all he needed before he saw the faces of the two men appear in the back window.

But as the time ticked by, the men didn't show.

He rounded on four men sitting in the row diagonally behind his own. "You four."

The men snapped to attention.

"Come with me."

Morovski led the way to the end of the cabin and paused to open the door. He considered removing the pistol from its concealed place in his coat, but doing so could alarm other passengers on board—and alarmed passengers could cause problems.

He reasoned that the two men he'd sent before had probably just stopped to snag a quick drink at the bar and lost track of time. His men were extremely disciplined, though, and he found it hard to imagine that was what happened.

If that was the case, they would get a good tongue lashing, but he could hardly blame the men. If circumstances were different, he'd have probably joined them in the bar and bought the first round.

The contingent entered the next car where six more of their men sat staggered in three rows. Half of them were wide awake, as Morovski expected.

He reached the men and roused the three from their shallow slumber. The men had been well trained. All three of them woke in an instant and reached for their sidearms. Then their tensions eased when they saw their comrades and leader standing over them.

All six men stood at attention.

"Is everything all right, Colonel?"

"I'm not sure," Morovski allowed. "But we are about to find out. You six take point. Weapons ready, but keep them concealed."

"What are we looking for?" a young soldier with a shaved head asked.

"He looks Italian. Maybe American. Dark hair. Came through earlier. Did you see him?"

"Yes, sir," one of the other soldiers replied. "I saw him. He went through here and into your car. Came back about ten, fifteen minutes later, sir."

"That's the guy," Morovski confirmed.

"I just thought he was lost."

"Me, too. Find him. I want to know what he's up to."

The men acknowledged with curt, simultaneous nods, then turned and marched to the end of the cabin. They didn't question their commander's motives or wonder if it was a wild goose chase. They simply obeyed.

They methodically checked the window into the interchange

tube, one after the other to make sure both angles were covered, then the one on the left reached over and opened the door. The men stepped out and over to the next door as the cold air seeped up from below despite the awning's staunchest protests.

They opened the next door and moved into the bar car, scanning the passengers as they passed.

Morovski followed with the other four behind him. He searched the faces in the chairs and at the bar, but none matched the man who'd walked through earlier.

The group continued through to the next cabin, repeating their deliberate trek toward the rear of the train.

None of the people in this cabin looked like the man either.

"He must be on the last car," Morovski said as the group reached the rear door. "When you see him, hold him down. I want to know what he's up to."

The men in front nodded and opened the next door. They moved through the tunnel as a single, cohesive unit and into the final car.

A handful of people slept in their seats, spread out throughout the cabin. The Russian soldiers slipped through the car with deadly stealth, each man checking the travelers they passed to see if any matched the description.

When the men in the lead passed the last row, they turned back to the colonel and shook their heads.

"He's not here, sir."

Morovski scowled at the news. He turned to the men behind him. "Check the lavatories."

They moved out immediately as the colonel strode to the rear door and looked around.

"He's here. He has to be."

He stood there for two minutes waiting for the men he'd sent to the bathrooms to return. He only had to wait three before the first of his scouts returned.

"Anything?" he asked, already knowing the answer. If they'd found the man, he'd have been in their charge.

"No, sir."

The others returned from the cars farther up the line. They, too, were empty-handed.

"That's impossible," Morovski grunted. "He couldn't have simply disa—"

He cut himself off as his eyes spotted something on the floor next to the last row of seats on the left.

He bent down and touched something dark and gooey on the burgundy carpet. Then he raised the index finger and looked at it.

A thick red liquid coated his fingertip. He rubbed his thumb on it as he examined it closely, but he already knew what it was.

"Whose blood is that, sir?" one of the men asked.

The colonel didn't answer immediately. He moved toward the back door and noticed another oddity. The window was cracked, as if someone had struck it with their head or hand. Maybe an elbow.

Morovski traced the spiderwebbed glass with the bloody finger, then opened the back door with an abrupt push.

He stepped outside, despite two of his men trying to take point and make sure the area beyond was safe.

He stopped at the railing and looked around. The train had reentered a forested area of the hills. But there was no sign of the stranger.

"That's impossible,' he said, half to himself. 'Unless…"

He rounded on the men. "Get back to our car. Now."

The colonel followed his men, keeping six in front and the rest in back. They wouldn't have had it any other way either. They pushed back through the next car, and the bar car, moving faster than on their initial sweep.

They didn't concern themselves with staying quiet, either.

Morovski didn't tell what concern racked his mind at the moment. And to them, it didn't matter. The order was enough. But they all thought the same thing.

Whoever this guy was had slipped by them somehow and could now be in their car with only a few guys left on watch.

DAK MOVED AS FAST as he could along the rooftop of the train without falling off. The wind up here felt twice as cold and slashed at his face like daggers. Behind him, the three members of his team did their best to keep their balance on the unsteady surface.

All of them kept their knees bent and crouched low as they moved up toward the train's engine.

Dak had seen scenes like this in movies—where train robbers or terrorists attempted to take over a locomotive. But he'd never expected in a million years to be trying anything like this.

The bitter cold clutched at his muscles. He felt stiff and tight but kept moving forward. They had to reach the front of the train to evade what he knew was coming.

The soldiers they'd thrown into the ravine had recognized Galyna. That left Dak and company with little choice. Killing the soldiers had only bought minutes at best. The moment the leader realized his men had been gone too long, he would send more to the back of the train to find out what was causing the hold up.

Dak and his crew had struggled with two of the soldiers, and they outnumbered them three to two—if he didn't count Galyna's not-insignificant contribution to the fight.

Questions loomed in Dak's head. Had he gotten rusty? Surely not. He stayed in good shape, worked out frequently, and trained as he always had. And his field operations—while different in nature to when he'd been in the military—had challenged his skills in new ways that would only make him a better warrior.

Still, those two had been tough.

As he crossed over the gap between cars, he knew for certain that whoever these Russians were, they were most certainly an elite force and would not go down easily.

Fortunately, Dak and his team had evened the odds a little more by taking out two more of the enemy. They'd be down to sixteen now, but it was that time in the chess game to make a play for the king.

Unless he missed his guess, the commanding officer would send three or four more men to the back. Maybe as many as six.

Based on his count, Dak figured that would leave ten guys in the car where the bulk of forces had been housed.

The moon shone down on the land from a clear, blue-black sky, shedding its light onto the mountains and hills, and onto the train's rooftop—which Dak was grateful for. Traversing this path would have been even more difficult in utter—.

The thought fizzled as he looked ahead.

They were almost to the car nearest the engine, but just ahead where the tracks curved to the right, Dak saw a new problem.

The train was about to enter a tunnel.

"Dak?" Will shouted over the immense sounds of wind and locomotion.

"I see it!" Dak replied back over his shoulder. "Everybody down low!" He motioned with his hand, pressing his palm down toward the rooftop like he was smashing a pancake.

The four dropped to their stomachs and held on tight as the train approached the hole in the mountain.

Dak hoped it wasn't one of those tunnels with a low clearance, but now it was too late to make that assessment.

The engine disappeared into the hole. Its forward lights reflected off the arched stone around it.

Then the first car.

"Here we go," Dak muttered.

With a loud woos, they plunged into darkness. The sounds around them amplified tenfold. The clacking of the rails, the squeaking springs, the grinding wheels—all rang so loudly that their heads throbbed. The smell of diesel exhaust didn't help things.

The tunnel seemed to go on forever, and it took enormous willpower not to let go of the tentative grip he had on a top rail to cover his ears to suppress the noise.

Then, just as suddenly as they'd been baptized in the blackish, loud hell, they were back out in the open again.

Dak sucked in a gulp of clean air and then looked back to check on his crew. Everyone was okay, at least for now.

Only one car to go, he thought.

He arrived at the next coupling between the trains and stopped to make sure his team was keeping up. They'd already risked shouting before, and that was only out of necessity. So he resisted asking if everyone was okay. If they hadn't fallen off at this point, that was good enough.

Dak climbed onto the accordion-like awning between the two cars. Then he heard the sound of something metal clank loudly. Then the train lurched, stretching out the awning in both directions.

"What the?" Dak wondered. The realization hit him a second later. "Oh no. They've uncoupled the train."

He turned to the others behind him. "Take care of the passengers!" Dak shouted back. He knew there wasn't time to say anything else.

Before the others could even register what he said, Dak dove toward the lead car just as the awning broke free.

He caught the top edge of the roof over the landing with both hands but only managed to slow his fall to the floor.

His boots hit the metal grate with a thump. Somehow, he'd landed on his feet. But as he looked around on the landing, he saw more pairs of feet. Dak didn't even have a second to congratulate himself on sticking the landing before a hard hand clapped down on his right shoulder.

He twisted and swung his opposing arm, but another firm fist wrapped around it. Dak felt his shoulder and pectoral muscles strain as he tried to simply overpower the enemy. But a third fist burrowed into his gut and drove the wind out of his lungs.

"The colonel has some questions for you," one of the men said in an ominous Russian accent.

Weakened by the gut shot, Dak felt himself dragged up by the armpits. Another shot to his middle back made things even worse, and he felt himself nearly vomit if not for immense willpower.

The men spun Dak around as another opened the door to the car. Dak grimaced as his feet dragged along the floor. All he could do was stare back at his friends on top of a train car as they gradually fell farther behind.

Then the door shut.

26

The men dragged Dak deeper into the train car and then stopped. Two men who'd been guarding the door moved in and searched him. They took the pistol out of his coat, then frisked him up and down, removing the phone from his pocket for good measure.

Then they spun him around just as he began to get feeling back in his legs and air into his lungs.

Eight feet away, standing in the middle of the aisle, was the man Dak had identified as the leader. The older Russian stared at him as he would a captured animal—curious but also disgusted.

"Who are you?" the man asked in clear, albeit accented English. He stood straight, with both arms tucked behind his back where his hands folded just above the belt.

There was no mistaking this guy was military. The civilian clothing couldn't hide the bearing and attitude of a battle-hardened commander. The way they stood. The way they spoke. Their body language. All of it betrayed the truth.

"Cable guy," Dak replied.

The leader inclined his head, raising his chin, and then nodded to one of the men close to Dak. A hard fist smashed down into the left side of Dak's face. His head whipped around, but the guy to his right caught it and set it back to center.

Pain shot through Dak's entire head, radiating from his jaw. He hoped he hadn't lost any teeth, but at this point that might be a foregone conclusion.

"Who are you?" the commander asked again. He spoke with the patience of someone who had all day to wait for the answer.

"Avon calling," Dak spat. A trickle of blood oozed across his lips.

The commander nodded again. Dak braced for the next punch, but it didn't come from the left as he expected. His right cheek exploded in pain as a fist from the other side drove into it. His jaw screamed in pain at first, then deadened to a constant, pulsing discomfort.

He worked his jaw back and forth, trying to rid himself of the feeling. The men delivering the punches on either side stood ready for more. There was no point in resisting. The men holding his shoulders weren't even letting him waver against the wobble of the train.

"My men will continue to hurt you until you pass out. But we will wake you up again. And start all over. So, you can either tell me who you are, or you can continue being punished until, ultimately, we kill you and leave your body in a ditch. The choice is yours. So," he brought his hands around and crossed them over his chest. "Who are you?"

Dak nodded as if he understood the gravity of the situation at long last. He peered at the man and then dropped his head, staring at the floor—defeated. "Your mom told me to tell you she said hi."

Dak couldn't stop himself from laughing as he said the words. The laughter ended abruptly with two punches, one to each side of his face in rapid succession.

The train car around him faded to a blur. It was all Dak could do to maintain consciousness, and he could only do so by the barest of threads.

"What were you doing sneaking around?" The leader pressed on despite Dak's recurring volley of snarky replies. "Are you a thief, American?"

Dak couldn't answer this time. Both sides of his face ached from the blows, and he felt his cheeks swelling. All he could do was breathe and try to hold on to reality.

The speaker reached over to a man next to him and took a pistol out of his hand. Dak recognized it even through the haze in his vision. It was his Springfield.

"I wonder," the commander pined, "what a thief would be doing with a weapon such as this."

"It's a crazy world," Dak argued. "Gotta protect yourself."

The man took a step closer to Dak, who raged on the inside—wishing he could tear away from the guards holding him back and pummel this guy into next week.

"I don't think so," the man said. "What are you? CIA?" He shook his head at that. "No, if you were, then you wouldn't tell me."

"Figure that one out all by yourself?" Dak teased. He felt the men to his right and left tense, ready to deliver more punishment. But the blows never came.

The commander stood with his hand out, halting their reactions.

"Then why were you snooping around the train? And why did you try to escape over the roof?"

"I wasn't trying to escape, moron. I was trying to get the drop on you and your... whatever you call this. Unit? I've seen better."

More tension on either side, and this time, the blows came, though not to his face. The men struck Dak in the middle of the back, right over the shoulder blades.

His head rocked back for a second as his torso fell forward. But he didn't fall far. The guards holding him down made sure of that.

"You shouldn't insult my men," the commander warned. "They have been unappreciated most of their lives. They don't take well to it."

"That supposed to make me feel pity?"

"It's supposed to make you show some respect. And you haven't answered my question."

Dak snorted, which actually hurt his gut. He realized laughing was probably a bad idea anyway. The tight pain in his abs only confirmed this.

"I answered three times already. Jeez."

"Do you know who I am?" the leader asked.

Dak sighed, exasperated and bleeding. He'd had enough of this guy. "You're the CO for this ragtag bunch you call a unit," he grumbled.

"I am Colonel Nikolai Morovski. And you are now my prisoner."

"Pfft. Not sure if you noticed, comrade, but we aren't in Ukraine anymore. Or Russia. Or Romania, for that matter. So, there's no war to fight here."

"Isn't there?"

Dak didn't like the way the man asked that last question, but he didn't have an answer. Instead, he kept quiet to see where this would lead. Sooner or later, they would reach the next train station, and then the colonel would have a decision to make.

If Dak could delay them long enough, he might still have a chance to get out of this alive.

"I sent two men to the back of the train after you walked by," Morovski continued. He looked to the right, out a window where the moon hung low over the western horizon. "Where are they?"

Dak feigned confusion for a second, twisting his lips up to the left as if in deep thought. "There were two of them?" he clarified.

"Yes."

"Kind of young? Maybe early, mid-twenties?"

"Yes."

"One blond and one with dark brown hair cut real short?"

The colonel leaned in closer, so close that Dak could smell the stale off-brand cigarettes from thirty years of smoking on his breath.

"Where? Are? They?"

Dak managed the slightest shrug. "Haven't seen anyone that meets that description."

The colonel stood up straight again and looked at the two men delivering the punishment.

"No. Wait. Wait," Dak said. "No more punching. Okay? I'm gonna level with you. Okay?"

"Talk."

"I saw two guys like that coming to my car through the windows between carriages. They looked scary, so I ducked out the back door and waited for them to leave. They're probably in the bar car..." Dak started laughing again. "Although you disconnected that, so they're probably sitting there a few miles back wondering what just happened."

A punch to the side stopped the laughter cold and replaced it with a fit of uncontrollable coughing.

When Dak was done with the racking cough, he looked down and saw splotches of blood mingling with the burgundy carpet.

The colonel saw it, too.

"Blood is a funny thing," Morovski said. "Very difficult to clean up once it's gotten on pretty much anything. And it sticks around a long time."

He crouched down low to set his eyes level with Dak's. "I found blood in the back of your train car. It appears there was a fight of some kind. And my men aren't in the bar car because we passed through it on the way to find you. Twice. So again, I ask, where are my two men?"

Dak stared down at the floor for several seconds—unwilling and unable to answer. Finally, he summoned the strength to push the words up through his throat and beyond his lips.

"I honestly don't know, Colonel," Dak said. "Last I saw the blond one, he was tumbling out of the train into a deep ravine. My guess is he's probably still down there somewhere. I didn't see what happened to the guy with brown hair, but it's a good bet he's in the bottom of that canyon, too. Although if you're going to go looking for him, you might want to take a mop. Probably messy."

The colonel listened patiently to the explanation, then abruptly swung the back of his hand across Dak's face.

The Russian's lower lip quivered with anger. "Those were loyal, good men," Morovski said. He stood and looked at the others. "Make sure their sacrifice is not in vain, brothers."

There were no shouts of agreement. No rallying cries. Only solemn nods.

"We'll be making an early stop, it seems." He went on, staring down at Dak, whose left cheek bled from a gash created by the ring on Morovski's finger. "It seems we've taken the train as far as we can."

27

"There has to be something we can do," Lesma said. "Some way we can find them."

Will shook his head while he stared at the worn hardwood floor. He scratched the back of his skull for several seconds as if that would pry an answer from the depths of his mind. Nothing but excuses emerged.

After the train was disconnected by the Russian soldiers, Will and the others managed to use the emergency brakes to bring it to a stop. The conductor happened to be in the bar car when things went awry, so he knew the procedures for such an event and immediately began to radio for help, and to let other trains in either direction know that they were stranded.

Teams arrived within thirty minutes to evacuate the train and get everyone safely to the nearest town.

Will and the other two found a hotel with vacancies. They rented two rooms, though Will had no intention of letting Galyna out of his sight. She insisted that she was fine and could take care of herself, but when he showed her the two queen beds in the room, and the fact that he wasn't going to take no for an answer, she surrendered to the idea.

The three met in Lesma's room, just across the hall, and they'd been sitting there for the last thirty minutes trying to come up with a way to find Dak and the rogue unit.

So far, no one had any clues other than they knew the thieves were heading to Budapest.

Will held his chin in one hand as he stood there in the center of the room. "Without knowing an exact location, I'm afraid there isn't much we can do, Les. We already tried tracking his phone. No signal. I assume they broke it and dumped it in a river."

Lesma exhaled loudly, flapping his lips as he did so. "Well, I can't just stand around here and do nothing. Perhaps the woman with the Axis agency, she can help us."

"Unfortunately, Dak was the only person with her contact information. I don't know if I'll be able to get through trying to contact her via Axis."

"It may be worth a try."

Will nodded. "Okay, that's a first step. What else?"

He thought hard, doing his best to imagine what Dak would do if the roles were reversed. Dak wouldn't give up. That much Will knew to be certain. But what action would he take?

"He would gather all the facts he could, all the knowns, and then add them together." Will spoke to himself, but everyone else in the room heard him.

"What?" Galyna asked.

"Sorry. I was just trying to think what Dak would do if he were here."

"Ah. Well, I'm sorry about your friend. I'm sure he's still alive." She didn't know why she said that and immediately wished she hadn't.

Will recognized the apologetic look on her face. "Don't worry about it," he said. "I know he is, too."

"I wish I had more information," she continued, standing up from the desk chair where she'd been sitting. She paced over to the door and back, then looped around again.

"German buyer," she mumbled. "Budapest." She turned to Will.

"Is there any way to isolate private flights coming into Budapest from Germany?"

"Sure," Will figured. "With the right connections."

"Do you have those connections?"

He didn't respond right away, instead pondering the list of contacts he dipped into from time to time.

Being a gunrunner for freedom fighters had its perks, and one of them was knowing several people with unusual career choices. Computer hackers were one of those careers, but in this instance, he wasn't sure that would work.

He needed someone on the inside of....

"Yes," he answered after the moment of deliberation. "I do think I know someone. His name is Richard. He's an air traffic controller out of Jacksonville, Florida. If there's anyone in my black book of contacts who could help us out with that, it's him."

"Then make the call," Lesma ordered.

Will checked his watch and shook his head. "I don't know. He keeps weird hours. And he's on East Coast time." Will paused for a second. "Then again, every minute that passes makes it harder for us to find Dak. It's worth a shot."

He took out his phone and entered the number while the other two waited, watched, and listened.

The phone rang three times before Will heard a tired, cracked voice on the other end answer. "Hello?"

"Dick. It's Will."

The man on the other end didn't respond immediately.

"Will Collins," Will clarified.

"I told you never to call me that," Richard complained. "And do you have any idea what time it is?"

"It's almost two in the morning here. So, I'm pretty sure it's still plenty early in Jacksonville."

"You know what time I go to bed, don't you?"

"I'm aware. Yes."

"And you know what I do for a living, right?"

"I thought you were quitting that gig to write novels."

Richard grumbled something unintelligible. "That's the plan. But the wife has expensive tastes, and the books don't pay for those things yet."

Will burst out laughing. "I hear that."

"How do you hear that? You're not married."

"True, but I've had some girlfriends who had expensive tastes. So, I can relate."

"Hmm. When are you going to get a real job, anyway? You know, 401(k). Health insurance. Benefits. You're still kind of young. Maybe it's time you settle down. Start a family."

"I'm sorry," Will said. "I didn't realize I called my mom. I must have dialed the wrong number."

"You could do with losing that smart-aleck attitude, too," Richard advised.

"Don't act like you don't like it."

The older man merely grumbled. "You didn't call me at bedtime to talk about my wife and to get career advice from me. Or did you?"

"Astute as always, Richard."

"Then what do you want?"

"Always blunt and to the point. Another reason I like you." Will smiled as he said it. "I have a problem. One that requires your specific expertise."

"Great. Since I'm only really an expert in one thing, let me guess. You lost a plane?"

"Actually, you're not too far off on that guess."

The older man huffed. "Seriously? I didn't even know you owned a plane."

Will twisted his lips into a wry, curled smirk. "I don't."

"Business been a little slow, huh?"

"Business is fine, Dick. It's not my plane I'm looking for."

"So, you know that giving out that kind of information is kind of against the rules, right?"

"I figured."

"And calling me that is also against my personal rule."

"Sorry. Yes, Richard."

The other two people in the room chuckled at the exchange.

"Are we on speaker?" Richard asked.

"Yes. Sorry. My team and I are currently in Hungary."

"Oh, so you have a team now. Look at you, making big strides. I thought you were the kind of guy who always works alone."

"I am. Mostly. Look, Rich, a friend of mine has been abducted by a group of rogue Russian soldiers. They stole a bunch of artifacts from a museum in Ukraine. Now they're AWOL. We tracked them into Romania and followed them onto a train going to Hungary. But we lost them."

"Wow. So, you're not doing this for personal gain?"

"No."

That seemed to wake the man on the phone up. He cleared his throat before he spoke again. "Okay, but I have one question."

"Shoot."

"You said you followed them on a train. Why are you trying to track a plane?"

"We think the Russians are going to try to sell the goods to a buyer in Budapest. I'm sure the rogue unit got off the train, or if they haven't, they will soon. Too easy to find them that way. So, we're not trying to track them."

"You're trying to track the buyer," Richard realized.

"Exactly. We believe he's coming in from Germany. If you can isolate private planes coming from there, we may still be able to find our friend before it's too late."

The phone went silent for fifteen seconds. Will waited patiently for another response. After twenty seconds, he broke his silence. "You still there?"

"Of course I'm still here," Richard said. "I'm just looking at the schedule to see who's working the tower tonight. I'm in bed."

"Sorry to keep you up."

"Well, I'm up now. Might as well go back to the office."

"I really appreciate this, Rich. Seriously. You're a good man."

Richard grunted. "Don't tell my wife. Would ruin her perception of me being a jerk."

Will laughed.

"Looks like Bill is on the tower tonight. He's a good guy. I can trust him. Knows how to keep a secret. Let me check with him and see what we can find. If there's a plane that meets your description and all that, Bill will find it."

"Thank you so much, Richard. I owe you one."

"You already owe me like three. Guess I'll just put it on your tab."

"Fair."

"I'll call you back when I have something. You'd better answer."

"Will do."

The call ended, and Will set the device on the desk nearby. "So," he said. "I guess we just wait. You two go ahead and get some shut-eye."

"What about you?" Galyna asked. "You need to rest, too."

"I don't think I can right now. My friend is out there somewhere, and who knows what kind of stuff those soldiers are doing to him? I wish there was more we could do, but for now all we can do is wait."

"How long do you think it will take for this Richard to find the buyer's plane?"

"No clue," Will said with a shrug. "First time I've done anything like this. Could be a few minutes. Could be hours." His face darkened. "They may not find it at all. People with the kind of money and the itch to buy black-market artifacts love their anonymity. They make it difficult to find them."

Galyna stretched her arms high over her head and yawned, signaling she was ready for some rest.

"I'll wake you two up when we know something. There won't be any trains out of here until early morning anyway. And that'll be our best bet to get there quickly. If the rogue unit got off their train, they'll have to take roads. We should be able to beat them to Budapest, locate the buyer, and set the trap for all of them."

28

Dak sat in the center of the middle row in an old Volkswagen fifteen-passenger van. He let his eyes wander from time to time, taking in the views through the windows—as much as he could trying to look past the Russian guards on either side of him.

He clenched his fingers several times. The zip ties around his wrists didn't allow for much circulation. He'd considered complaining to his Russian escorts but figured they wouldn't do much about it. Still, he thought it would be funny.

Turning to the guy on his left, he said, "Would you mind loosening these a little? They're kind of tight."

His answer came in the form of a thump on the back of the head from one of the guys behind him.

The Russian contingent had abandoned the train during the dark hours of morning, just prior to it reaching the station. The engineer had resisted stopping, but his mind was easily swayed by a pistol pointed at his head.

Not that his change of heart saved him. The Russians executed the man the instant the train halted.

Dak regretted the unnecessary death, but there was nothing he could do to stop it.

He turned to the right, looking straight at the guard's cheek. "I've never really seen the Hungarian countryside before. Have you?"

The soldier said nothing.

"It's much prettier than I realized," Dak continued, rolling his head back to the guy on the left. "You? You ever been here before? I should really think about taking a vacation here sometime."

Another thump to the back of his skull sent a concussive pain all the way through his eyeballs.

"Hey, cut that out," he ordered. "Last thing I need is to be in concussion protocol. I've got stuff to do."

"If you don't shut up," Morovski said from the front passenger's seat, "we have other ways of making you quiet."

Dak thought about it for a second, then pushed back against the urge to fling a half-dozen wisecracks back at the guy. Things were bad enough. He didn't want a gag in his mouth. Or worse.

The colonel turned around and looked out the windshield again, and the van interior returned to the steady moan of the engine and the rumble of the asphalt under tires.

Dak looked at the clock in the center of the dashboard for the umpteenth time in the last several hours. It would have driven him mad were he not trying to keep up with how long they'd been in there and how much farther they had to go to reach Budapest.

He wondered where Will and the others were, but Dak had no grand delusions about them coming to his rescue. How could they? Now that the Russians were off the train, locating the group would be nearly impossible.

Sure, the stolen vans might become an issue at some point, but the colonel had been clever in selecting their transportation.

The three vans belonged to a rental company and had been parked in the back of the lot. The vehicles didn't have modern amenities such as navigation systems, and they were certain to lack any kind of tracking system for the police to use if they ever went missing.

Even if the rental company manager realized the vans were

missing—which likely wouldn't be for hours or even days—they'd have to rely on using license plates to track them down. The colonel took care of that on the first stop for fuel, ordering his men to change out the plates for others they found on parked cars near the refueling station.

The colonel was smart; Dak had to give him that.

"I'm just wondering what you plan to do with me, Colonel," Dak said again, breaking the ordered silence.

The man didn't respond.

"It's just, I'm not really a valuable asset to anyone. So, I don't see where this is going."

"You may be more valuable than you realize, Dak Harper."

Dak nodded slowly, dramatically. "Oh, I see. You went through my things. Not cool, man. I don't read your unicorn diary about your secret crushes. By the way, I don't know who Peter is, but he sounds dreamy."

The guy to Dak's right snapped his head around. He peered at the American, confusion dripping from his eyes.

Morovski simply chuckled. "He's trying to goad you. But it's funny. We need some humor to pass the time. We are still several hours from Budapest."

Dak looked at the man to his right, a young soldier with a baby face and fierce blue eyes. "Let me guess. Your name is Peter."

The man frowned back.

Dak leaned closer. "He likes you." Dak lifted his hands and pointed as best he could toward the colonel.

The guard merely scowled back, then looked the other way out the window.

"Ignore it if you want to, big guy. But you have a secret admirer."

Morovski's laughter swelled. "My men are beyond any sort of teasing you could offer them, Dak."

"Oh, is that a fact? Well, how did I know about young Peter here? Huh?"

"It is a common Russian name. Much like in your country Jack or

John is often used." He directed the next comment to the guard. "He got lucky, Peter. Odds are one of you was named that."

Dak shook his head, never taking his intense gaze off the young soldier. "Don't let him fool you, Pete. He's into you. All those cold nights during ops. Tents. Warm blankets. Army-green cots. You know what I'm talking about."

Another thump to the back of Dak's skull quieted him down. This one really hurt, and it only made the headache from the previous ones that much worse.

"Jeez, take it easy back there," Dak groaned. "I already said I don't want to be in concussion protocol when I have to kill you guys."

"Yes. The killing part," Morovski said. "It would seem we all have that in common."

Dak shut down the humor for a second and replaced it with genuine curiosity. "What's that supposed to mean?"

"You were in the American military, no?"

"No," Dak scoffed. "Military? Me? I don't think so. I couldn't hurt a fly."

"Interesting. Because our intel says that you were in the Army. Your record was a little hard to uncover, which means you were probably special ops. Much like the rest of us."

Dak looked around at the men in the van. He already knew about their background, their training, and assumed many of their operations—like his—had been clandestine in nature.

"You don't know me," Dak defended, but his tone betrayed the truth.

"Oh, you're wrong about that, Dak. We know enough. I do have a question, though."

"Yes. I already have a date for prom. Her name is Abigail. She's a starting forward on the basketball team."

Peter jabbed him in the ribs with his elbow, which sent a fresh pain up through Dak's torso.

"My question, Dak, is what you were doing on that train? And why did you try to get away?"

Dak shrugged, which stretched the new bruise on his right side in a painful way. "Seemed like a logical thing to do. A couple of sociopaths coming through the train, looking for trouble. I figured there would be more."

"Ah yes. My two men. The men you killed. I find it difficult to believe that you were able to overpower them alone."

"What can I say," Dak argued, "American training is better than Russian."

Peter started to send another elbow into Dak's ribs, but Morovski raised his left hand to stop the blow. "Let him think what he wants, Peter. We know better."

Dak leered at the guard again. "Yeah. That's right. Heel. If you're good, maybe later he'll give you a treat." He leaned closer. "He wrote about that in his diary, too."

The soldier could only glower back.

"However well trained you might be, Dak, you must have been quite lucky to catch my men by surprise. But again, that begs the question, why you would in the first place? Have you been tracking us?"

"A girl's gotta keep *some* secrets."

"I am certain you have many of those. But this is one I have been very curious about. My men would not have attacked you, which means you struck first."

"Han shot first."

Morovski didn't get the reference and so went on. "Which tells me you were following us, and perhaps you got scared when the two of them appeared in the back of the train."

"I don't scare easily," Dak fired back. "If you knew anything about me, you'd know that." The sense of humor abandoned, he pushed forward. "I sensed your two men meant trouble. I'd seen them on my first pass through the train. I was minding my own business. Just on vacation. I went to have a look around at the rest of the train, and then went back to my seat. A few minutes later, they started harassing me."

"Harassing you?"

"Yeah. Asking me for my papers and stuff like that. I knew they weren't Romanian or Hungarian. No mistaking that Russian accent you guys throw around."

"Interesting."

"When one of them grabbed me, I defended myself."

"And threw them both off the train," Morovski finished.

"Strangest thing," Dak explained. "I shoved one back, which knocked the door open. Then the other guy tried to hit me. I managed to kick him into the other guy, and they both fell out over the railing. Somewhere in there, I guess I must have busted one of their noses. It's all kind of a blur, really."

"Fascinating. What are the odds that a former military special operator like yourself would be on the same train as us." Morovski turned around and stared into Dak's soul. "I suppose it doesn't matter now. Soon, we will be in Budapest. And there is someone there who is extremely interested in seeing you again."

Again? What did he mean again?

"It would seem," the colonel went on, "that there is a significant bounty on your head, Dak." At the obvious surprise on Dak's face, he lifted one shoulder as if it was of no matter. "Of course I keep tabs on the mercenary network. Several of my men have gone on to careers in the private sector, bounty hunting and things like that. It turns out, you have been a very bad boy."

Dak did his best to keep from squirming. "What are you going to do, send me to the principal's office?" The quip did little to settle his growing nerves.

The Russian commander didn't understand the reference; not that he would have addressed it in the first place.

"You served in the Middle East. Quite the distinguished record, until you betrayed your comrades."

This guy did have intel. A few key points were faulty, but he'd done his research—and quickly.

"That isn't how it went down," Dak defended. "It was the other way around."

"And then, in the course of the following year after you abandoned your post, those men who served with you ended up dead or missing. I suppose you don't know anything about that."

A chill shot through Dak's spine. Up until now, no one had ever made mention of the killings.

"Who told you that?" He stared into the Russian's eyes.

"It would seem that our worlds are more connected than you realize, Dak." He cocked his head to the side, offering mocking pity to his prisoner. "When we captured you, we immediately ran a check to see who you really are. The information was easy for my men to obtain. For all your efforts to stay in the shadows, eventually the light found you."

"What are you talking about?" Dak growled.

"We were surprised to find so many people—mercenaries, bounty hunters, assassins—searching for you," Morovski said. "So many resources put to use. And you fell right into our lap. Now we have two buyers. One for the treasure... and one for you."

Dak didn't want to ask. He didn't want to know the answer, but deep down he already did.

"Who would want to buy a retired old soldier like me?"

"Don't devalue yourself so, Dak. I assure you, Colonel Cameron Tucker is willing to pay top dollar for your head."

The name sank like an arrow into Dak's chest.

Morovski turned around and faced forward one more. "But when he found out we had you alive, he told us he'd pay extra for the privilege of killing you personally."

29

Will's phone rang only twice before he answered it. The other two were asleep in seats across from each other on the train, both leaning against the window. He'd dozed off a few times to the monotonous sound of the clacking underneath the carriage.

He checked the number before hitting the green button and putting the earpiece to his right ear.

"Did you find it?" he asked.

"Did I find it?" Richard grumbled. "Seriously? Would I be calling you right now at this unearthly hour if I hadn't found the plane?"

"Sorry. We... didn't hear from you the rest of the night, so I was starting to wonder."

"Well, I did. And it wasn't easy. Let me tell you." Richard paused. "What in the sweet fancy Moses is that noise? It sounds like you're in a factory or something."

"We're on a train headed to Budapest."

"Oh. Well, good, because there are two private jets leaving Frankfurt this morning headed to Budapest."

"Did you get a look at the passenger manifests?"

"What do you think this is, amateur hour? Obviously, I checked to see who was flying on the planes."

Will wanted to laugh at his grumpy friend's antics, but he refrained—albeit with tremendous effort.

"I'm sorry," he managed. "Go on."

"Took a bit of digging, actually. Both planes are owned by corporations. One of the companies is a tech outfit. They make microprocessors and things like that. Their CEO is flying to Budapest right now. That one was easier to find since she's apparently going to Hungary for some merger talks."

"That doesn't sound like our buyer."

"I had a feeling you'd say that. The second one was trickier. The company that owns this plane is called Runfeld."

"Never heard of it."

"I'm not surprised. They don't do anything."

Will's forehead tightened at the comment. "What do you mean they don't do anything?"

"Just what I said. They're a shell corporation. A bottom-feeding vacuum for the rich jerks who own it." Richard cleared his throat. "Just so you know, doing this sort of investigation isn't really my thing."

"I'll bring you a good bottle of bourbon the next time I'm down Duval way."

"Yeah, well get me some Jags tickets, too, while you're at it."

"I didn't think those were hard to come by."

"Luxury box, son. I want a suite for the lack of sleep."

Will chuckled. "I'll pull some strings. Tell me about this Runfeld."

"I'm only partially kidding about the luxury box. Truth is, this is interesting stuff. I'd prefer to do it while sitting on the can midmorning, but whatever."

"Thanks for the visual."

It was Richard's turn to laugh. "Turns out, Runfeld has never turned a profit. They're the company that takes most of the losses so the other ones above it can use various international tax laws to their advantage."

"Sounds like a pyramid scheme."

"It isn't all that dissimilar, actually. And it's extremely clever. They have so many companies built into this thing, it would take an army of accountants to process all of it."

"You figured it out," Will noticed.

"Oh, seeing the family tree is easy enough. But the amount of paperwork it would take to track down every nickel that filters through all these things would be insurmountable. Not only that; you can bet your sweet tuchus they're running dozens if not hundreds of cash-based businesses that help clean the money the old-fashioned way."

"Laundering?"

"Exactly."

"Okay, so with all these companies connected, who's the big umbrella?"

"I was hoping you'd ask that. It's Meridian."

Will's breath caught in his throat. "Did you just say Meridian?"

"Did I stutter?"

"No. It's just that—"

"Heh. Bit of a mind job, ain't it, kid? I thought that would probably shake your socks a little."

Will couldn't say anything for what felt like ten minutes. Meridian was one of the largest media corporations in the world, with dozens of national news outlets in more than a dozen countries. In the United States alone, they owned two mainstream news companies, the largest sports news network, multiple streaming service providers, film production companies, and probably more that Will didn't even know about.

They were a multibillion-dollar entity, and one of the largest corporations on the planet.

"Who's on the plane?" Will asked, getting right to the point.

"That's the big question, ain't it? Unfortunately, all I got was a bunch of John Does, if you know what I mean."

"No. What does that mean?"

"With some of these groups, they want to be as anonymous as

possible. Leave no paper trail. That sort of thing. Whoever is getting on that plane doesn't want the rest of the world to have the slightest chance of figuring it out."

"They must be a big player."

"The biggest, if I had to guess."

"But why go to all that trouble to conceal their identity for a trip to Budapest? High-level CEOs do that sort of thing all the time. Like the one from Runfeld. Why not just concoct a story like that and fly under the auspices of a merger meeting? Those big companies are always acquiring smaller ones. It just doesn't make sense unless—" He stopped in midsentence, the answer suddenly appearing to him like fireworks in a dark sky. "Unless they were making a big purchase of illicit goods. Like stolen artifacts from the Ukrainian museum of history."

"Bingo."

"That means someone high up in the company is dealing in the antiquities black market."

"Can't have that on the front page. Not that it would be since they own at least four major newspapers in the United States alone, not to mention ones overseas. This company is a juggernaut, Will. If you're gonna go after this person, whoever they are, you need to tread carefully. With the amount of detail that's gone into hiding their name, I'd say it's gotta be someone near the top of the corporate food chain—if not the owner of the company himself."

"But they're a publicly traded corporation," Will reasoned.

"Sure they are. And you probably think that your vote actually has sway in the elections, too."

Will's lips curled.

"Yes, the company is publicly traded, but there are still majority owners, and then there are the shell owners. Just like with the shell companies underneath the big one, wealthy elites use puppets to buy up more shares. Find the majority shareholder, and you probably find the person who's on that plane."

Will felt his senses tingle at the thought, and a surge of adrenaline pulsed through him. "And who is the majority shareholder of Meridian?"

"I thought you'd never ask. His name is Karl Niemann. And he's based out of Berlin."

"So, he's the buyer," Will whispered.

"More than likely. I'd say the rabbit hole goes deeper, but that's as far as I could get tonight. I worked all day so I need to get some shut-eye. I'm just glad I have tomorrow off."

"I really appreciate all this, Richard. Seriously."

"Don't mention it. I mean, you still owe me. But don't mention it. Now, the plane is supposed to arrive in Budapest later this afternoon at four local time. I hope that train you're on can get you there soon enough."

"Fortunately, we're on one of the faster ones, so we should get to Budapest about one. That should be plenty of time to figure out our next move."

"I'd get to figuring now if I were you. Not sure how you're going to take on a group like this. They'll have a ton of security with them. No way you'll get to them in the airport, so maybe your best bet is to tag along behind them if you can, catch them if and when they let their guard down."

"You're starting to sound like someone who's done a little of this kind of thing before. There something you're not telling me, Rich?"

"Just thinking out loud, kid. I hope you find your friend. And the artifacts. Just be careful.'

"Thanks for caring. We'll figure something out."

"One more thing, Will. I wouldn't call the police about any of this. People like these run the show. I mean the whole show. They're likely connected with the feds here, international police agencies, you name it. Unless you know someone you can trust, I'd keep this in-house."

"I think I may know someone who can help."

A chuff came through the speaker. "You'd better be sure, kid. That's all I'm going to say. Now, if you'll excuse me, I have to go to bed.

I'm sending you the flight information via text. If you have any more questions it'll have to wait until after I take a nap."

"Thanks again, Rich. Big time."

"Yeah, yeah."

The call ended abruptly. A few seconds later, Richard's text message popped up on the phone screen. Will briefly looked over the flight details and then opened up his contacts.

He had another call to make.

30

W ill climbed out of the cab and passed an extra ten to the driver. Then he thanked the man and closed the door.

Will, Lesma, and Galyna stood outside of what looked like an American dive bar—except in the middle of Budapest. A green-and-white-striped awning stretched out from the old brick façade. Four tinted windows lined the wall on either side of the front door. Neon beer signs hung in two of them.

The bar sat on the corner of a busy street, but the entrance faced the adjacent street, which seemed to get much less traffic, both pedestrian and vehicle.

If someone didn't know better, they'd think the owner had designed a place they didn't want people to visit.

That wasn't too far from the truth.

"What is this place?" Lesma asked. "I've been in some questionable bars before, but this one looks like a...." He struggled for the word.

"Americans would call it a dump," Galyna offered.

Will took their comments in stride. "In the US, some of the best bars look just like this one."

"If that is the case, then I can see why you left," Lesma half joked.

With an eye roll, Will opened the front door and held it so the other two could enter. They hesitated.

"You say a friend of yours owns this place?" Lesma asked.

"Yes. Now get inside. We don't have much time."

The two obeyed, and Will followed them into the dimly lit pub. Sports pennants hung from the wall near the ceiling, wrapping around the entire place. A rectangular bar stood in the center, surrounded by round, green-upholstered vinyl stools with wooden backs. A loop of booths encircled the bar, lining the walls. A Pac-Man arcade game in the back corner rang with the familiar theme music.

Three men sat at the bar, each sitting alone with a few stools between them. One middle-aged couple occupied a booth to the left, chowing down on a couple of Philly cheesesteaks. Two other couples —all with gray hair—sat in a booth to the right around the middle of the wall. Each of them also had a cheesesteak and fries plate between their elbows.

Every person in there had a tall glass of beer in front of them.

Every person but one.

A woman with blonde hair pulled back in a ponytail sat facing the door on the other side of the bar. She held a glass of ice water in her right hand, staring at the three as they loitered in the entryway.

"There she is," Will announced in a hushed tone.

No one except the bartender seemed to notice the three new visitors. The man beamed under a bushy beard and greeted Will with a nod.

Will walked over to the bar and stepped into the walk-through to give his friend a hug.

The man in a beige fabric apron and black bow tie returned the gesture, clapping Will on the back.

"Been a long time, my friend," the barkeeper said.

"What's it been? Four? Five years?"

"Try six."

"Wow, Matty. That's a long time, bro."

"Yep. Well, I only remember because that's when I quit Interpol and started my own business." His Eastern Pennsylvania accent rippled through the room.

"Matt, this is Galyna and Lesma." He pointed to the two who'd followed him over to the bar.

Matt shook both their hands, starting with Galyna.

"Matt here makes the best cheesesteaks this side of Philly," Will bragged.

"It's okay to say it, buddy," Matt countered. "Best in the world."

Will laughed. "You know I can't disagree."

His eyes diverted over to the blonde woman who sat at the counter still holding the water in her hand.

"Thanks for letting us meet here. I knew your joint would be safe."

"No problem," Matt replied. "*Mi casa es su safe house.* Or however they say safe house in Spanish."

Will chuckled again and started toward the other side of the bar. "Get us three of those cheesesteaks, too."

Matt nodded. "You want fries with that?"

"Always."

"You got it."

Will sidled up next to the blonde woman, who continued to stare at the door. "You certainly make a scene considering you're trying not to draw attention, Will."

"Sorry about that. Haven't seen Matty in a while."

"Yes. I heard. Six years. So did everyone else in here."

Will looked around the room, analyzing every face until he returned to hers. "Hungarians who like a good American dive bar in their town. They don't care."

"Two of them are American expats," the blonde said. "Or did you not see their clothes and the waters next to their beers?"

Will looked across the bar, beyond the three tiers of liquor in the center, at the couple in the booth by the window. "What about their waters?"

"There's ice in them," she explained. "That's a predominantly

American thing. Most Europeans I've met don't drink beverages with ice."

"Maybe they're progressing."

She finally ripped her gaze from the door and passed a weary, sidelong glance at him.

He held up his hands in surrender. "Okay. Okay. Point made. I was just kidding. But seriously, thank you for meeting us."

"You called Tommy. He called Emily. Emily called me."

"Did you get a chance to talk with Liz?"

"She briefed me on what's happening. She would have come here herself, but I was closer—operating on the western side of Hungary."

"What were you doing over—" Before he finished the question, the *back-off* look she gave him cut off his words. "Right. I guess I'm not supposed to know that."

She flicked her head toward the back corner at an empty booth near the hallway. A green-and-white sign pointed the way to the restrooms deeper into the corridor. "Let's go somewhere quieter."

Will and the others followed her to the booth, where she stood and motioned to Galyna to take the seat nearest the wall.

The curator didn't argue and slid in, waiting for her cue to speak.

The two men stood next to the seat staring at each other for several seconds.

"Go ahead," Will offered.

"No, I insist," Lesma protested.

"I'd prefer to—" Will stopped when he caught the stubborn glare from the big Russian. "You know what? Fine. I don't mind the inside seat. But if I need to take a leak, you'll have to get up."

"Is risk I'm willing to take," Lesma said with a crooked grin.

The blonde woman slid in next to Galyna and rolled her eyes at the two men. "You two idiots figure it out yet?"

"Uh, yeah. Yeah, we're good." Will scooted close to the wall to get some space between himself and Lesma. Then he held out his hand to introduce the woman to his companions. "Lesma, Galyna, this is June Holiday."

June didn't offer to shake hands. Which made things awkward for

Lesma as he offered his, then held it there for a few seconds until he realized the gesture wasn't being returned. He withdrew his hand and wiped it on his pants.

"June is—"

"Here to help you guys take down an elite Russian army unit that robbed Galyna's museum," she said, giving him the *don't say too much* stare.

"Right," Will corrected course quickly. "Were you able to locate the plane?"

"It's on its way now," she said. "Lands in two hours."

"Awesome. Were you able to cordon off the airport?"

She looked at him like his eyes were melting. "No. Maybe you don't realize this, but agents in my organization are few and far between."

"So I've heard. I just thought you might have leveraged some local connections."

"As little as possible."

"Wait a minute," Galyna protested, speaking up for the first time since walking in. "You're saying we're going to try to take down this buyer and the Russians, just the three of us?"

Will shook his head just as Matt walked up to the table with three beers in his hands. "These are on the house," he said, setting them down on the edge of the table.

"Nope," Will answered Galyna. "That's where my old pal Matt McClath comes in."

Matt crossed his arms and nodded. "My guys should be here soon," he said. "Good people. I trust 'em. And if I trust 'em, you can, too."

"Guys?" Lesma wondered.

June was also curious about this, as evidenced by the skepticism on her face.

"Some of my old Interpol buddies from here. They come in on Thursdays most weeks."

The smell of onions filled the air as if to emphasize why Matt's friends came by.

"How were you in Interpol?" Galyna asked. "You must be a citizen of one of its member countries. You don't sound like you're from one of those."

"I'm not from any of them. But I have citizenship here in Hungary. Have for a long time."

"He came here in college to find himself," Will explained, using air quotes with the last two words. "Never wanted to come home."

"Something like that," Matt semi agreed. "My only regret is that I never caught a clever gunrunner smuggling weapons to freedom fighters in struggling nations." He cast Will a disdainful glance.

"Oh, it's like that?" Will asked.

"No. Not really. Anyway, the three guys I mentioned are legit. And if you're right about all this, they want to stop this group of Russians as bad as you. Maybe doesn't hurt that it would be a big bust for them."

"Hmm," Will laughed. "I wish we had more than three. But we gotta make do with what we got."

"If we try to bring in too many people, then there's a higher risk of a mole catching wind of things. From what you told me, the buyer is well connected in Europe."

"He is," June said, finally finding a wedge to cut into the conversation. "Karl Niemann is one of the most powerful men in Europe, and the world. His media conglomerate controls a massive share of every market imaginable. According to my sources, there have been several suicides and accidental deaths around him."

"I've heard of stuff like that back home," Will chirped.

"Also," June continued, "many of the company's holdings under his administration have skyrocketed in value."

"That could just be good leadership," Matt offered.

"Perhaps. Or it could be that high-level players are pumping the stock. We're talking major institutional money. Money that has been scrubbed so many times you could eat off it. It's the money that prints more money, and that can never be tied to anyone."

Will didn't say anything for a second, instead taking in her words like a kid listened to a ghost story by the campfire. "You almost sound like a conspiracy theorist," he managed. "Except I know you know your stuff."

"I find it's best not to think too much about some of the things I know," June answered. "Better to just make what little difference we can, and try to enjoy what time we are given."

Lesma sat there dumbfounded. "I didn't realize we were starting philosophy club here. Any chance we can stick to telling everyone the plan?"

Will let out a short laugh and nodded. He glanced over at the door, then began as he folded his fingers together.

"When your guys get here, we head to the airport, follow the buyer to the rendezvous, surround both parties, and the cops call in the cavalry."

"That's it?" Matt asked. "That's the plan?"

Will shrugged. "Unless you got something better."

June shook her head, looking down at the table as she processed her own ideas. "No. These guys won't be taken into custody. And there will be too many of them for us to take out all at once."

Galyna sat up straight. She'd been silent for much of their time in the bar. "What if...." She stopped, as if uncertain she should say anything.

"Yes," Lesma pressed. "You have an idea?"

She tilted her head to the side, still unsure. "It's just that... if you can't outgun them, perhaps you can cause them to turn on each other."

Will's eyebrows lifted, and he looked to June for her thoughts.

"Yeah," she said. "Now that's a good idea. We just have to figure out how to do it."

"I have been in situations like this before," Lesma confessed.

Matt and June both looked at him with mock surprise.

"Neither party will trust each other. You can use this."

"That's true," Will confirmed. "Whenever I'm in a"—he looked to Matt for a second and tweaked his words—"business meeting, you always have to be on high alert. Can't trust a criminal."

Lesma pretended to be hurt. "Seriously?"

"Okay, sometimes you can." Will looked around at the others. "None of you has to do this. So, I appreciate the help."

"I have to do this," Galyna stated. "Those artifacts are my country's heritage. Our history."

"Dak is my friend," Lesma added. "And I don't have many of those I can trust."

"You know I'm down to help," Matt said. "And you can count on my Interpol buddies."

June raised her glass of water and smiled. "I'm just here for the cheesesteaks, but whatever."

The comment sent a trickle of laughter around the group.

"Well," Will said, "thank you. It's going to be dangerous. I don't want anyone getting hurt, but that outcome is likely."

"Not if we can get them to turn on each other," June disputed, bringing everyone back to the plan.

"Right. Now the only trick is how to make that happen."

31

The sound of jet engines filled the cool afternoon air. Evergreens swayed in the breeze next to the fence surrounding the airport.

Will watched the entrance from a hundred yards away, binoculars pressed to his eyes.

"You guys see anything yet?" he asked into the radio clipped to the inside of his shirt collar.

"Nothing here," Matt answered first.

"All clear on my side," June said.

Within five minutes of meeting Matt's friends at the bar, the group had loaded up and headed for the airport.

Those three remained together in one vehicle. June brought Lesma and Galyna with her, and watched the airport exit from another angle in their black SUV parked next to an old factory a few blocks down and across the airfield.

Will and Matt stayed together, keeping an eye on the exit from their position, parked behind a clump of bushes straight down the street from the airport exit.

With everyone in their respective vehicles, the group could mobilize fast—and would need to.

If they lost sight of Niemann's convoy, Dak and the treasure were as sure as gone.

"According to the flight plan," Will said through the radio, "they just landed. Probably that G6 that just touched down a few minutes ago."

"Is that the kind of plane this guy uses?" June asked.

"That's what Richard said. So I don't think we'll have to wait much longer."

They'd been in position for ninety minutes, and Will was starting to feel the tug of doubt on his paranoid mind. *What if we missed them already? What if the Russians already killed Dak?*

He shook off the thoughts and focused on the exit.

"Remember, we have all three streets that lead away from the airport covered," Will said, partly to keep his mind clear of negativity. "If they pass, you—"

"We become the lead tail," Pierre said, cutting him off. "Yes, we know the plan."

Will hummed a laugh to himself. Pierre—a vain Frenchman with carefully coiffed brown hair—was as direct a person as Will had met, and the one who seemed to be in charge of the Interpol squad. Pedro, from Spain, seemed the quietest of the three and was the smallest, though Will knew that probably meant the man was all the more lethal.

The largest of that bunch—a Croatian named Luka—carried himself like an NFL linebacker, and had a high degree of intelligence. He spoke little at the initial meeting at the bar, but Will could tell the man was absorbing everything, observing everything, and processing everything.

"Right," Will confirmed into the mic. He felt the need to do more, say more, but everyone knew the plan. Now it just came down to waiting.

"Don't sweat it," Matt said to his friend from the driver's side of the car. "I'm sure your buddy is fine. And we're exactly where we need to be."

"You sure?" Will asked, rubbing his legs to rid himself of the swelling anxiety.

"Uh, yeah. It's a good plan. Three directions out of here, and we have them all covered."

"Unless they went through the normal terminal and exit."

Matt sighed. "Yeah, I'm sure there's a guy in a black tuxedo waiting in the terminal with a little sign that says Niemann on it." He reached over and shook Will by the shoulder. "Relax, man. We got this. These kinds of guys don't take the normal passenger route through the airport. They're coming out through that gate. And when they do, we'll follow them."

Will had gone over the plan twice with everyone, just to be sure. It was simple enough in concept, but it was in the execution where everything could go haywire.

Depending on which direction Niemann's group took, the car closest would be the lead tail, and the other two would hang back, following at a distance until they knew the location of the buy.

The lead tail would be the most dangerous, and most difficult, to execute. Get too close to Niemann, and his security detail would get spooked. Stay too far back, and they'd lose them altogether.

"We have visual on the convoy," June said. She was in the best position to see through the fence and across the tarmac. "I count...." she stopped for a second. "Wow. Five SUVs. Mercedes-Benz."

Will wanted to ask how many guys Niemann had in the security detail, but he kept his mouth shut, knowing that information would come soon enough.

On cue, June added, "There are twenty of them."

She didn't sound disappointed or concerned by the number, though Will felt his heart sink a little at the revelation.

"That's a lot of dudes," Will said to Matt.

"Gotta like those odds," Matt responded cheerfully, though with a macabre sort of sentiment in his tone.

"Make that twenty-one," June added.

"Noted," Will said to himself but still loud enough for Matt to hear.

A flicker of dread shot through Will's chest. "Going to be tough against that many."

"You sure are Captain Positivity today," Matt drawled. "Have a little faith, my friend. The numbers don't matter. As long as we get them to turn on each other. And we know exactly how to do that."

"Yeah," Will said, though he didn't sound convinced. "Let's hope so."

"Loading up the convoy now," June interrupted. "Everyone stay ready."

Matt revved the engine to life and waited with both hands gripping the steering wheel, while Will watched the exit gate.

Will felt the tingle of anticipation pulse through him. It was a mix of battle energy and fear—the compounds that created courage or cowards.

"Here they come," June said.

Will peered through the windshield, waiting. He'd always wondered what the term bated breath meant. Now the realization suddenly hit him as he couldn't have inhaled if he wanted to. Every nerve ending was on a hair trigger as his eyes locked on that gate.

Then he spotted the first of the convoy's SUVs. It pulled up to the striped gate bar and waited for a security guard inside the shack to come out.

A man in uniform exited the guardhouse and walked over to the vehicle. The man held a tablet in his hand as he approached the driver's door.

The guard bobbed his head a few times, then pointed back to the SUVs behind the lead one. Then he nodded again and checked the tablet. Will assumed the guy was checking off a list of names.

"Come on," Will said.

Finally, the guard nodded and waved the convoy through. The striped bar lifted as he ambled back to the guardhouse, and the SUVs drove onto the street and continued straight ahead—right toward Will and Matt.

"Looks like you two are the lucky winners," June said. "Team Three, move out and fall in behind us. Team One, we'll be behind you even though you won't see us."

"Copy that," Will said. "Here we go."

The convoy rumbled by, engines zooming then fading repeatedly like a dulled-down NASCAR race.

Will watched the line turning left at the next street. When the last of the SUVs disappeared from view, he turned to Matt. "Punch it, left at the next intersection."

"Roger that," Matt chirped.

He spun the steering wheel and mashed the gas. The black sedan whipped around to the sound of squealing tires, then charged ahead.

At the intersection, Matt turned onto the next street and slowed down at the sight of the convoy two blocks away.

"You tracking us?" Will asked into the radio.

"Yep. We got you, Team One," June confirmed.

"Same here," Pierre said.

"Okay, gang," Will muttered, "let's see where this leads."

The convoy continued away from the airport, snaking its way southeast from the city. Rolling hills of green and brown rippled before them as the vehicles left the industrial part of the city behind.

Within ten minutes, the traffic thinned, as did the homes dotting the land around the ancient city. Patches of trees grew denser the farther they drove. And the hills continued to rise.

"Leaving the city," Will whispered—half to himself, half to Matt.

"Yeah, I wondered what their play would be." He kept his eyes on the last SUV, making sure to stay far enough back to not arouse suspicion. "Abandoned warehouse in the city? Junkyard? Empty parking garage?" He rolled his shoulders. "I didn't even think about the countryside. Makes sense, especially if you're a high-profile baller trying to keep a low profile."

"Yeah," Will agreed. "Fewer people means fewer potential witnesses. Best to keep things quiet. And nature is real quiet."

"Getting too quiet on the road, though, pal. Aren't too many cars out this way. We'll need to rotate soon."

"You're right." He pressed the button the radio. "Team Two, rotate up."

Within thirty seconds, Will saw the headlights of another sedan appear in the rearview mirror. The other car caught up within another fifteen seconds, and when June's vehicle was only ten car lengths back, Matt flipped on his blinker and turned right at the next road.

June and Galyna zoomed by as Matt and Will waited for Team Three to pass. They didn't have to wait long. As planned, the other two cars stayed close together, and a mere ten seconds after June's car passed, the third one—another gray subcompact—followed.

With the other two cars ahead, Matt turned the wheel again and did a U-turn, then merged back onto the main road.

"We have visual on the target," June said through the radio.

"Copy that," Pierre's voice confirmed.

"Your fish now, June," Will announced.

Will watched the SUV closely until it disappeared around a bend in the road, blocked by dense forests.

He looked down at his phone to make sure the tracking beacons were still working on the other two vehicles. The blue dots blinked, melting that worry immediately. Not that it was any real relief. Will still had plenty to be concerned about.

Just because they could follow the buyer didn't mean they would be able to implement the plan. There were many moving parts in this scenario, and most of them were moving against him.

Ten minutes passed before June's voice broke the frail silence. "Looks like they're taking the exit to Gomba," she stated. "Rotate up, Team Three. I'll take the opposite direction of the target once we leave the main road. Then I'll swing back into formation."

"Understood," Pierre said.

"Moving up now behind Team Three," Will added.

The road opened up again, clearing through the trees and hills, to an open stretch of highway.

The sun hung in the sky to the west, dipping ever closer to the horizon. When that happened, darkness would make following the buyer even more difficult—if for no other reason than their own headlights could give away that they were following the convoy.

Will hoped it wouldn't take that long.

"What's in Gomba?" he asked, keeping his eyes straight ahead.

"Not much," Matt answered. "I mean, it's a nice village. Real quiet. Some nice buildings. Couple of good places to eat."

"Village. So, not a lot of people." It wasn't a question.

"Right. There are some farms around this area, as you can already see. But lots of forests and hills. Plenty of good places to do a shady deal out here."

"They're turning right, away from the village," June said through the radio. "We're going left and will fold back in behind Team One."

"Copy," Pierre and Will echoed.

Ahead on the exit, Will saw the line of Mercedes SUVs meandering to the right, heading toward a rolling forest. He saw June's vehicle veer left toward the heart of the village that cropped up against the waning afternoon sun.

"We're in pursuit," Pierre announced.

Will saw the SUV turn. Matt followed twenty seconds later.

The dots on Will's screen still blinked, and now he watched as the one marking Pierre's vehicle broke away from the one indicating June's ride, which fell back into line a minute later.

Neither Matt nor Will could see the convoy beyond the bends in the road. And at the moment, Will felt completely helpless. The three men from Interpol he'd just met a few hours before now had total control over whether or not Dak would live or die. It was a hard thing to accept, but he had no choice.

"Relax," Matt said, as if he could read his friend's thoughts. "My guys got this."

Will took a deep breath and sighed. "Yeah. I know." He nodded, hoping that would help him believe it.

Three more minutes had passed when Pierre's voice crackled through the radio.

"They're turning off the road onto a gravel path. Dropping tracking beacon to mark the spot."

"Roger that," Will said.

"Copy," June chimed.

Will watched his phone screen. The blue dot indicating Team

Three's position continued blinking. Then it stopped moving.

"Okay," Will said. "The beacon stopped. Should be just ahead."

Matt guided the sedan around the next curve. Shadows and sunlight danced through the foliage and into the car windows.

"Almost on top of it."

The road straightened and stretched down a long corridor cut through the forest. Another road cut off to the left just ahead.

"That's gotta be it," Matt figured.

"It's where they dropped their beacon."

Matt slowed down and turned onto the gravel road—if it could be called that. Tall grasses had grown up along both sides of the path, and shorter patches in the middle.

"Looping back around," Pierre announced.

Will saw June's car come around the bend and slow down to join them on the side of the road.

Matt stopped the car fifty feet off the main road. June pulled in behind them. Then a minute later, Pierre's SUV rolled up in the back.

Will climbed out of the car before Matt could kill the engine. He scanned the map on his phone.

The others left their vehicles and huddled around the lead car.

"This path doesn't go anywhere," Will said, pointing at the screen. "Just into the forest. Must've belonged to someone."

"Or still does," June hedged.

"Right. Either way, there's only one path in and out of here. We should probably keep going on foot. No telling how far they've gone."

"That could be problematic," Pierre theorized. "If this road goes too far, we'll never catch up."

"It doesn't look like it goes far," Will said. "It's a dead end."

Everyone looked at him with concern in their eyes.

"You could have chosen a different way of saying that," Matt joked.

June forced a smile. "I was thinking the same thing."

Will snorted. "We'll be fine. Just stick to the plan. We can use the forest to our advantage." He met every pair of eyes in the group before he continued. "Here's what we're going to do..."

32

Dak peered out the window from his middle seat as the three vans rumbled to a stop in a clearing in the forest.

"Oh, nice choice," he said. "This is the perfect place for an execution. No one around to hear the screams or gunshots."

Morovski opened his door and stepped out. He looked back into the van as he rechecked his pistol for the fifth time in twenty minutes. "I'm glad you approve since it's your execution."

"Hey, if you're gonna do it, do it right."

The Russian didn't seem to comprehend the joke. He slammed his door shut as the others emptied out of the van, ushering Dak with them.

"Easy," Dak said to one of the nearest guards. "Hard to keep my balance with these zip ties on my wrists."

"Shut up," one of the soldiers said and shoved him in the back.

Dak stumbled away from the vehicle and into the clearing. As he regained his footing, he surveyed the immediate area. Here, in the heart of the forest, a meadow opened up and filled the space with tall grass. A single, wide tree stump stood in the center. Dak wondered what offense the tree had committed, and who would have done the cutting.

"Form up, men. On the other side facing the road."

The Russians moved ahead as a single unit, with the exception of Kostya, who lingered behind with his commander.

"You think the German might try something?" he asked.

"You never know," the colonel answered. "Better to expect it and be pleasantly surprised."

"You guys sound worried," Dak cut in as one of the soldiers shoved him toward the middle of the meadow. "I know I would be if I were you."

Morovski and Kostya followed the rest of the men through the tall grass. The afternoon sun barely shone through the forest to the west, stabbing diminishing rays of sunlight between minuscule openings in the canopy.

Once the men were on the far side of the meadow, they formed a wide semicircle around the stump in the center.

And there they waited.

Dak stood there with his hands folded in front of him. He bounced up and down with nervous tension. He had no delusions of rescue or some miracle that could save him from his fate. While he didn't fear death, he didn't look forward to it, either.

His mind wandered to Istanbul, where his ex-girlfriend, Nicole, was probably just getting home from work. Perhaps she was making dinner.

Dak's biggest regret in all of this was that he couldn't be with her, right now, right there in her flat in the city.

It was the one thing he wished he could change.

He'd tried. *Blast it, I tried.*

Everything he'd done in the last few years was to keep her safe, and to eradicate any future threat to her safety.

But that security had eluded him at every turn. And soon, he would come face to face with the end result of his failure.

The sound of more engines rumbled through the woods. Dak looked off in the direction of the gravel driveway. He saw the headlights first—poking in and out between the trunks amid the dense forest.

"Friends of yours?" Dak prodded.

"Actually," Morovski corrected, "one of them is a friend of yours."

Right. Way to soft-toss him one, Dak.

There'd been a million moments where Dak had considered what he might say to Col. Cameron Tucker should he ever find him. Some of the ideas were real zingers. Others came off like an A-minus action movie cliché. Ultimately, Dak had decided not to say anything to him—to let the moment and the bullet take care of all that.

But these were the kinds of circumstances he'd allowed to roam his imagination. In those vivid and victorious daydreams, he took out the one man who stood between Dak and a peaceful, almost normal life.

Instead, he was the prisoner of a bunch of rogue Russian soldiers who were going to sell him to his fate. Dak knew Tucker would spare no expense to personally end his life—*but the money. Where was the money coming from? Was it the German buyer these guys were meeting?*

Dak wrestled with that last bit. *How would Tucker have met the wealthy German? What could he have possibly offered to someone like that?*

The answer was there, just beneath the murky surface.

The first in the convoy of SUVs pulled onto the grass in the meadow. Then another and another until the entire line created a similar semicircle to the one the soldiers had formed.

Dak pressed his lips together and watched as the doors to the vehicles opened and men in suits piled out.

He snorted a derisive laugh. "You guys could take these bozos, man. Don't let them intimidate you."

Morovski stood resolute for a second, then cast a questioning eye at Dak. He said nothing, though, and turned back to the German's entourage as they set up a formation in front of their vehicles.

Every one of the men was armed—some with pistols, some with submachine guns.

"I like the H&Ks those guys are toting," Dak commented. "Quality firearm." He indicated the guns by tilting his head forward.

"You'll probably meet your end with one of those," Morovski sneered.

Dak knew he was getting on the man's nerves. That was the plan. He'd been needling the guy the entire uncomfortable trip to Budapest. Now Dak just needed to come up with the second phase of the plan, but time for that was quickly evaporating.

That, and no reasonable ideas came to mind. To say things looked bleak was a huge understatement. Dak wasn't about to beg. He didn't have that in him. Sure, he wanted to live, but he wasn't about to give these guys the satisfaction of seeing him plead for his life.

A man in an expensive gray suit stepped out of the middle SUV. Dak didn't recognize him but figured he was the buyer. The man's wavy blond hair brushed against his ears as the breeze blew through the forest.

But it wasn't the man's hair that drew Dak's focus. He merely noticed it. What held his attention was the other guy that climbed out of the SUV and walked around the front. It was the face Dak had been both avoiding and searching for the last few years.

Colonel Tucker's skin displayed a deep tan. Chrome aviator sunglasses blocked his eyes from anyone else's view. As he walked, the black cargo pants swung with each step, which meant he was one of those people that used all his pockets for something—a fact Dak had witnessed many times. The navy-blue coat he wore likely concealed at least one firearm and possibly two, plus a blade of some kind.

Tucker was always armed, and Dak didn't believe for a second that time out of the military had purged those habits from his core. And if he believed he was going to have a chance to rid Dak Harper from his life for good, well, he'd bring extra toys.

He and the buyer walked toward the center of the circle with four guards—two on either side. Two of the guards carried metal brief-cases, probably filled with cash.

Morovski looked over at Dak, then at a soldier behind him, and nodded.

Dak felt a sudden push in his back and stumbled forward, nearly tripping over a particularly thick patch of grass. Four of Morovski's men stepped forward with the colonel and his lieutenant colonel in the middle next to Dak.

The men marched to the stump in the center of the meadow and stopped there.

For a few seconds, no one said a thing.

Dak decided to do the honors.

"Okay, boys. Let's have a good clean game here today. Who wants to call the coin toss? Morovski? You're the road team here. Actually, I guess none of you are from here so—"

"Good to see you haven't changed, Dak," Tucker interrupted. "That's going to make this so much sweeter."

"It's just a coin toss, Cam," Dak said, refusing to call him by his rank. "Everybody makes way too much out of the toss."

He shut up when the butt of a gun thumped into his kidneys and dropped him to his knees.

Dak grunted and wobbled, trying not to fall over in the grass, but that balancing act proved difficult. As he righted himself, he looked back at the solider who'd delivered the punishment. "Not cool," he breathed through gritted teeth. "If I end up pissing blood later, I'm blaming you."

The man merely stared back at Dak with unfeeling, vapid gray eyes.

Tucker laughed and looked over at the man in the suit. "He was like this when he served with me in the Army. Never could learn, this one. Ain't that right, Dak?"

"You know what they say about old habits, Cam."

"I sure do, son. I sure do."

"I don't mean to interrupt this little reunion," the man in the suit said, "but we're here to conduct business." He looked to Morovski. "I trust you were able to bring the artifacts, Colonel?"

"Only if you brought the money," Morovski replied coolly.

The German's lips parted ever so slightly in a skeptical grin. "You should know money is no object to me, Colonel. It's right here." He motioned to the men with the briefcases, and they stepped forward, set the metal containers on the ground, and flipped them open.

Stacks of US Treasury bonds and euros overflowed from the cases.

"There are four more just like those in my car," the German said. "Totaling over five hundred million in various liquid assets."

Tucker whistled at the statement. "Man alive, that's a lot of coin. You could have had a part of this, Dak, had you just learned to play ball."

"I don't play with people like you."

Tucker bent down while Morovski turned to his men and motioned them to bring some of the items forward.

"You always played ball, Dak. You just didn't know it." Tucker removed his sunglasses and winked at him, then slid the glasses back on.

The Russians lugged four oversize duffle bags into the middle of the clearing. The men set them down carefully, though a few of the metal items within clanked.

"Careful, boys," Morovski cautioned in an unsteady voice. "We didn't bring those priceless artifacts all this way just to have them damaged now."

The men nodded at their commander and stepped back once they'd unzipped the bags.

The German nodded to two of his men, who immediately moved forward and inspected the contents. One of them pulled out a bronze helmet. The other held up a golden half-moon necklace.

"I'm impressed, Colonel. Your resourcefulness knows no bounds."

"It wasn't easy," Morovski said. "We encountered some trouble along the way."

"I'm not surprised. But you seem to have come through unscathed."

"We lost a few of my men. Good soldiers."

Dak sensed what the Russian colonel was doing. He was trying to ply the buyer for more money.

Tucker paid no attention. His focus was on Dak.

"I guess you never really knew what was going on, did you, son?" Tucker asked.

Dak looked back at his former CO, searching him for an answer he felt was right in front of him. "What are you talking about, Tucker?"

"All that gold and loot these guys brought from Ukraine... Reminds me of another treasure I've seen before."

Dak lowered his eyebrows, still not catching the answer. It wasn't until Tucker stood up straight again that Dak realized the truth.

"It was you. It was you all along, wasn't it?"

Tucker held out both hands as if to say, "You got me."

"You knew what was in that cave all along. You sent us in there to take out terrorists, but the enemy had nothing to do with it. You were after the gold."

"Ding, ding, ding." Tucker looked around as if playing to an audience. "Look at that. He finally figured it out. Only took you a few years."

Dak's breathing ramped up. Adrenaline pumped through his veins, and he felt a blinding rage take over. He surged up from his knees, willing to bite the man to death if he had to.

But a strong hand clamped down on his shoulder and pulled him back down to the ground. Within a second, he felt another nauseating blow to his lower back, and his legs gave out. He fell forward onto his face, barely cushioning the fall with his elbows, and there he stayed for what seemed like a lifetime.

His breath blew out in bursts of cloud into the cool air, illuminated against the dying light of day.

"Easy," Tucker warned. "Don't damage the merchandise. That's what I'm paying you guys extra for."

He reached into his back pocket and pulled out a wad of cash wrapped in rubber bands. He tossed it to Morovski, who snatched it out of the air.

"Twenty grand," Tucker said. "As promised."

He bent down again and pulled Dak up by the hair. Tucker peered into Dak's eyes with disdain. "I woulda paid twice that." He leaned closer. "In fact, I have. But somehow you've managed to evade every merc and assassin in the network. Not sure how."

"Maybe they weren't as good as you thought."

Tucker nodded, half agreeing. "Perhaps. Or maybe you're just better than I remembered." He shrugged as if it were of no consequence. "Doesn't matter now, Dak. You're mine. And I'm going to enjoy killing you myself."

He shoved Dak's head down and drew a pistol from within the confines of his coat. "But first, I'm going to make this hurt."

"Please, Colonel Tucker," the German said in his thick accent. "May we conclude our business before you have your fun?"

Tucker looked disappointed. "Sure, Herr Niemann. I've waited this long. Few more minutes couldn't hurt."

"Niemann," Dak muttered. "Karl Niemann. I knew I recognized him from somewhere." He looked over at the blond man. The guy was pushing sixty but didn't look a day over forty-five. Only a few wrinkles stretching out from his eyes betrayed the years. Other than that, he looked like he was in the prime of his life.

"You're just figuring out all kinds of things today, aren't you?" Tucker taunted.

Dak sighed. "Why don't you cut these zip ties off of me, and maybe you'll learn a few things too, Colonel."

Tucker laughed. "Don't take this the wrong way, Dak, but I'm not scared of fighting you."

"Then let me loose, and let's settle this once and for all."

"I'm also not stupid."

Morovski raised his right hand and flicked his fingers forward. More of the Russian soldiers brought sacks full of loot forward.

Niemann turned and looked over his shoulder at two more men and nodded. The two brought out the remaining cases of money and set them down in the center of the circle while the Russians finished offloading the artifacts.

"You are a man of unusual tastes, Herr Niemann," Morovski said, using the man's proper name for the first time.

"Oh, these aren't for me," Niemann corrected. "There is someone else who wants these things very badly. I have no need for such trinkets."

Trinkets? The word struck Dak as a funny way to describe priceless historical artifacts connecting a nation to its ancient past. *Who is this guy?*

Dak had heard the name. Most people had. Karl Niemann was the head of a massive media conglomerate. The guy's net worth was in the billions, and not just barely in the billions, either. His total assets were in the hundreds of billions.

"So, you are selling these?" Morovski asked.

"Of course," Niemann answered. "Is that a problem?"

Dak heard the questions. He'd always understood how to deescalate a situation; it had been part of his training. But reverse techniques could also be applied to ramp things up.

"That's interesting," he said, aiming his comment at Morovski. "If the buyer has a buyer, then I guess that makes you the low man on the totem pole as far as profits go."

The Russian colonel looked over at Dak. It was only for a second. But in that brief moment, Dak saw the seed had taken root. It was written in the man's expression.

"Yep," Dak went on, "if he has a buyer, that means you're not getting the top dollar you thought you were, Colonel." He flashed a look at Tucker. "Him, not you, Cam."

Tucker's eyelids narrowed in an instant, and he raised his pistol, aiming at Dak's right leg.

"You should know when to keep your mouth shut, Harper," Tucker warned.

"This buyer," Morovski said to Niemann. "Who are they?"

Niemann chuckled. "What does it matter to you, Colonel? You've been paid the money I promised. You will live well the rest of your days and never have to take orders from anyone ever again. What does it matter to you what I do with these relics?"

Morovski clenched his jaw. "I suppose it doesn't matter," he said.

But Dak knew better. The seed of discontent had already blossomed into a venomous, all-consuming monstrosity. Now all he needed to do was tip the scales a little more.

"You know," Dak said. "I—"

"I think you've said just about enough," Tucker cut him off. "Don't listen to him, Colonel," he cautioned the Russian. "He's just trying to get under your skin, turn you against our friend here." He indicated Niemann with a tilt of the head. "Isn't that right, Dak?"

"Just seems like—"

Tucker brandished the gun, bouncing the sights back and forth between Dak's legs. "Which kneecap do you want me to blow off first, Dak?" Tucker asked. "Or did I forget to mention I was going to make this hurt? A lot."

"Pretty sure that was implied," Dak drawled.

Tucker turned to the two leading men. "Would you two mind if I go ahead and do this?"

Morovski hesitated. Reluctance dripped from his eyes. Dak knew the man wasn't happy about the deal now, despite the incredible sum of money awaiting him in the metal briefcases.

But there was nothing he could do, and Morovski knew it. Nothing short of demanding more at gunpoint.

"Yes," the Russian colonel said finally. "We are good."

Dak looked up into the barrel of the pistol waving back and forth above him.

"Well, Dak. Looks like your time is up. You've been a worthy adversary. I'll give you that. But now, it's time for you to die."

Dak didn't look away. If this was it, he'd go with pride. The only thing he didn't look forward to was the pain he was about to face. He knew it would be excruciating. And he hoped he could endure it with a sliver of dignity.

Tucker's lips curled to the right side in a wicked grin. "Time to pay the piper, Dak."

A loud pop echoed through the forest.

33

A bullet zipped through the air. A thump immediately followed. Blood splattered onto the grass around Dak's feet. Then one of the Russian soldiers fell prostrate next to him.

Dak turned his eyes to the dead man and the grotesque exit wound in the back of his skull.

Morovski reacted immediately, drawing his pistol and raising it toward Niemann.

Tucker's head snapped left and right as he tried to determine where the shot came from.

"Do not move!" a voice with a distinct Russian accent shouted from the woods.

"That voice?" Dak breathed so only he could hear it. The voice in the shadows sounded familiar. He couldn't fully place it, but it reminded him of... "Lesma?"

"You are surrounded! By order of the Russian Army, drop your weapons and put your hands up!"

"You!" the Russian colonel yelled as he tensed, ready to fire his weapon.

Niemann's eyes were wide with confusion and fear—two

emotions the man clearly wasn't accustomed to feeling. "Stop!" Niemann shouted as he fell back. "What are you doing?"

"Thought you could ambush us? Take the money and the gold? I don't think so, Herr Niemann."

Tucker shuffled backward slowly, away from both men. He, too, felt the wave of uncertainty.

"That is not one of mine," Niemann declared even as his men took defensive stances, gripping their weapons with both hands. Several of them in the front began shuffling their feet backward. A few of the Russians did as well. None of the men in the cluster felt comfortable at such close range, no matter the training or experience.

The tension escalated so quickly, even the trees seemed to rustle.

Again, the voice shouted from the trees. "I said put your weapons down! We have you surrounded!"

"How do I know you didn't orchestrate this?" Niemann demanded as he continued to inch back from the front line. "He's Russian."

"They just killed one of my men."

"Because you betrayed them. Your kind will turn on each other in a moment's notice."

"What is that supposed to mean?" Morovski insisted, his eyes burning with rage. He didn't notice his men slowly retreating.

"We both know what it means, Colonel. You Russians cannot be trusted."

"How dare you insult us like that," Morovski roared. His trigger finger tensed. "You are the one who set a trap for us."

"Put your guns down!" the voice from the woods warned again.

Neither of the groups was willing to do so since both believed the other responsible for the betrayal.

Tucker kept backing away. Where he'd stood before was in the center of potential crossfire. He'd only managed to gain a few feet toward safety with Dak still close and on his knees.

"Why would I be working with the Russian army?" Niemann questioned. "How would I even make that work?"

The query sent a sliver of doubt through the colonel's mind, and Niemann saw it.

"Do you have any idea who I am? The money I agreed to pay is nothing to me."

"Is that supposed to make me feel better about the deal?" Morovski countered.

"This is your last chance!" the Russian voice blared from the woods. "I will give you to the count of three to drop your weapons. If you do not, we will have no choice but to open fire."

Morovski's focus flashed to the right where the voice had come from. He noticed Tucker drifting backward away from the argument. He felt the temptation to order the man to stop moving, but he didn't take his aim away from the German and brought his attention back to Niemann after the briefest moment.

"If they are not with you," Morovski said, "why did they kill my man?"

"Because you betrayed them," Niemann answered. "You and your men went AWOL. And you've led them straight to me. Your recklessness has caused this. I should have known better than to trust you with such a mission."

"One!" cried the voice in the woods.

Niemann took another wary step back.

Morovski brandished his gun. "Where do you think you're going, Herr Nieman?"

The German held his hands up at shoulder height. "Don't do anything rash, Colonel."

"You have insulted me and my men. And my people. Now you will pay for your insolence."

"Two!"

"Don't be a fool, Colonel," Niemann retorted calmly. He realized how dire the situation truly was. His weapon was still holstered. While the men surrounding him were ready to fire at the drop of a hat, he was unprotected and currently unarmed. Deescalating the situation was his best chance at survival.

"Now you beg for your life like a coward. So typical of men like you. You sit in your fancy homes drinking expensive wine and eating expensive food. Your life of luxury has made you soft, Herr Niemann."

"Three!"

The German immediately stepped back as the guard to his right stepped in front of him with a pistol in his hand. The guard tried to raise his weapon to Morovski's eye level, but the seasoned Russian commander didn't hesitate, giving no time for the man to even come close to getting off a shot.

He fired, and at such close range, striking the man in the kill triangle was too easy. The round went through the tip of his nose and out the back of his head, sapping the life from him before he hit the ground.

Another pop echoed from behind the Russian side. Another of Morovski's guards fell, clutching the base of his throat on his way to the ground. It was too late.

The Russian soldiers' instincts kicked in. The men immediately raised their weapons at the same time as Niemann's men while every one of them withdrew toward their respective vehicles.

Another gunshot popped from the forest. This time, one of the German's guards fell to his knees, grabbing at his gut.

Morovski lost focus for a single second, turning his attention in the direction the shot had come. In that instant, Niemann drew a pistol from his coat as he retreated toward the convoy and aimed at the Russian leader's head.

Kostya saw the move and lunged in front of his commander just as the firearm discharged.

"Colonel!" Kostya shouted as he moved to protect his commander. The round snapped through the air and struck the diving lieutenant colonel a blink before it hit Morovski.

The Russians returned fire as the German's guards retreated into a protective formation around the rich man, ushering him backward to his SUV.

Dak watched the chaos erupt in a matter of seconds. And he knew exactly how to use it to his advantage. He dug one knee into the ground and swung his other leg around as Tucker focused his attention on the three closest Russian soldiers.

By the time Dak's leg struck Tucker's left heel, the colonel had already taken out two of the Russians—one with a shot to the forehead, and the other with a shot to the gut, then face.

Tucker felt the impact of Dak's kick before he realized what was happening. The force knocked him off balance, but he had enough presence of mind to use his right foot to spin over in a twisting corkscrew as he fell to the ground.

He rolled away from Dak and rebounded to his feet, raising the pistol to take out his nemesis with the next shot, but one of the three Russians he'd targeted a moment before fired a round straight into the center of Tucker's chest.

The colonel stumbled backward and dropped to the ground with his head hitting a clump of grass.

Dak looked over at the Russian soldier who'd just killed his enemy. Part of him wanted to thank the guy, but before he could do that, or retreat from the gunfight, the soldier took a round to the left shoulder and fell to the ground.

The meadow filled with the sounds of gunfire as men blasted each other from close quarters. Several of the remaining German's guards retreated as they returned volleys with the Russians. Dak noticed the distinct pop of long rifles continued to join the fray from the edge of the forest.

Dak dove toward one of the fallen Russians and slipped over the man's torso, pulling him up on his side by the arm to use him as a shield. As the soldier absorbed the rounds, Dak slipped a knife from the man's hip, and sliced away the bonds that had kept his wrists together. With his hands free, he scooped the soldier's pistol.

He crouched behind the dead man for a second, noting the nearest soldier who'd taken the round to the shoulder still standing there firing into the enemy ranks.

The man only stood for another second before a round caught him in the right side of the chest and spun him around. He dropped to his knees, determined to keep fighting, squeezing off two more shots before a third bullet struck him in the gut.

He doubled over, keeping his pistol leveled until a fourth round bore into his forehead and emerged out the back.

Dak had been in more firefights than he cared to remember. But in every single one of them he knew whom to shoot at. It was never a question.

This one marked the first such instance where he wasn't sure which enemy to fight. That meant he had to fight all of them.

With Tucker dead a few yards away, and opponents on both sides cutting each other to shreds, Dak's experience kicked in.

Eliminate the closest threat. Work your way to the back.

34

The remaining Russians fell back with one of the men dragging Morovski with him. Only nine men remained, with one of them limping from a gunshot wound to the leg. Within two seconds of Dak counting the enemy ranks, that man received another round—this one to the center mass. His body jerked backward, then he stumbled forward with his weapon extended, firing the remainder of his magazine's contents before catching a third bullet—again to the chest. He collapsed to his knees and then tipped over onto his face. His legs twitched for a few seconds before the body went entirely still.

Eight left. But how many of the other guys?

Dak kept the corpse-shield against his right shoulder and aimed at the next Russian in the formation. The men were thirty feet away now, and as good as Dak was, anything beyond twenty-five feet in the swirling chaos of a gunfight made for a difficult shot with a sidearm.

He lined up the sights with the nearest target, adjusted for the guy's movement, and fired. The shot missed; Dak figured wide left. He readjusted and shot again. The round struck the soldier in the side and spun him around.

More shots popped from the forest. Another of the soldiers fell two men away from the one Dak targeted.

The Russian soldiers dove for cover, finally reaching their line of vans. One of them climbed into the driver's seat of the center van, but when he tried to start the vehicle, a plume of white smoke seeped out of the hood.

Dak's target limped toward the next truck in line. Now more than thirty feet away, Dak knew the shot was nearly out of range. He lined up his sights in the middle of the man's back and fired three times.

At least one of the rounds found the mark because the man's knees buckled and he fell over prostrate into the grass where he writhed in agony, clawing at the ground to try to pull himself to safety.

Dak looked at the vehicle the man had tried to start and realized what had happened. Someone had pumped a bunch of rounds into the hood, and from the looks of it, they'd done the same to every one of the vans. The tires, too, were flat.

It was unclear who'd immobilized the vehicles—the German's guards or the shooters from the forest. One thing was certain: if the Russians escaped, they'd have to do so on foot.

Dak took aim at another of the soldiers and fired three more rounds, but only managed to scare the man as he ducked behind the first van.

The others had already reached the back side of the convoy, though gunfire continued to pepper vehicles from the German's ranks and, Dak presumed, from the forest.

If the Russians in the trees have everyone surrounded, though, why haven't they moved into the clearing?

Tactically, it made a certain level of sense for them to keep their positions behind the cover of tree trunks. And why move forward into the meadow if they could simply pick everyone off one by one from the shadows?

But one key component of it didn't make sense unless his suspicions were correct. *Could it really be Lesma out there?*

If so, that meant Will was there, too. *But how? How have they managed to track me down to this random place in the middle of nowhere in the Hungarian countryside?*

Another piece of evidence needled Dak's brain. They hadn't shot at him. Or if they had, they'd missed—possibly many times.

He looked to the left; eyes narrowed to better focus his long-range vision. He spotted the silhouette of a rifle and half of the person holding it.

Dak risked looking over the body he lay next to and saw the German and his men falling back behind their vehicles, just like the Russians. And just like the enemy, their tires were all flat. Dak assumed the radiators had been punctured as well, perhaps even some of the electrical wiring—with a little luck.

Now all of the remaining forces would have to attempt to escape on foot, which looked as though it was the plan all along.

Meanwhile, the artifacts and the cases of money still sat in the center of the clearing—abandoned by both sides.

Dak wasn't about to make a play for any of it, not until every last one of the enemies was either dead or had surrendered.

But first, he needed to get out of the meadow.

The shadow in the trees could have easily picked him off multiple times but hadn't. Based on that, and the familiar sound of the voice he'd heard, Dak made his decision.

As the steady staccato of gunfire slowed to intermittent pops, Dak shoved the corpse over and sprang from his spot. He scooped up another pistol from another nearby body as he crouched and moved toward the edge of the clearing.

A bullet cracked the air near his head, but he saw the muzzle flash from the rifle in the shadows. The shooter must have aimed in the direction of the first shot because no more followed—meaning the sniper had either eliminated the other gunman or sent them reeling for cover.

It also reassured Dak that the guy in the woods was on his side.

Dak raised up slightly to gain more speed, pumping his legs as he sprinted through the acrid-smelling fog of gun smoke that hung over the grassy meadow.

The dying rays of sunlight disappeared over the hills to the west as he neared the trees. Now, hitting any targets would be extremely difficult, and that challenge would only be made tougher as darkness deepened.

The gunman in the shadows fired again, Dak assumed to suppress another shooter.

"Hurry!" the voice commanded.

"Will?" Dak shouted back with ten yards to go to the figure.

"Shut up and run, man!" Will ordered.

I am running, Dak thought.

With fifteen feet to go, his toe caught a clump of grass and he tripped. Dak felt his balance give way, and he tumbled forward onto the ground, hitting it hard with his right shoulder.

A gunshot popped from somewhere behind him a second after he fell. The bullet thumped into the tree trunk next to Will, shattering a chunk of the bark into splinters.

Will returned fire with another shot. "Get up, Dak!" he yelled.

Dak rolled to his feet. His shoulder screamed from the blow it had taken from the ground, but it could have been worse.

He scampered the last ten feet and then slid behind the tree trunk next to his friend. He gasped for air, catching his breath as he leaned his back into the tree, craning his neck downward as if he'd just run a 400-meter race in the Olympics.

Will ducked behind the thick trunk and inspected his friend, brushing loose grass and dirt from Dak's shoulder.

"You okay, man?" Will asked.

Dak nodded, still taking air into his lungs in huge gulps. "Yeah. I'm good."

"You clumsy idiot. You almost got yourself shot tripping over nothing."

Another nod between gasps. "Yeah. Thanks for noticing."

"You should be thanking me for the cover fire."

"Hey, he made it!" another familiar voice exclaimed from somewhere to Dak's left. He looked over his shoulder and saw Lesma standing in the shadows with a rifle butt against his shoulder, the barrel pointing low into the meadow.

Dak spotted two more figures beyond the big Russian—female figures. Then he looked to the right and saw another male figure in position behind an oak.

"Okay, so Galyna I recognize. And I'm not sure why you brought her. But who are the other people?"

"We'll have time to discuss that later," Will explained. "Right now, we need to get out of here."

Dak shook his head. "No way. Not without the artifacts. And not before we take down Morovski and Niemann."

Will sighed. "I had a feeling you'd say that." He looked over to his right at the guy firing toward the Russian convoy. "That's Matt. Former Interpol agent turned bar owner."

"Interpol?"

"Long story. Well, actually, not such a long story."

"And who's the other woman?" Dak asked, motioning to his left.

"Oh, you know her."

Dak's forehead tightened in a confused frown. "I do?"

"Yeah. That's June Holiday. From Axis."

"How in the—"

"I made a call to your pal Tommy Schultz with the IAA. He took care of the rest."

"Tommy?" Dak processed the information in seconds.

"She was close by. Let's leave it at that," Will said. "Actually, she wouldn't tell us what she was up to."

The two women approached, skirting the edge of the clearing by overlapping one another until they reached the two men.

"More like can't tell you," June corrected. Apparently, she'd heard the last part of the conversation.

"Right. Can't."

"We wouldn't be the Shadow Cell if we let everyone know what we were up to."

Lesma joined the group next. Then the guy to the right made his way toward them. "How in the world did you guys find me?" Dak asked no one in particular.

"It wasn't easy," Will admitted. "But we can talk about that later. If you're dead set on getting the artifacts back, that's the easy part."

"What?"

"The two groups of bad guys are on the run," Will said, indicating one direction then the other with a bob of his head. "It's the second part of your plan that's going to be tricky."

The guy on Dak's right had a phone to his ear. He was speaking French; a language Dak only knew to a slight conversational extent.

The man ended the call and slid the phone into his pocket. "That was Pierre. He said Interpol is sending a team right away, but it will take some time. They'll set up a perimeter around all the roads in the area."

"We have three Interpol agents with us," Will explained, noting the beleaguered look on Dak's face.

"Three?" Dak asked then spoke to Matt. "I appreciate you guys coming to help me. You didn't have to do that."

"Don't thank us," Matt replied. "Not yet anyway. My buddies took up positions near the end of the driveway. We figured if they tried to get away, we could block off their escape. We didn't expect them to be on foot, but my guys can handle it."

"Interpol agents, June from Shadow Cell, Matt...How many people did you bring with you?" Dak asked Will.

"Enough."

"With the Russians making a break for the road" he said, jerking his thumb in that general direction, "Pierre and the other two can block them from reaching the road. But we should still pursue, catch them in the crossfire. If we go through the woods over here, we can cut them off before they try to retreat back here."

Dak agreed with a nod. "Then let's go after them." He turned to Galyna. "You think you can secure the artifacts and all those metal cases out there?"

She nodded. "That's why I'm here."

"Good. There's roughly a hundred million in those briefcases." He turned to the Interpol guys. "I assume you don't have a problem with her confiscating that to help with the war relief efforts, do you?"

Will whistled. "Did you say a hundred mil? Man, that's a lot of dough."

"Yeah. Don't get any ideas."

"Wouldn't cross my mind."

Dak rounded on Matt. "You want June to go with you, or you want to help your pals alone?"

"I got this," Matt said. "Take them with you. It'll even the odds."

"Okay." Dak turned to Will. You're with me, brother." He looked at June. "You, too. Lesma, stick with Galyna?"

"It would be my honor. Is least I can do as a Russian considering what my people have done to hers."

Galyna's hardened expression softened. "You're a good man, Lesma Lebedev."

He chuckled. "Don't tell anyone. After all—"

"I know. You have a reputation to keep."

His head bobbed. "Go," he said to the others. "We will be fine."

"Right. Good hunting, y'all," Dak said. "Let's finish this."

35

Morovski ran through the forest. Every other step, it seemed, he glanced back over his shoulder to see if he was being followed. After years as a hunter who'd instilled fear across the world, Morovski was now the prey—and he was panicking. He hadn't felt fear like this in decades, not since he was a skinny new recruit all those years ago.

Each time he felt the momentary relief of seeing no one behind him, that feeling faded the second he heard the rustle of a leaf, the snap of a twig, or even the slightest noise from the animals in the canopy above.

He tripped on a root and tumbled forward, landing hard on the ground. He had the presence of mind to stick out his elbows, though in this instance that caused more temporary pain than it might have had he used his hands instead. The clumsy crash jarred the pistol from his right hand.

It took him a second to right himself and get back on his knees. Then he immediately began searching for the weapon.

"Are you okay, Colonel?" one of his men asked.

At last count, only six had survived the firefight in the meadow, not including himself.

"Yes, I'm fine. I... dropped my gun." He ran his hands over the leaves around the area where he fell.

The soldier bent down and started to help.

The other five hadn't seen their leader fall and continued running ahead toward the road.

To the east, the moon climbed through the cool night sky. The eerie, pale glow did little to assist the colonel in finding his weapon on the ground. It was dumb luck when the fingers on his right hand passed across the pistol's barrel.

He traced down to the grip and picked it up, brushing off a leaf that clung to the sights.

"Found it. Thank you for stopping, Vasilii."

"Of course, Colonel."

The commander looked ahead, peering into the darkness. The other five were already out of sight, each of them plunging through the trees.

Morovski swiped his left hand across his chest and pants, knocking off the rest of the debris that clung to his clothes from the fall. "We should keep moving, Vasilii."

"Yes, sir."

The two men pushed ahead, though the colonel moved slower this time. His right elbow hurt, as did his right hip. He hadn't realized it at the time, but he must have landed on a rock or a root. He counted himself lucky the elbow hadn't struck a harder surface and shattered the bone.

They continued on for another minute, but the sharp, throbbing pain shooting through Morovski's hip grew to the point of unbearable. He stopped and leaned against a tree trunk, bracing himself with his elbow.

"Colonel? Are you all right?" Vasilii asked.

Morovski nodded. "Yes. I'm fine. Just bruised my hip. Go on ahead. I'll catch up."

The young soldier shook his head in defiance. "No, sir. I will not leave you."

He was a good and loyal warrior. Of that there was no denying.

Morovski's thoughts drifted to another loyal soldier—his friend Kostya.

The colonel had watched his friend die before his eyes, diving in front of a bullet meant for him.

Morovski had seen countless men die in the field of battle—both ally and enemy. It was part of the job, and one he'd grown almost callous to in many ways.

The first time it happened—when he was a young soldier—it had bothered him. It haunted his dreams for more nights than he could count. The face of his comrade that had perished at the hands of an Afghani bullet seemed it would never leave his mind's eye, but eventually it did—melting away into the sands of time.

This one, though... This one would never leave him.

Kostya had been by his side in more battles than anyone he'd ever served with and had become the best lieutenant colonel a commander could hope for. He was not only loyal, though that much was without a doubt as proven by his final act. Kostya had been a brilliant strategist.

Now he was gone. Right on the precipice of their freedom from the Russian military, a freedom that had been stripped away by the treacherous German, Karl Niemann.

"Come," Morovski said, believing the pain in his hip had subsided enough for him to continue. "We must hurry."

The two moved ahead, albeit slower than before. Even as he picked his way through the moonlit forest, Morovski turned his pain into a vengeance-fueled rage.

Wild, fanciful plans developed in his mind—plans that would end with him squeezing the life out of the German, or perhaps simply putting a bullet through his head. After he tortured him to the point of death, of course.

That was assuming Niemann made it out of the battle, which Morovski was nearly certain to be the case. Men like Niemann weren't warriors. But they were certainly lucky, seemingly able to dodge bullets—both literal and metaphorical.

The colonel wondered if the German's convoy of SUVs had been disabled as his vans had been. So far, skirting along the edge of the driveway toward the road, he'd not seen any headlights or heard any engines that might indicate the contrary.

He wondered how much farther he and Vasilii had to go before they reached the road. On the way in, it hadn't seemed that far through the woods and into the clearing, but now it felt like he'd run forever with no end in sight.

As he ran, his mind kept running the other way—to his fallen comrade, Kostya. Morovski had been forced to retreat in an instant, never getting the chance to help his friend no matter how much he might have wanted to.

He knew too well that in the field of battle, enemies used that tactic to their advantage. They would often shoot a target in the center mass—preferably the gut. Then an ally would inevitably come to help the fallen soldier, and then they would also get picked off.

Most militaries around the world operated in such a manner.

Morovski hadn't succumbed to the strategy he himself had employed many times in the theater of war, but that did little to suppress the feelings of sadness, regret, and anger.

"It should have been me," he muttered through hurried breaths.

"I'm sorry. What, sir?" Vasilii asked.

"Nothing, Vasilii. Keep going. We should be to the road soon. From there, we will flag down a car and take it. We must get out of here."

"Where will we go next, Colonel?"

Morovski shook his head. Breath spewed out of his mouth in bursts of cloud. "I don't know. Not Romania. Wouldn't be a good idea to return there. Perhaps we push north. Or to the west. Find a place to lie low for a little while until the heat dies down on all this."

"Yes, sir," Vasilii agreed.

The pain continued to course through the colonel's hip, pulsing up through his right side and into his lower back. It shot down his leg, too, which made moving excruciating.

He'd been injured in multiple ways throughout his life—both in battle and otherwise, but this was a new kind of pain he'd never felt before. And the timing couldn't have been worse.

"Stop!" a voice shouted from somewhere ahead. They'd yelled in English.

Morovski skittered to a stop and braced himself against a tree with his left hand.

Vasilii likewise halted in midstride and shuffled quickly over to a tree next to the colonel. The two men listened carefully, peering through the dark forest to see where the order had come from.

"This is Interpol. We have you surrounded, and the road blocked. Put down your weapons, or we will be forced to fire."

The colonel scowled at the order.

"Is that really Interpol?" Vasilii whispered. "How did they find us?"

"I have no idea," Morovski answered, keeping his voice so low only Vasilii and the nearest tree could hear. "How *would* they? Interpol doesn't know we're here."

But his tone of voice gave away a twinge of doubt. *Do they?*

Myriad questions surfaced in his mind. *Had we been spotted on camera at one of the train stations? If so, how were we tracked to this place?*

Even though he spoke the words, they mirrored the lack of conviction in his heart.

The two men watched from their positions behind two trees, listening for a response from their comrades. An eerie silence settled over the forest, made more ominous by the half-moon glowing brightly in the sky, stabbing rays of light into the settling fog through openings in the foliage above.

"I said put them down!" the voice shouted again. This time the order was in Russian.

For the first time since he'd joined the military decades before, Nikolai Morovski didn't know what to do. The seasoned veteran in him told him to advance forward and attempt to flank whoever was threatening his men. The human inside Morovski begged him to run the other way, perhaps west through the hills.

He couldn't abandon his men. *Could I?*

They'd gone on ahead without him. Only Vasilii had remained by his side. Was it because they didn't know he'd fallen? Or had they broken through years of training and battle experience to return to base survival instincts?

"Wait," Morovski ordered, holding up his hand as he peered into the fog.

Why aren't they firing? The question looped in his brain. The only reason he could think of was that his men couldn't see the enemy. In these conditions—darkness, fog, trees everywhere, there was no telling where the enemy was hiding.

He cursed to himself at the thought. *Did I make a mistake? How could this have been prevented?*

In his military career, he'd made a name for himself by always being prepared, never leaving a stone unturned when it came to planning and tactics. He was a commander that could not be ambushed because he had a strategy for every situation.

Until now.

He'd been desperate to get to the rendezvous point. That desperation had been driven by necessity.

The situation at the border, the incident on the train, and even switching transportation modes multiple times had all pressed him against the clock. He'd allowed the German's demand of being here promptly override his thinking.

Normally, he would have reconnoitered an area like this, inspecting it for vulnerabilities, points of attack an enemy could use against him. And he would have taken appropriate actions against such.

Instead, he and his men had rolled onto the driveway and into the forest, totally exposed to attack from all around.

"Drop them!" the voice demanded in Russian. "This is your last chance."

Morovski pinpointed the location this time. It came from his left, probably fifty meters away.

He looked to Vasilii and motioned with his finger, indicating the general area where he believed the speaker hid.

Vasilii nodded. Every one of Morovski's men could communicate silently that way. They'd operated together in many situations where total silence was required and the use of hand signals the only means of communication.

The young soldier shifted, then swept behind the colonel, moving through the darkness in a loop toward where the voice had come.

Morovski followed, creeping through the undergrowth, crouching low.

Both men picked their footsteps carefully. The forest presented a million ways to signal their approach. A snapping twig, rustling leaves, the brush of a low-hanging branch against the fabric of a coat —all could be heard by the enemy.

They'd maneuvered only twenty feet when they heard the first gunshot echo through the woods.

Shouting immediately ensued. Some of it from Morovski's men. Some from the voice who'd issued the warning.

More gunfire erupted.

The colonel saw the muzzle flashes this time. *One, two, three.* He counted silently in his head.

The nearest one came from about forty meters straight ahead. The others appeared to be wrapped around the driveway, which was fifteen meters to his right.

Vasilii aimed his weapon into the fog as he pushed forward.

Morovski followed close behind, moving to a tree, stopping for a moment, then moving to the next one in their path to the shooter.

The colonel didn't have to wonder what instigated the gunfire. One or more of his men must have made a sudden move. He doubted they'd tried to run. That wasn't a quality any of his soldiers possessed. More likely, they'd attempted to get to cover based on the location of the voice.

Initially, that would have been to the right, but upon seeing the shape of the muzzle flashes through the fog, he realized that would have been futile.

More flashes blinked from just ahead and slightly to the right near the driveway. His men were returning fire, though Morovski wondered how they were seeing anything in the blurry darkness.

The moonlight didn't help much. In fact, the diffused glow in the fog seemed to make things worse. That meant if the Interpol agents were willing to take shots, they had a close and clear view of the Russian soldiers.

The loud pops of weapons discharging grew louder with every step Morovski and Vasilii took.

Through the mist, he saw the outline of the shooter in front of them.

Ten meters away, Vasilii shifted to his left—a maneuver intended to allow him to sneak up on the gunman from behind. It was a standard play, and would allow for an easy kill.

Vasilii pointed his pistol forward as he rounded the next tree and pushed ahead. He moved faster this time than he had been, hoping to close the gap quickly to ensure the accuracy of his shot before the other gunman realized what happened.

As he crept ahead, though, he missed a stick on the ground in his path. To a trained agent, the sound of his boot cracking the wood might as well have been someone banging on a drum to draw attention.

Morovski cringed and ducked down as he saw the gunman swivel toward Vasilii.

The latter saw it, too, and realizing his mistake knew he had no choice but to take the shot.

Vasilii fired first, and the gunman with the rifle staggered back. It was nearly impossible to tell where the bullet found purchase, but Vasilii didn't wait for that confirmation. He shot again and again.

The sniper spun around behind the tree as Vasilii pushed ahead.

Ahead to his right, he saw silhouettes of his other men now, each returning fire at the enemy positions. He counted four.

Sentiment and emotion couldn't—wouldn't—be allowed in. But he still felt the stab of pain in his chest at having lost so many.

He'd long since washed away thoughts of regret from ever losing a man due to his command, but in this instance doubt lingered. *Have I been too greedy? Wanted too much?*

No.

He forced himself to think only of the battle. Doubts led to mistakes. And he'd made enough that night.

Vasilii kept pressing ahead. He moved toward a tree to his left, circling around behind the gunman's flank.

But his move was too aggressive, too predictable.

The sniper shifted around the tree where he hid and raised the rifle again. Vasilii saw the move too late, adjusting his aim to compensate.

The gunman's rifle flashed with a loud bang. The high-velocity round's impact knocked Vasilii off his feet and landed him on his side.

Fury burned through Morovski like a wildfire through a dry field after harvest. He lined up his sights with the shooter, who now stood in the clear, not realizing there were two enemies to deal with.

The colonel squeezed the trigger as he stepped forward on the balls of his feet, keeping the weapon steady as it discharged once, twice, three times.

The sniper caught every round. One in the left shoulder. Then as he twisted around to meet the attack, two more in the chest.

He dropped to his knees, feebly trying to raise the rifle with his one good arm. But it was too late as Morovski approached, only a few meters away, and took aim at the man's head.

A single, final shot ended the Interpol agent's life—the bullet exiting the man's skull into the tree behind him.

The second he fell onto his face, Morovski turned to Vasilii, who writhed on the ground, his legs kicking aimlessly like a rag doll gone wild.

The colonel knelt next to the young man and put his hand on his shoulder to keep him from moving, but it did little good.

He saw the bloody wound on the left side of Vasilii's chest, and he knew it was over. The round hadn't found the younger man's heart, but it surely hit an artery or something else vital.

"Easy, son," Morovski soothed. "Easy."

Vasilii grimaced, looking into his commander's eyes.

The colonel knew, based on what he'd heard, what Vasilii was experiencing now. The gunfire muted in the man's ears, tunneling through his senses. His vision would blur next as he searched Morovski's face for reassurance.

"It's okay, Vasilii."

"I... I don't want to die, Colonel."

It was a common thing to say, and words that Morovski had heard before.

"I know," the colonel managed. "I know."

Vasilii swallowed.

Morovski tore his eyes from the dying man as he reached down and gripped his hand to ease the suffering. He scanned the battlefield to make sure the enemy wasn't moving in on him, but they were preoccupied dealing with the other four.

Vasilii squeezed his hand tighter than any of the firmest handshakes he'd ever felt, and he knew the young man was on the threshold.

"It's so cold," Vasilii said. "So cold."

"I know."

"I... I don't want—"

He swallowed again and then let out one last gurgled breath. Then his body went limp, and the hand Morovski held lost its grip.

The colonel sighed. He let go of the dead hand and closed the eyelids of his loyal soldier as the eyes stared blankly up into the canopy.

Morovski looked toward the next enemy gunman, picked up Vasilii's weapon, and stalked ahead.

There would be no retreat this night.

36

D ak and his two allies hurried through the woods, circling around the clearing toward Niemann's convoy.

They moved together but split apart by five to six yards —a distance that fluctuated depending on the terrain and available cover from the trees.

Dak doubted they would encounter the enemy until they were beyond the line of SUVs parked on the edge of the woods. The German and his men had retreated and would likely continue heading north until they felt they'd gained enough separation from the Russians to allow a change of direction, possibly toward the country road that divided the forest.

It made sense in his head, but Dak knew from experience not to make such assumptions, and to be ready for anything.

A plan was a good thing to have, to be sure, but sticking to one blindly could create devastating problems.

The three crept between the trees, overlapping each other while the other two provided cover.

Dak took point, moving ahead to the next position of cover, then stopped and aimed into the general direction they were heading while Will moved forward and passed him. June did the same once Will was in position, and then Dak repeated the process.

They maneuvered without speaking, and the only sound came from their feet stirring the leaves on the ground or the occasional dead stick.

In some ways, Dak knew they had the advantage of being the hunters. With the German and his guards on the run, they would be susceptible to attack from the rear. On the other hand, if the enemy decided to stand their ground and take defensive positions, Dak and company could run headlong into a deadly trap.

The fog didn't help things any, cutting the field of vision down to twenty or so yards. That was still good enough to spot a target but not if they were moving too fast. A shooter from that distance could spot them, too, and with the advantage of being ready and likely behind cover, it could be a bloodbath.

The three Americans kept moving, though, one overlapping the other as they pursued Niemann and his men.

They reached a point in the forest where they were even with the line of SUVs. In the point position, Dak stopped at a pine tree and held up a fist to signal the others to stop.

They did as instructed, and he stole a glance to the left at the line of vehicles. He searched the area for anyone lagging behind—either taking cover from another attack from the Russians or laying an ambush for anyone trying to chase the main group.

When Dak saw no threat loitering by the SUVs, he lowered his fist and wagged his finger.

Will took the signal and moved ahead, now curling around the bend along the edge of the woods.

He stopped at a wide oak, aimed his rifle forward, and waited for June to take her turn in the lead.

Dak listened for any sounds the enemy might make as they retreated—clumsily, he hoped—through the dark forest. So far, all he heard were the quiet sounds, not even noises, he and his allies made as they crept their way toward the enemy.

Having to move so cautiously had its own disadvantages, a fact

Dak was acutely aware of. While the German and his men could run, Dak and crew could move at half the speed, and that was being generous.

Dak moved forward once June was in position. This time, he stretched out their formation, creating a wider gap between himself and her. They needed to go faster. He'd still be careful, but there had to be a balance between speed and stealth.

With the SUVs to his back, Dak hurried to another tree and pressed his shoulder against it, pointing the pistol in his hands toward the direction he'd seen Niemann run.

There was no sign of the enemy, which didn't surprise him, but it didn't make him happy, either. An unseen adversary was the worst kind.

Will looped around in front of him, understanding the play Dak had in mind. He separated himself from Dak by fifteen yards this time and then waited for June to do the same.

She pressed forward, keeping her wide line to create a U-shaped formation with the other two. Moving in a column would put the point person in greater danger—a basic fact all three of them understood.

With June in the lead, Dak sprinted this time, rushing north.

The terrain along this part of the forest was relatively flat, with only slight undulations rising and falling. Hills rose on either side of them, creating a sort of valley where they chased the enemy. Dak was fully aware of yet another distinct disadvantage. He'd had no way to survey the area, so the topography remained a total mystery to him outside of what he could see and hear. He hoped none of the bad guys had thought to take that higher ground.

Nothing I can do about that, he thought.

The three continued their maneuvers, each taking turns moving to the point in their pursuit. Minutes continued to pass, and Dak started to wonder if the German and his guards had veered off toward the road. If that were the case, Dak and his team were exposed on the right flank, where June was.

He knew she could handle that, but that didn't mean he had to like it. In any combat scenario, Dak always wanted it to be him in the line of greatest danger.

On his next turn moving to the front, he saw some mass crumpled on the ground between two evergreens. When he was thirty feet away, he saw clearly what it was.

One of the German's guards lay on his side, unmoving.

Dak kept his weapon trained on the body until he reached it, then held up his fist for the other two to stop.

He inspected the man, pressing two fingers to the guy's neck.

Blood soaked the man's coat and pants from a wound in the upper abdomen. Lifeless eyes stared off to the west into the fog.

Dak looked north.

They were heading in the right direction, and it seemed the two hills on either side were funneling Niemann and his men straight ahead.

Dak motioned with his finger, and Will took off from his position, hurrying forward in the center of their formation.

He didn't stop to see what Dak was looking at. He could tell from his close range. If Dak said it was clear, that was good enough for Will.

Encouraged by the sign, when it was Dak's turn to take the lead, he moved faster and farther ahead, chewing up more real estate to close the gap between him and the enemy.

The three pressed on for another five minutes, leaving the meadow far behind. If Niemann was going to veer off toward the road, he'd have done it by now. Any change of direction at this point would make for an uphill climb—which would give the Germans the high ground in a fight but also slow them considerably.

Five more minutes passed, and Dak found himself nearly on the other side of the two hills. A hundred yards ahead, he spotted something unusual in the terrain.

The forest thinned and then appeared to end abruptly.

Is that a cliff?

June moved up and then waited.

Dak sprinted forward, keeping his pistol ready for anything. As he suspected, the forest floor came to an end fifty feet away and dropped off into a foggy oblivion.

He didn't dare hope that Niemann and his men had accidentally tumbled to their deaths. Plus, Dak had no way of knowing how far down it went just yet.

He stuck out his hand and flicked his fingers at Will to signal his friend to use caution.

As Will moved up, Dak peered through the hazy light of the moon, sweeping his gaze from left to right and back again. If the German and his guys had come this far, they either went one way or the other.

Unless they split up.

Dak couldn't rule that out. Once June reached the edge of the cliff, Dak moved ahead and joined her, then covered her left flank as Will hurried to their position.

The three of them caught their breath, each taking quick, deep inhales. They'd moved fast to catch up to the enemy, but there was no way to know if they'd made it. Another looming question hung in Dak's mind. He had no way of knowing how many of Niemann's guards were left.

There'd been a handful who died in the initial firefight at the clearing, plus the one they found in the woods. Conservatively, there could be as many as ten of them left. A dozen at most, but he felt certain it was ten or less.

"Which way do you think they went?" Will asked between breaths. The three crouched low next to a boulder.

Dak shook his head. "No way to know."

"Do you think they split up?" June asked.

"Maybe. If they did, it would be as a diversion. No way a guy like Niemann would give up the majority of his protection."

"True."

The decision for Dak was an easy one. "You two go that way. I'll go this way."

"You sure?" Will asked. "What if you find the whole group on your own?"

"I'll be okay," Dak said with confident smirk. "And if I do find them, I'll let you know."

Will took his meaning with an understanding nod. "Okay, man. Be careful."

"You, too."

He turned his back to the two and took off into the fog along the cliffside. He understood the danger of going alone and finding the German and his men, but in his mind, Dak hoped that was the case.

He preferred it that way.

If it came down to him finding the enemy or the other two, Dak wanted the ball in his hands at the buzzer.

37

M orovski crept toward the next enemy shooter. To his right, he heard one of his men yelp. Only distracted for a second, the colonel looked that direction and saw the soldier fall onto his side, grasping around the area of his clavicle.

The sight only heightened the colonel's resolve as he approached the next shooter. The man with the rifle turned his attention to the next of the Russian contingent and fired again, forcing the solider to retreat behind his cover.

The colonel took the opportunity to circle around farther to his left, putting the sniper's back toward him.

He stopped and leaned into a tree, taking aim at the gunman. He was still a good fifteen meters away, too far to reliably hit the mark.

So Morovski waited until the shooter fired again and used the reverberating pop to make his next move and advance closer. He closed the gap to within ten meters this time—a much more reasonable distance for a sidearm, and again pressed his shoulder into a tree to steady his aim.

He looked down the pistol sights at the gunman, targeting the man's exposed neck. His trigger finger tensed. He let the sights drift to the right, then back to the center of the target, then squeezed.

The muzzle flashed, and the report echoed around him. The round burrowed through the target, exiting the man's neck on the other side.

The Interpol agent immediately dropped his gun and pressed both hands to the wound. It was futile to hope he could stem the bleeding, and within seconds, the man slumped down against the tree trunk.

Morovski darted from his hiding spot and slid to the ground next to the dying man as his eyes rolled up and back down.

"May the gates of hell take you," the colonel said as the man's head lolled to the right shoulder and went limp.

More gunshots echoed through the misty woods. The smell of gunpowder filled Morovski's nostrils as the hazy blue smoke mingled with the wet air.

He quickly stuffed his sidearm into its holster and picked up the dead man's rifle. He pressed the button to release the magazine and looked it over. There were still several rounds inside. Upon further inspection, he noticed two full magazines in the agent's belt—more than enough ammunition for the colonel.

To his right, one of his men grunted and fell. Then another.

Whoever these agents were, they must have been good to take out his men.

But as of yet, they hadn't noticed him.

He slid the magazine back into the well and stepped over the dead man, scooting toward the front of the tree.

Now the two remaining enemies maneuvered away from him, converging on the last of Morovski's unit.

The thought struck him in the chest. *The last of my men.*

All of them were dead. The entire group he'd assembled years before, the men he'd served with in more battles than he could recount, the warriors who'd obeyed him no matter the circumstances —all of them were dead but one.

Morovski set the butt of the rifle against his shoulder and aimed through the scope. *No wonder the Interpol agents were so accurate.* It was a thermal scope.

He found the nearest target and readied to fire, but the man disappeared behind a tree as he maneuvered around to flank the last Russian soldier.

The colonel cursed under his breath but stood up and crept to another spot, where he raised the rifle to his shoulder again and looked through the scope.

The two colorful targets crouched low as they scurried in between the trees, their multicolored figures dipping in and out of view.

Morovski lowered the rifle in frustration. He needed to get behind them.

He turned, keeping the enemy at his right side, and retreated toward the main road as the gunfire intensified. He felt the pressing need to hurry. The last soldier under his command was in the fight of his life.

The colonel heard him giving the Interpol agents everything he could, but he was outnumbered two to one, and against those odds his chances of survival were slim—despite his training and experience. These agents had already taken out several of his men, which proved their mettle several times over. *Who had ever heard of civilian cops wiping out a special forces unit?*

Morovski hurried, bearing down on the opening where the driveway cut a path through the woods. The muzzle flashes to his right continued intermittently as the agents exchanged fire with the lone soldier.

He stopped behind a tree stump and rested the body of the rifle on the edge, steadying it with his left hand as he placed his finger on the trigger. Once more, he looked through the scope and spotted the next target on the right.

The man lowered his weapon and started to walk out toward where Morovski's last soldier had been. If the gunman was taking such a lax approach, that could mean only one thing.

The lone remaining member of Morovski's unit was dead.

He calmed his nerves against the rage filling his heart and tensed the trigger against his finger.

"This one is for you Kostya. For all of you, my comrades."

He squeezed.

After the loud report, the colorful figure in the scope fell forward onto his knees and then over onto his face.

Morovski didn't watch to see if the man got up. He'd planted the round squarely in the center of the target's back. Immediately, the colonel turned his focus to the last enemy. But inexplicably, the gunman was gone.

A chill snaked across his skin.

He looked across the rifle with his naked eye, and then back through the scope again, turning left to right. There was no sign of the last shooter.

"Where did you go?" he whispered.

He continued to search to the left but saw no sign of the man. *That's impossible. He couldn't have simply disappeared. And if he'd gone that way, he'd have been out in the open, exposed in the driveway with nowhere to hide.*

He must have gone to the right, perhaps farther back toward the meadow, possibly to check and make sure all of my men are dead.

The colonel hesitated. One of the few times in his life he didn't act decisively. Doubt reared its ugly head in his mind. He felt a paralysis unlike anything he'd ever experienced in recent memory.

He swept the rifle to the right again and this time caught a glimpse of the multicolored figure. The gunman hid behind a tree, barely revealing himself. Only edges of his arm and back displayed through the scope, not enough to target.

Morovski waited patiently for the gunman to make a mistake—to lean out and aim his way, but the man remained hidden.

"Come on," he muttered. "Show yourself, and I will give you death."

Still, the enemy remained behind the tree trunk, unwilling to risk the shot.

"Move, coward."

The colonel waited for a minute, then another.

Why isn't this man moving?

The only explanation in Morovski's mind was fear. The other

shooter must have seen that his comrades had been taken out, and now as the lone opposition, along with not knowing where the deadly gunfire was coming from, he remained in place under the assumption that the enemy had attacked from behind.

A gentle breeze wafted through the forest, stirring the gun smoke and fog in little swirls through rays of moonlight. Something made a sound to his right, and he turned his head to face the danger.

There was none, and he cursed himself for taking his eye off the target. When he brought the weapon back around, though, the man was still there, cowering behind the tree.

Must have been a small branch falling from the trees, he thought. *Or a blasted squirrel.*

He swallowed and pressed his eye to the scope, keeping his sights locked on the enemy. Morovski knew it was only a matter of time until the guy had to move. After all, he couldn't stand there all night.

Then the figure moved. It was only slight, but for a brief moment the gunman's side was exposed.

Morovski rushed the shot, squeezing the trigger in a hurry.

The multicolored target shifted back behind the tree as the bullet sailed by him.

He swore under his breath at the careless shot. He'd let his emotions get the better of him, and hurried when he should have remained patient, waiting for the perfect opportunity.

On top of that, he'd given away his position. That could be quickly rectified, however. If the enemy was determined to stay put, Morovski would shift to his right and flank him. From this distance, the man would only see him clearly if he was looking through his scope. Based on what the colonel could see, that wasn't what he was doing.

"Very well, coward," he whispered. "If you want to die there, I'll let you."

He started to get up from his kneeling position when he heard a stick crack to his left.

"Hey, idiot," a voice said in an American accent.

Morovski swiveled in that direction, but it was too late. He saw the gunman in the mist, standing in the open only forty feet away with a rifle against his shoulder and his eye to the scope.

The muzzle flashed a second before the report reached the colonel. The round struck him in the center of the chest and knocked him backward off his feet and onto the ground where he lay staring up at the canopy.

He gasped for air but only gurgled and coughed. Terrible pain radiated from his chest. Instinctively, he put his hands over the wound to stem the bleeding—an effort in futility. He felt the warm, thick liquid spilling through his fingers.

How had this happened? It's impossible! He was the only man left. Unless....

The American approached carefully, his weapon trained on the dying Russian commander as fits of coughing racked his body.

The enemy stopped short of Morovski's feet and looked down at him.

"You know," the American said, "I should put you out of your misery. But after everything you pulled, I think I'm just gonna let you suffer this one out."

The colonel couldn't respond, no matter how much he wanted to.

As the darkness closed in around his field of vision, he saw the faces of all his men he'd lost on this endeavor—this mission he thought would set him free. In a way, it had done just that. It had freed every last one of them.

With that final, poetic, and brutal notion, Morovski laid his head back on the ground and stared at the stars until they vanished in the darkness.

38

Dak worked his way along the edge of the forest, keeping to the shadows amid the fog. The cold air brushed across his face, tickling his skin. He heard every sound, felt every shift in the temperature, and smelled the different varieties of trees that filled these woods.

The only sense that wasn't operating at peak performance was his vision. But the mist would cause the same problem for the men he pursued.

He considered that as he stalked forward, moving quickly on the balls of his feet. Fortunately in this part of the forest, the leaves on the ground were few, which made his pursuit faster without the risk of alarming his quarry.

Dak wished he knew how many of them there were. Niemann and his remaining men had managed to escape the fray before Dak could even get a quick scan of that side of the battlefield.

His gut told him that the German's forces lost more than the Russians. The latter had been in combat more recently than anyone in private security, Dak figured, and despite their top-rated civilian training, nothing was a substitute for real bullets flying at you.

Dak's mind had slipped to the Interpol agents and Matt. He'd heard distant gunfire as he and Will and June pursued Niemann, but there was no way to know what was going on. Without knowing much about Matt's background, he didn't want to think too much about it. He had to focus on the task at hand.

The rough path between the forest and the cliff curved back and forth, undulating its way around the hill to Dak's left. In the distance, the light pollution of the nearest city dimmed the twinkling stars. The moon, however, shone bright in the clear sky.

If he hadn't been in a life-or-death situation with extremely dangerous enemies, he would have sat down on the rocks to his right and enjoyed the serenity of this spectacular night.

Dak breathed steadily, pushing onward faster than a jog but not quite at a sprint. From the looks of Niemann, he was in decent shape, but Dak figured if it came down to a couple of miles' worth of running, he could catch up to the German. Dak's exercise regimen kept him in peak condition, which paid huge dividends in moments such as this.

After ten minutes in the chase, however, he wondered if his calculation had been correct. There was still no sight of the enemy, and no sound either.

The air felt like it was getting colder, and as it did the mist settled lower to the ground, rolling over the precipice to his right like a thick, slow-motion waterfall.

Two more minutes into the pursuit, his patience was rewarded.

He heard the sound first—rustling in the leaves, small rocks being kicked, twigs breaking underfoot.

Niemann's men were probably former military of some kind, but they were being extremely clumsy in their desperation for escape.

Dak spotted a guy in a suit at the rear of the group. The man ran along the path in the open, illuminated by the moonlight. Another was in front of him and a third to the left running next to the forest's edge.

As he closed the gap, Dak spotted the man in front—Niemann.

I should have known he'd survive that firefight, Dak internally complained.

He narrowed the distance between them, making sure he didn't do anything stupid like trip over a rock or a tree root, or break a dead branch and signal he was behind them.

It might not have mattered. Niemann's group was hardly being quiet in their escape. Dak didn't know where they thought they were going, and maybe they didn't know, either. Getting away from danger was the only objective. And a man like Niemann, driven by utter fear, would have done anything to get to safety.

Dak didn't need a strategy for a situation like this. The plan dictated itself.

With the three guards at Niemann's back, Dak simply needed to take them out, and then the German.

In his mind, it sounded simple, but anything could go wrong—especially with everyone moving so fast.

He found it surprising the men kept up their pace—especially Niemann. Dak moved faster, though, and closed the distance to a mere fifteen yards. Then twelve.

When the last man in the group was only ten yards away, Dak raised his pistol. He'd kept the other one in his belt as a little insurance.

He took aim at the last guard nimbly skipping through the trees. Even with his considerable marksmanship, hitting a moving target while he himself was moving would be incredibly difficult.

Just a little closer, he thought. Before he took the first shot, Dak wanted to make certain he didn't miss.

His finger tensed on the trigger as he placed the middle of the nearest guard's back in his sights.

Then something snapped under his right foot.

Dak winced at his mistake, and he knew what would come next.

The last guard heard the stick break and reacted instantly.

He stopped running and turned around with a submachine gun braced against his shoulder.

Dak shot first, though his aim had shifted slightly. The round missed but caused the guard to duck out of instinct despite there being nothing to hide behind.

He returned fire, but Dak ducked behind a tree before any of the rounds came close.

The men shouted at each other in English, and Dak knew his tenuous plan had crumbled.

A lull settled over the trail, which meant Niemann's guards were probably spreading out to take care of the problem.

Dak had only two options: retreat and regroup or go on the offensive before the other guys could.

He gripped the pistol firmly, holding it in front of his face, took a deep breath, and spun.

The gunman he'd fired at first was only twenty feet away now, creeping toward Dak's position.

The move caught the guard by surprise as Dak fired three rounds. The quick succession of pops reverberated through the forest. Two found the mark—one in the chest and one in the abdomen—and felled the guard where he crouched. The man only managed to get off a few wild shots as he hit the ground, sending bullets sailing into the woods and then the night sky.

The other two guards saw Dak and immediately opened fire, but Dak ducked back behind the tree and waited for the volley to cease. They would split up to flank him, and creep up on either side. It's what he would do if he were in their shoes.

He couldn't retreat now; doing so would open up the shooting angles for the two remaining guards, and they would cut him down as he scrambled to separate himself from them.

Dak had only one option left, and he didn't like it. But there was no choice.

He drew the other pistol from his belt. Holding a gun in each hand, he closed his eyes, took a deep breath, and steadied his nerves.

If he was going to go down, it would be shooting not running.

Keeping the pistols high and close to his cheeks for two seconds, he waited until he figured the men were well within range.

One.

Two.

Three.

Dak pivoted and drop-stepped backward away from the tree, lowering both pistols in two directions. He had only a split second to both spot the men and line them up—a nearly impossible task for anyone.

But the two guards had overplayed their hands. Both were in the open—each with a pistol gripped in their hands at full extension.

As Dak fell backward, he aimed roughly with both guns at the two men and fired.

His trigger fingers twitched rapidly, sacrificing volume for accuracy. His aim, however, was true, and the bullets bore into the two guards as they desperately returned fire.

Their rounds found tree trunks and dirt but not the target.

Both men dropped to their knees with multiple bullet wounds to their torsos. Dak hit the ground on his backside, and the thud knocked his aim off for a second. The wounded men tried to muster another defense, but Dak unleashed two more shots at each of them, and they fell where they knelt.

Dak swallowed and held his breath for two seconds, keeping the guns trained on the two men. Then he breathed hard, sucking in huge gasps of air as the adrenaline pumped through him.

"Didn't think that would work," he muttered.

Beyond the dead men, he saw Niemann in the moonlight just as the German disappeared around the next bend in the trail. Before he vanished, Niemann glanced back over his shoulder. Even at a distance of thirty yards, Dak saw the look of abject fear in the man's eyes.

Now, the German was on his own. Dak knew the odds were now in his favor.

39

D ak scrambled to his feet and hurried forward. He tossed the two pistols aside as he reached one of the guards and pried the man's weapon from his dead hand.

He sprinted by the other guard lying on the trail and slowed down when he reached the turn. As he suspected, Niemann had stopped about forty feet away and held a pistol at full extension.

The muzzle flashed four times. Dak ducked down and returned fire, but at that range it was more suppressing than anything. He barely had time to aim and missed with four rounds of his own.

Niemann turned and kept running, momentarily satisfied he'd kept his pursuer at bay for the time being.

Dak took off after him again, counting the spent rounds in the magazine. He'd fired four but couldn't recall how many the guard had used. *Three? Six?* He didn't have time to slow down, eject the magazine, and count them.

He pumped his legs harder now, and based on the clumsy way the German was running, knew he'd catch up soon.

The trail undulated up and down, left to right along the cliff's edge. When it straightened out and he didn't see Niemann ahead, he knew something was off.

A gut instinct raised a red flag, and Dak immediately ducked to the left just as Niemann popped out from behind a tree thirty-five feet away. The German popped off four more shots, one coming dangerously close to Dak as it cracked the air near his right shoulder.

He dove for cover behind a rock outcropping to his left and waited for a second. Then he peeked around the edge of the stone with his pistol and looked in the direction his quarry had fired from.

Niemann was on the run again, looking back over his shoulder intermittently as he tried to escape.

Again, Dak pushed forward, as fast as he could make his legs go. This time, though, he cut through the woods. The trail ahead bent to the right and then back to the left, creating another blind turn. He had no intention of running headlong into another of Niemann's little traps.

Navigating through the trees was a little slower than the rough-hewn trail, but based on the hill to his left, he figured the path wrapped around that direction. If he was lucky, he could cut Niemann off at the pass.

Dak dipped and swerved through the trees, using his left hand to slingshot himself forward with a few of them. For the most part, kept his eyes focused straight ahead but checked to the right, where he saw the forest end at the cliffside.

Within a minute, he spotted Niemann again, and now Dak was nearly parallel to the German. Renewed energy pulsed through him, and Dak maxed out his speed, lifting his knees high as he darted through the low-hanging mist.

Soon, his prey was behind him to the right, constantly looking back to see if the hunter was catching up.

Dak allowed a grin to cross his face as he cut on an angle to the right. As he suspected, Niemann turned around the other way and looked back down the trail behind him, aiming his pistol where he thought Dak would emerge around the bend.

Slowing down to ensure stealth, Dak moderated his pace—careful not to make the slightest sound. He kept the pistol in his hand at the ready, aiming it loosely toward the German as the man stood there thinking he'd laid the perfect trap.

Dak slowed to a stalking pace, keeping his knees bent and making sure he didn't make the same mistake he made before when he stepped on that branch.

He neared the edge of the forest and crept closer. The German was only ten yards away now, nearly within easy range for Dak's abilities. He neared the last tree in a sharp bend, and started to step out, but Niemann abruptly turned around and spotted him.

Panic shot through the German's eyes, and he fired rapidly. Dak stepped behind the nearest tree—a thin, barely suitable pine—and hoped it would be enough. Bullets chipped bark from other trees around him as the loud discharge of Niemann's pistol echoed in Dak's ears.

Then the shooting stopped, and Dak heard the most reassuring sound he could imagine in a scenario like this—a click-click-click signaling the enemy had run out of rounds. That sound felt like a warm, cozy blanket wrapping around Dak in the dead of winter. He stepped out from hiding with his pistol raised and pointed at the beleaguered German. In three steps, Dak closed the gap to twenty feet—easy pickings for him.

"It's over, Niemann," Dak said. "Nowhere to run. And all your men are dead."

The German glared back at him, nostrils flaring as they pushed out clouds of breath. He inclined his head proudly and tossed the useless gun aside.

"What are you going to do now, Dak Harper? Kill an unarmed man?"

"Thought crossed my mind. And please, you can stop with the using-my-full-name routine. I get that maybe you think it makes you sound more threatening, but it just doesn't."

Niemann didn't seem to understand the comment, as evidenced by the confused twitch of his nose and the lowering of his eyebrows.

"What is your plan, Dak? You think you can kill a man like me?

You have no idea what will happen if you do that." He took a step forward.

"Stay right there, Karl," Dak warned. "I don't think I have to tell you how good I am with this thing, especially with an easy shot like this one."

Niemann only paused for a second, then took another step forward. "I can pay you," he offered. "You let me go, and you'll never have to work another day in your life."

"I don't need your dirty money."

"Perhaps." Another step forward. "But imagine what you could do with all that cash sitting back in the meadow. A hundred million. You'd be able to disappear."

Dak snorted in derision. "We already have a plan for that money. But thanks. Now stop, or I'll have to put one in your knee. You ever been shot in the knee, Karl? I heard it's pretty painful."

The German stopped this time. Dak saw the consideration streaking through his eyes.

"So, what's your plan if you're not going to kill me?" he asked. "Are you going to arrest me? Is that it?" He laughed—a chuckle at first that swelled into a disturbing bout of guffaws. "Surely, you realize a man like me is never going to do a minute of jail time, even if you had the authority to take me into custody. People like me? We own the governments. We run the world!"

"I'm still thinking about it," Dak answered. "That kneecap is still in play, though."

"We own the police, I told you," Niemann snarled. "We own everyone."

"Who is this we?"

A wicked smile creased Niemann's lips. "Oh, that is the great question, isn't it? We are everywhere, Dak. Kill me, and there is nowhere you can hide from the retribution that will follow. And if you try to take me in, I will make certain you are dead within the week. This is a game you can't win, unless you cooperate."

Dak considered the man's words, not because he was actually

thinking about taking the deal but because he needed more information.

"Yes," Niemann prodded, and took another step closer. "That's right. The only way for you to win is to join me. I could use someone like you. Clearly, you are better than anyone else I had working for me."

"You don't get it, do you, Karl? I don't side with the bad guys. And you're definitely a bad guy. Especially considering you were in bed with Tucker."

Niemann laughed again. "Ah yes. Your former boss. He spent a tremendous amount of money trying to find you, trying to kill you. He used every resource he could muster, and yet you escaped every trap. Come with me, Dak, and you can kill Tucker yourself."

It was Dak's turn to chuckle. "Yeah, not sure if you noticed, but I'm pretty certain he's already dead."

The words had no effect on the German, not even the slightest hint of surprise.

"I suppose with him gone, you'll feel safe again."

"I won't miss him if that's what you're saying."

Another step forward.

"Okay, if you take one more step, I'm going to blow out your kneecap. No more tennis for you. Capisce?"

It was as if the warning never reached the German's ears. "Of course," Niemann continued, "there is always your lady to consider."

Dak felt a shiver ripple over his skin like a hundred tiny spiders. "What did you just say?"

"Nicole, I believe it is. Yes?" He arched his right eyebrow. "I can see from your body language I've struck a nerve with that one. I suppose you think now that Tucker is dead, she will be safe. But I assure you, Dak, she is not. If you kill me, my organization will come after you, and take her down as well. Do you want that on your conscience? Knowing that she died because of you?"

Dak swallowed back the anger burning like an inferno in his chest. "Shut your mouth, Karl."

"Ah, but you've already given it away. Do you think we can't find her? That we don't already know where she is? She can be safe, Dak. All you have to do is put down the gun and come with me."

"You're bluffing."

"Is that a chance you're willing to take?"

Dak's heart raced like a cheetah. For a second, he considered asking the man where she was located but thought better of it. Part of him didn't want to know if Karl knew.

Karl's confidence swelled. "Join me," he said, taking another step forward. "And she'll be safe. You have my word."

Dak pulled the trigger with the sights aimed squarely at the German's right knee. But instead of the expected report and kick from the pistol, it merely clicked.

Karl's eyes widened with a sinister sort of surprise, and he rushed forward to attack.

Dak threw the pistol at the man's head, but it flew by harmlessly as Karl ducked to the right. It was a clumsy, reckless charge, with both fists raised.

Dak adjusted his stance and waited. Karl reached him in a second and swung his right fist in a desperate attempt to land a heavy blow.

Instead, Dak dipped to his left and grabbed the German's wrist. Using the opponent's momentum against him, Dak pulled hard and swung Karl around toward the cliff's edge only three yards away.

Terror swept across the German's face as he realized he'd made a mistake. He stumbled toward the precipice, unable to stop himself as he twisted in one last attempt to keep from falling. His heels slipped on a patch of loose dirt and rock on the lip of the drop-off, and then his feet went over.

He shoved out his hands as his legs disappeared from Dak's view. The German's hands smacked against the rock, and his jaw slammed into it, but he didn't go completely over. Somehow, he'd managed to cling to the edge, clawing at the rock with his pale, bony fingers.

Dak stepped over to him, looking down at the vile man.

"Help me," Niemann pleaded, all confidence in his voice replaced with undeniable fear.

"One second you want to make a deal. The next you want to bum-rush me like a drunken idiot at an all-you-can-drink cheap beer night. Which is it, Karl?"

Dak stopped with his boots mere inches from the man's fingers.

"How are you doing that, anyway?" Dak asked. He shifted to the right and looked over the edge. "Oh. Wow. That's a long drop. I didn't realize they had cliffs like that here. Must be a few hundred feet down, Karl. But hey, at least there are plenty of pointy rocks to break the fall."

"Shut up and help me. I'll pay you whatever you want."

"And we're back to this again. Karl, if I passed on a hundred million, what amount makes you think I would change my mind?"

"If you let me die, you and your woman will follow. I can promise you that."

Dak ignored him. "Oh, I see. You managed to find a little ledge down there for your toes. That was lucky."

The German swore at him.

"That's not nice," Dak said. "Even for someone like you, Karl."

The man's right foot slipped, and he scratched at the rock while trying to find purchase once again.

"I'll do whatever you ask," he pleaded. "You and Nicole will be safe. I swear. I won't let them get you if you just help me."

"Yeah," Dak said, standing up straight again. "See, I don't think I can trust you, Karl. One minute you say one thing, then you contradict yourself the next with some kind of threat. I think maybe I'll just wait and see if you can pull yourself up."

Fury streaked through Niemann's eyes. "Then we both die." There was no hiding his thoughts in that moment. He reached out toward Dak's ankle with his left hand and tried to grab it in one last desperate attempt to take the American down with him.

He swiped hard but missed as Dak took a quick step back.

The move threw off Karl's razor-thin balance, and he lost his grip with the other hand. As he fell backward, he slapped his hands at the rock ledge again, but this time they merely bounced off it with a smack.

He yelled as his other foot slipped from its narrow perch and felt the sickening sensation of nothing but air beneath him.

His screams faded as he plummeted downward, his body tumbling until it hit the rocks below. Then all fell silent.

Dak lingered there for a few seconds, staring down at the still figure of the man he knew had been the cause of so much suffering, so much trouble for so many. In truth, Dak didn't know the extent of just how far Niemann's deeds went. But he had a few ideas.

He'd been unable to extract more information about this mysterious group Niemann claimed to be a part of, but one thing was certain: if he knew about Nicole, then their reach was far greater than he could have previously anticipated.

Dak turned away from the cliff and started back toward the fork in the trail. He heard the sound of footsteps pounding toward him.

More goons? he wondered.

Without a weapon, Dak braced himself in a defensive stance and waited for the enemy to show themselves.

Relief flooded him as Will and June appeared around the bend. He lowered his fists and slumped his shoulders.

"I thought you might be more of Niemann's guards," Dak said.

Will and June trotted to a stop next to him. "We didn't find any the other direction," Will said. "Then when we heard gunfire this way, we turned around to come help."

"I'm afraid you're a few minutes too late."

"We saw the bodies of the guards," June added. "What about Niemann?"

Dak turned his head toward the precipice. "He's gone, too." Then he added, "Man, I really wanted to throw in a catchy one-liner like they do in the movies, but I got nothin'."

"Like, he had to catch some air?" Will asked.

"That's terrible. Come on," Dak said, slapping his friend on the shoulder. "We need to go check on Lesma. I hope he hasn't been hitting on Galyna the whole time."

Will's brow wrinkled. "You think he likes her?"

"Isn't it obvious?"

40

When Dak reached the clearing, he and the others found Galyna and Lesma standing guard over the bags of artifacts and the briefcases.

The two waved at them as they approached, glad to see they'd survived.

Matt stood next to them with another guy, who sat on the ground wincing in pain.

The fact there were only two told Dak everything he needed to know, but he still had to ask as he arrived in the center of the meadow.

"The other two?" he asked Matt.

Matt merely shook his head. Then looked at the guy sitting on the ground. "Pierre here was lucky. Took a round to the back, but his vest stopped the bullet."

"It still hurts like Hades," Pierre complained. "I hope you killed that son of a—"

"He's dead," Dak cut him off.

"You killed him?"

Dak shrugged. "He kind of did it to himself. Fell over a cliff."

"But you're certain he's dead."

"Oh, I'm certain. Two-hundred-foot drop with a sudden, rocky stop."

"Good." Pierre spat on the ground.

"Looks like you're going to get all your artifacts back, Curator," Dak said to Galyna. "I'm not sure where you're going to take them right now with all that's going on in your home country."

She flicked her right eyebrow. "I was hoping you could help with that."

"Me?"

"You're friends with Sean Wyatt and Tommy Schultz, yes?"

Dak forced a chuckle. "June is Tommy's wife. If you want to reach out to him, she's the one to talk to."

Galyna faced her with an idea written on her face. "I would like to ask that the International Archaeological Agency take custody of these artifacts until the war in my country is over. Do you think your husband would be willing to do that?"

June smiled back at her. "It would be his honor to help with that. I'll call him right now. I don't know which of their agents is closest to here right now, but I'm sure they can get someone to Hungary within the next twenty-four hours."

"Thank you." Galyna met the eyes of everyone else one at a time. "Thank all of you. You all risked your lives to save me. And I will never forget it."

"Our pleasure," Dak said. "Just glad we were able to get to you before it was too late."

"What will you do now? Return to America?"

Dak thought about it for a second before responding. "At some point, yeah. But I have something I need to take care of first." His mind wandered to Nicole's face, the way she'd looked at him the last time they saw each other.

"What about you?" Galyna looked to Will.

"I don't really know. But I think I'll stick around the area for a while." He looked around the meadow. "I hear there's a country close to here that needs guns. Maybe I know a guy who can help."

Everyone looked at Will in surprise.

"What?"

"You're a good man," Dak said, clapping his friend on the shoulder blade.

"I will be returning to Mumbai," Lesma said. "I must make certain my businesses are running smoothly." He looked at Galyna. "If you need a place to go, you can come to Mumbai, too."

Dak cast a sidelong glance at Will and June. "Called it," he whispered.

"Thank you," she said, "but I need to make sure these artifacts are safe. And then there's the issue of the money. This will go a long way to helping the people of Ukraine, if you still want to use it for that."

Everyone nodded in agreement.

Dak took a deep breath and sighed. This chapter of his saga was over. Tucker was dead, and it felt like a huge weight had been.... He looked over toward the spot where Tucker had fallen, but the man wasn't there.

Dak's head twisted back and forth as he searched the forest edge around them.

"What?" Will wondered. "What's the matter?"

Dak walked over to where he'd seen Tucker's body. "Where is he?"

"Where is who?" Lesma asked.

"Colonel Tucker. He was right here. I saw him—" Dak cut himself off. "I saw him die." He realized in that moment: he'd seen Tucker shot, but there'd been no way to confirm the man was dead.

He looked back at Pierre, who still sat on the grass, nursing what must have been a massive bruise on his back. "He must have been wearing a vest, too."

The feeling of victory fell away like waves receding from the shore, replaced by an empty, unsatisfying feeling.

When Dak spoke, his voice sounded hollow. "I guess it's not over after all."

41

Colonel Cameron Tucker sat in the back corner of a café with a steaming cup of coffee in front of him. His eyes remained fixed on the door. He picked up the cup and took a sip, then set it back down again.

His cell phone sat near his left hand with the screen facing up.

Patrons chatted as they enjoyed their coffee and pastries. Outside the glass windows lining the outer wall, pedestrians walked by on their way to work. Tourists blended in with them like oil and water, easily spotted against the backdrop of locals with their cameras and fanny packs, book bags, and clothing.

Tucker took another sip and checked his watch. It was nearly nine in the morning local time.

He rubbed his chest where a three-inch-wide purple bruise scarred his skin. He'd been lucky. Tucker knew that.

In all the firefights he'd been a part of in his time with the military, he'd never been shot, and he was fortunate that this time just happened to be in the chest. The vest he'd worn saved his life, and he swore to himself he wouldn't waste the second chance.

He would kill Dak Harper if it was the last thing he did.

His eyes wandered from the door down to the phone again. Still no response.

He'd sent the message twenty minutes before. He reminded himself that these things could take some time, but if the organization was so powerful, it should have been instant—in his opinion.

There'd been no word out of Niemann after the battle. It was safe to assume the man was dead. If not, they'd be reunited eventually. And if the German was, in fact, dead, it wasn't a problem. Tucker had no attachment to the man other than in business, and there were others like him in Niemann's organization.

The German had been coy about what they were called, only referring to his secret handshake collection of uber wealthy people as the Syndicate.

These folks were beyond the one percent. Their assets and money were hidden in more shell corporations and secret bank accounts than Tucker imagined possible. But who they were, on an individual basis, was unknown.

He'd only been given a number for a person called the Secretary. Tucker had never talked directly to this mysterious persona, only connecting via text. And it was a text from the Secretary on which he waited.

A young blonde woman pulled open the front door to the coffee house and walked to the counter. She wore a light blue coat and black leggings.

She was attractive, Tucker thought, but he dismissed the distraction and returned his attention to the door and any potential threat that might enter. The blonde wasn't that.

The phone abruptly vibrated, jerking his focus back to it. He picked up the device and opened it, then selected the encrypted messaging app. After entering his passcode, he read the one-word message.

"Well, well, well. Lookie what we have here. Gotcha."

His lips curled with wicked delight as he stared at the white text on the black screen.

Istanbul.

THANK YOU

I just wanted to say thank you for reading this story. You chose to spend your time and money on something I created, and that means more to me than you may know. But I appreciate it, and am truly honored.

If you want to have some fun with like minded readers, get access to exclusive contests and giveaways, and more, join the Ernest Dempsey's Hunters and Runners Facebook group: https://www.face book.com/groups/dempseyshuntersandrunners

Be sure to swing by ernestdempsey.net to grab free stories, and dive deeper into the universe I've created for you.

I hope you enjoyed the story, and will stick with this series as it continues through the years. Know that I'll be working hard to keep bringing you exciting new stories to help you escape from the real world.

Your friendly neighborhood author,
Ernest

OTHER BOOKS BY ERNEST DEMPSEY

Sean Wyatt Adventures:

The Milestone Protocol
Where Horizons End
Adriana Villa Adventures:
War of Thieves Box Set
When Shadows Call
Shadows Rising
Shadow Hour
The Relic Runner - A Dak Harper Series:
The Relic Runner Origin Story
The Courier
Two Nights In Mumbai
Country Roads
Heavy Lies the Crown
Moscow Sky
The Adventure Guild (ALL AGES):
The Caesar Secret: Books 1-3
The Carolina Caper
Beta Force:
Operation Zulu
London Calling
Paranormal Archaeology Division:
Hell's Gate
Guardians of Earth:
Emergence: Gideon Wolf Book 1
Righteous Dawn: Gideon Wolf Book 2
Crimson Winter: Gideon Wolf Book 3

ACKNOWLEDGMENTS

As always, I would like to thank my terrific editors, Anne and Jason, for their hard work. What they do makes my stories so much better for readers all over the world. Anne Storer and Jason Whited are the best editorial team a writer could hope for and I appreciate everything they do.

I also want to thank Elena at Lɪ Graphics for her tremendous work on my book covers and for always overdelivering. Elena definitely rocks.

A big thank you has to go out to my friend James Slater for his proofing work. James has added another layer of quality control to these stories, and I can't thank him enough.

Last but not least, I need to thank all my wonderful fans and especially the advance reader team. Their feedback and reviews are always so helpful and I can't say enough good things about all of them.

AFTERWORD

Printed in Great Britain
by Amazon

11075033R00181